THE PENGUIN CLASSICS

FOUNDER EDITOR (1944–64): E. V. RIEU

COUNT LEO NIKOLAYEVICH TOLSTOY was born in 1828 at Yasnaya Polyana in the Tula province, and educated privately. He studied Oriental languages and law at the University of Kazan, then led a life of pleasure until 1851 when he joined an artillery regiment in the Caucasus. He took part in the Crimean war and after the defence of Sevastopol he wrote *The Sevastopol Stories*, which established his reputation. After a period in St Petersburg and abroad, where he studied educational methods for use in his school for peasant children in Yasnaya, he married Sophie Andreyevna Behrs in 1862. The next fifteen years was a period of great happiness; they had thirteen children, and Tolstoy managed his vast estates in the Volga Steppes, continued his educational projects, cared for his peasants and wrote *War and Peace* (1865–8) and *Anna Karenin* (1874–6). *A Confession* (1879–82) marked an outward change in his life and works; he became an extreme rationalist and moralist, and in a series of pamphlets after 1880 he expressed theories such as rejection of the state and church, indictment of the demands of the flesh, and denunciation of private property. His teaching earned him numerous followers in Russia and abroad, but also much opposition and in 1901 he was excommunicated by the Russian holy synod. He died in 1910, in the course of a dramatic flight from home, at the small railway station of Astapovo.

PAUL FOOTE was born in Dorset in 1926. He is a University Lecturer in Russian and Fellow of The Queen's College, Oxford. His publications include translations of Lermontov's *A Hero of Our Time* (Penguin Classic) and Saltykov-Shchedrin's *The History of a Town*.

LEO TOLSTOY

MASTER AND MAN
and Other Stories

TRANSLATED AND
WITH AN INTRODUCTION
BY
PAUL FOOTE

PENGUIN BOOKS

Penguin Books Ltd, Harmondsworth, Middlesex, England
Penguin Books, 40 West 23rd Street, New York, New York 10010, U.S.A.
Penguin Books Australia Ltd, Ringwood, Victoria, Australia
Penguin Books Canada Ltd, 2801 John Street, Markham, Ontario, Canada L3R 1B4
Penguin Books (N.Z.) Ltd, 182–190 Wairau Road, Auckland 10, New Zealand

—

This translation first published 1977
Reprinted 1980, 1982, 1984

—

Copyright © Paul Foote, 1977
All rights reserved

—

Made and printed in Great Britain by
Hazell Watson & Viney Limited,
Member of the BPCC Group,
Aylesbury, Bucks
Set in Monotype Bembo

CONTENTS

INTRODUCTION

THE three stories in this volume date from the last two decades of Tolstoy's life. *Father Sergius*, begun in 1890, was worked on at intervals until 1898. *Master and Man* was completed between September 1894 and January 1895. *Hadji Murat* was written in the period 1896–1904. Only *Master and Man* was published in Tolstoy's lifetime (in 1895); *Father Sergius* and *Hadji Murat* first appeared in 1911 and 1912 respectively in an edition of Tolstoy's posthumous literary works.

The stories belong then to that period when Tolstoy had largely turned away from literary work and become preoccupied with writing on religious, moral, philosophical, and social problems. In 1897 he expressed in *What is Art?* his moral utilitarian aesthetic, which required of fictional works that they should be morally improving and accessible to the widest possible public. Sophisticated literature, including his own earlier work, he viewed now with disapproval. Yet, more than once in these later years he expressed in his letters and diary the urge to write 'something artistic' – something that would combine moral teaching with the old style of his previous fiction. The stories in this book are some of the works written in response to this urge. Tolstoy's later works (from which one might except *Hadji Murat*) are more strongly didactic and generally more sombre in tone than his well-known early works, but all show the familiar features of Tolstoy's fiction – clear-cut narrative, firmly drawn characters, and convincing observation of man, society and nature.

Father Sergius and *Master and Man* present a familiar Tolstoyan theme – a man's discovery, through experience, of the 'truth' of life and how to live. In the case of Father Sergius, the society man turned monk, the discovery comes only after many years in the monastery, where he has lived a life of outward sanctity, though inwardly torn by temptations and doubt. The crises in Sergius's life are moments of sexual temptation, in which he is first triumphant and then defeated. The story is often considered together with *The Kreutzer Sonata* and *The Devil* (both published in 1890, the year *Father Sergius* was started) as making up a trilogy on the destructive power of sexual passion. However, the sexual theme in *Father Sergius*, though it provides the most dramatic moments in the story, is of only secondary importance. 'The struggle with lust,' Tolstoy wrote to Chertkov in 1891, 'is . . . only a stage; the main struggle is with worldly fame.' It is pride which stands between Sergius and the true life; he is proud of his saintliness, proud of his good works, proud even of what he thinks is his humility, and he is ripe for salvation only when he has succumbed to fleshly lust and thus utterly debased himself in the eyes of men and, more importantly, in his own eyes. At this moment of degradation the truth comes to him and it comes, as it does to so many Tolstoyan seekers, through the example of an inconspicuous and unpretentiously righteous person. In Sergius's case it is his ageing childhood acquaintance Pashenka who shows him the way – not consciously, for she considers her own life (as it might well seem) totally unsatisfactory, but by her example of humility and devotion to the needs of others.

Master and Man is a more compact story. It relates the events of a single day: the merchant Brekhunov (the 'master' of the title) sets off on a short business journey with his man Nikita; in a blizzard they lose their way and are forced to spend the night in the open. It is in this crisis that Brekhunov, the brash, confident, self-made man, discovers the vanity of wealth and worldly success and learns the satisfaction of sacrifice and service to others. Nikita, like Pashenka in *Father Sergius*, stands in contrast to his proud master. Nikita's life is unsuccessful and he is no moral paragon, but he has simple qualities and skills and possesses the self-sufficiency of a man who, through a life of want and toil, has never indulged in worldly illusions or lost sight of his personal dependence on God.

Of these two rather similar stories *Master and Man* must be reckoned the more successful. The concentrated action, the clearly drawn characters of Brekhunov and Nikita (not to mention Dapple, the horse, another of Tolstoy's convincing animal portraits), and the impressive descriptions of their journey through the blizzard, all contribute to its effectiveness. *Father Sergius* is more ambitious. Like *Resurrection*, it combines the story of an individual's moral quest with social criticism and satire on a broad scale – witness the wide range of social types introduced in *Father Sergius*: tsar, high society, soldiers, ecclesiastics, merchants, higher and lower professional classes, peasant pilgrims. Perhaps in the story Tolstoy attempts too much for, despite the interest of Sergius's development and some powerful moments in the narrative, it is hard to escape the awareness of Tolstoy's manipulating hand in the conduct of the characters.

Hadji Murat stands apart from these two stories, as it does from all of Tolstoy's later fiction. The story of Hadji Murat takes us back to the colourful years spent by Tolstoy with the Russian army in the Caucasus (1851–4), which had provided him with material for his first military stories – *The Raid* (1853), *Wood-Felling* (1855) – and for the most important of his pre-*War and Peace* work *The Cossacks* (1863; translated by Rosemary Edmonds in Penguin Classics). To the nineteenth-century Russian the Caucasus offered attractions similar to those of India and the North-West Frontier for an Englishman of the same period – majestic scenery, strange peoples, the mystery and excitement of an exotic world, and opportunities for adventure and death – an attraction alike for the world-weary and the man of spirit. Russian novels and stories set in the Caucasus, even the most sophisticated, have a *Tales from the*

Outposts ring about them, and Tolstoy's early tales are no exception. They are all stories of action. At the same time they contain a moral point in the contrast drawn by Tolstoy between nature and the works of man, between the integrity of the natives' elemental life and the distortions of civilized existence. As the reader will see, these basic ingredients are to be found too in *Hadji Murat*, written fifty years later.

Hadji Murat is based largely on historical events. Hadji Murat was one of the chief lieutenants of Shamil, who led the native tribes in resisting the Russian occupation of the Caucasus in the nineteenth century (for a brief account of Russian policy and involvement in the Caucasus, see the note preceding the translation of *Hadji Murat*, pp. 129–32). The events described in Tolstoy's story – Hadji Murat's surrender to the Russians, his subsequent flight and death – took place between December 1851 and April 1852, soon after Tolstoy's own arrival in the Caucasus (Tolstoy was in fact in Tiflis at the same time as Hadji Murat, though he never saw him). Tolstoy paid careful attention to the accuracy of his depiction of these events and the characters involved in them, reading memoirs, historical and ethnographical accounts of the Caucasus, interviewing and corresponding with participants and eye-witnesses of the episodes described, and making use of published documentary sources – indirectly in the case of Hadji Murat's narrative to Loris-Melikov (in chapters 11–13) and directly in the case of Vorontsov's letter to Chernyshev (chapter 14).

Like all of Tolstoy's more substantial works, *Hadji Murat* has several themes. Central, of course, is the story of Hadji Murat himself, the man of action torn and destroyed by the conflicting pull of loyalties and hostilities within him. In 1898, when working on *Hadji Murat*, Tolstoy referred to his interest in the 'fluidity' of human character and his wish to depict man in the many facets of his nature, alternately villain and angel, sage and idiot, strong man and weakling (Diary, 21 March 1898). A diary entry of the same date referred to the need to treat Hadji

Murat in this way, to show him as a husband, as a religious fanatic, and so on. His finished portrait of Hadji Murat partly reflects this preoccupation, though the diverse aspects of his character make no striking impression of incongruity on the reader, whose sympathies, prompted by Tolstoy, are engaged entirely in Hadji Murat's favour. Interwoven with the story of Hadji Murat is the theme of power, which Tolstoy investigates in the two adversaries – Nicholas I and Shamil – whose plaything Hadji Murat becomes. In his depiction of these two rulers, to each of whom he devotes a chapter (chapters 15 and 19), Tolstoy presented what he considered to be the European and Asiatic faces of absolutism. If different in style, in substance they were the same: arrogant, arbitrary power is the mark of both Nicholas and Shamil, as we see in their identically harsh resolutions and identically spurious pretence of guidance by some higher wisdom. The military scene is depicted in familiar Tolstoyan manner: characteristic episodes are described – sentry-watch, march, skirmish, punitive raid; numerous well-observed, carefully detailed characters are portrayed, ranging from the commander-in-chief to the regimental dog. Tolstoy has done all this before, but never with more economy and skill than in *Hadji Murat*. Using the death of a conscript soldier as pretext, Tolstoy introduces a further theme in a chapter on peasant life in Russia, digressing on such matters as threshing, peasants' work obligations and the disruptive social consequences of conscription. Here Tolstoy takes us a good way from Hadji Murat, but even as digression the chapter is a model of compactness, giving in a few pages both a general view of peasant life and a defined picture of a particular household.

A feature of *Hadji Murat* (even, arguably, one of its strengths) is its lack of a Tolstoyan positive hero. Nobody in the story undergoes a moral crisis, seeks perfection, or proclaims a truth. The story is didactic, but didacticism is not the major concern. Where it occurs, it comes blatant and sharp in Tolstoy's thrusts at Russian state institutions and historical figures; it is not conveyed through the soul-searching of an Olenin, Levin, or Nekhlyudov. First and foremost, *Hadji Murat* is the story of a man of action, and the chief stimulus to its composition was not a moral purpose, but the simple admiration inspired in Tolstoy by the strength, courage, and dignity of a man whom he saw, like the thistle in the prologue to the story, as an embodiment of the life-force of nature itself.

At different times while writing *Hadji Murat* Tolstoy referred guiltily to the story as being unworthy of the time and attention he devoted to it. He wrote in 1903 of working at it 'on the sly from myself', and Biryukov records that in 1905–6 Tolstoy confessed to being engaged on *Hadji Murat* with an expression of pleasurable guilt on his face such as a schoolboy might wear when speaking of a cake he has eaten. It was a piece of self-indulgence for which no reader of the story would wish to reproach Tolstoy.

*

The translations have been made from volumes 12 and 14 of the edition of Tolstoy's works published in Moscow in 1960–65 (*Sobranie sochinenii v dvadtsati tomakh*, Izdatelstvo 'Khudozhestvennaya literatura').

A number of people have kindly given me advice and information on various matters. I would like in particular to acknowledge the help of Professor R. F. Christian, Marina Fennell, Emma Shotton, my daughter Susan, and I. N. Gilinsky of Leningrad through whose good offices I had the benefit of a most helpful reply to a query from the great-grandson of Hadji Murat, M. B. Khadzhi-Muradov, to whom I would like to express my special thanks. I am also indebted to Patricia Lloyd for her skilful conversion of manuscript to typescript.

PAUL FOOTE

FATHER SERGIUS

1

In the 1840s there took place in St Petersburg an event which caused general surprise: a handsome prince, commander of the sovereign's squadron of a regiment of cuirassiers, whom everyone expected to become an *aide-de-camp* and have a brilliant career at the court of Nicholas I, a month before his marriage to a beautiful lady-in-waiting who enjoyed the special favour of the empress, suddenly resigned his commission, broke with his fiancée, made over his modest estate to his sister, and retired to a monastery with the intention of becoming a monk. To those who knew nothing of the circumstances the whole thing was odd and unaccountable, but for Prince Stepan Kasatsky himself it was all so natural that he could not conceive of any other possible course of action.

Stepan Kasatsky's father, a retired guards colonel, had died when his son was twelve. Much as the boy's mother regretted sending him away, she felt obliged to carry out the wishes of her late husband, whose instructions were that in the event of his death his son should not be kept at home but sent to the cadet school. So she entered him at the school and with her daughter Varvara moved to St Petersburg in order to be near her son and to take him out at holidays.

The boy was remarkable for his brilliant ability and colossal ambition, qualities which took him to the top of his class both in his school work (particularly in mathematics on which he was especially keen) and in drill and horse-riding. Although more than usually tall, he was lithe and handsome. In conduct, too, he would have been a model cadet, had it not been for his quick temper. He did not drink or go in for debauchery; he was remarkably upright in character. All that prevented him from being a paragon was that he was given to outbursts of anger in which he lost all control of himself and became like a wild animal. On one occasion he practically threw another cadet out of a window for poking fun at his collection of minerals. Another time he almost came to grief: he threw a dishful of cutlets at the catering officer, attacked him and, it was said, struck him because he had gone back on his word and told a barefaced lie. He would certainly have been reduced to the ranks had it not been for the head of the cadet school who dismissed the catering officer and hushed the matter up.

When he was eighteen Kasatsky passed out as an officer and joined an aristocratic guards regiment. The Emperor Nicholas had known him when he was still a cadet and continued to take notice of him now that he had joined his regiment, so it was predicted that he would become an imperial *aide-de-camp*. And this was Kasatsky's own earnest desire, not just because he was ambitious, but also – and chiefly – because ever since his days as a cadet he had passionately – literally passionately – loved the emperor. Every time that Nicholas visited the cadet school (which he did often), as soon as his tall, military-coated figure with swelling chest, aquiline nose, moustache and trimmed side-whiskers strode in and boomed a greeting to the cadets, Kasatsky felt the rapture of a lover, the same feeling he experienced later on meeting the woman he loved. Only his rapturous affection for Nicholas was stronger. He wanted to demonstrate the utterness of his devotion, to sacrifice something, his whole self, for him. And Nicholas was aware that he aroused this ecstasy and purposely evoked it. He played with the cadets, gathered them round him, and varied his treatment of them, being one moment boyishly simple, then friendly, then solemnly majestic. After the recent episode involving Kasatsky and the officer Nicholas said nothing to him, but when Kasatsky came near he theatrically rebuffed him, frowned and wagged his finger. Then, as he was going, he said:

'Understand that I am aware of everything. Certain things, however, I do not wish to know. But they are here!'

He pointed to his heart.

When the cadets appeared before Nicholas on passing out, he made no further mention of this, but said, as always, that each of them could approach him directly, that they should loyally serve him and their fatherland, and that he would always be their best friend. They were all, as always, moved by this, and Kasatsky, recalling the past, shed tears and swore to serve his beloved tsar with all his strength.

When Kasatsky joined his regiment, his mother and sister moved first to Moscow and then to the country. Kasatsky gave half his property to his sister, keeping for himself only sufficient to pay his way in the smart regiment in which he served.

Outwardly Kasatsky appeared to be a perfectly ordinary brilliant young guards officer making his career, but within him there was an intense and complex process at work. Ever since childhood he had had this impulse; it had taken various apparent forms, but basically it was always the same – the urge to attain perfection and success in everything that it fell to him to do and thus attract the praise and wonder of other people. If it was a matter of study and learning he buckled down and worked until he was lauded and held up as an example to others. Once one object was attained, he took on something new. So it was that he made himself top in his class; so it was that, when still a cadet, having noticed on some occasion how awkwardly he expressed himself in French he taught himself to speak it as perfectly as he did Russian; so it was that later, when he took up chess, he became an excellent player, though still only a cadet.

Apart from his general vocation in life, which was to serve the tsar and his country, he always had some set purpose to which, however insignificant it was, he would devote himself wholeheartedly and live only for the moment of its achievement. But no sooner had one aim been achieved than another immediately took shape in his mind and supplanted the one before. This urge to excel, and to achieve the aims he set himself in order to excel, dominated his whole life. So when he was commissioned he made it his object to achieve a complete mastery of his duties and soon became an exemplary officer, though he still suffered from the same uncontrollable temper which in his service life too caused him to do things which were bad in themselves and prejudicial to his career. Once, later, when conversing on some social occasion, he had been conscious of his lack of general education, so he determined to make good this deficiency, got down to his books and achieved what he intended. He decided then to win for himself a brilliant place in high society, became an excellent dancer, and was soon invited to all the society balls and to certain receptions as well. But this did not satisfy him. He was used to being first, and in the social world he was far from that.

High society at that time consisted (as, indeed, I think it consists at all times and in all places) of four kinds of people: (1) the wealthy who attend court; (2) the not wealthy who nonetheless have been born and brought up in court circles; (3) the wealthy who fawn on those at court; and (4) the not wealthy, unconnected with the court, who fawn on those in the first and second categories. Kasatsky did not belong to the first group, though he was readily received in the last two circles. On his very first entry into the social world Kasatsky set his sights on forming a liaison with some society lady and, contrary to his expectations, it was not long before he succeeded. But he very quickly saw that the circles in which he moved were the lower circles of society and that there were circles above these and that, though he was received in these higher court circles, he did not belong there. People were polite, but everything in their manner made it clear that he was not one of their set. And this Kasatsky wished to be. But for this it was necessary to be an *aide-de-camp* (which he had hopes of becoming) or to marry into the circle. And that is what he decided to do. The girl he selected was beautiful and one of the court circle; she was not only part of that society which he wished to enter, but

someone whose acquaintance was actually sought after by all
the highest and most established members of this higher circle.
She was the Countess Korotkova. It was not merely on
account of his career that Kasatsky began courting her: she was
extraordinarily attractive and he was soon in love with her. At
first she was distinctly chilly towards him, but then everything
suddenly changed. She began to show signs of affection and
her mother became particularly pressing with invitations.

Kasatsky proposed and was accepted. He was surprised how
easily he had won such happiness; he was surprised, too, by
something peculiar and odd in the behaviour of both mother
and daughter towards him. He was deeply in love and blinded
by his feelings and so was unaware of what practically everyone else in the city knew: that the year before his fiancée had
been Nicholas's mistress.

2

Two weeks before the day fixed for their wedding Kasatsky
was sitting at his fiancée's summer villa at Tsarskoe Selo. It was
a hot day in May. The engaged couple had been walking in the
garden and now sat on a bench in the shade of a lime avenue.
Mary was looking more than usually pretty in a white muslin
dress and seemed a picture of innocence and love. She sat with
lowered head, looking up now and then at the great handsome
man who was talking to her with particular tenderness and
caution, fearing that his every word and gesture might injure
or defile the angelic purity of his betrothed. Kasatsky was one
of those men of the 'forties – not met with today – who, while
consciously allowing themselves to be unchaste in sexual
matters and inwardly seeing nothing wrong in it, nonetheless
expected their wives to possess an ideal celestial purity; they
assumed this quality to exist in all the girls of their society and
behaved towards them accordingly. There was much that was

false in this attitude and much that was harmful in the dissolution indulged in by the men, but as far as the women were concerned this attitude – so different from that of young people today who see in every girl a female looking for a mate – was, I think, beneficial. Seeing themselves worshipped, girls actually tried to be more or less like goddesses. This attitude towards women was shared by Kasatsky, and it was thus that he regarded his bride-to-be. He was especially in love that day; he felt no sensual attraction towards her, but regarded her rather with tender awe as something unattainable.

He rose to his full height and stood before her with his hands resting on his sabre.

'It is only now that I have discovered how happy a man can be. And it is you, you – my dear,' he said with a bashful smile, 'that I have to thank for this.'

He was still at the stage of being unused to addressing her affectionately, and to him, conscious of his moral inferiority to this angel, it seemed terrible that he should do so.

'I have come to know myself through you, . . . dear, and I have found that I am better than I thought.'

'I have known it long since. That is the reason why I love you.'

A nightingale trilled nearby; a sudden breeze rustled the young leaves.

He took her hand and kissed it. Tears came into his eyes. She understood that he was thanking her for saying that she loved him. He walked a little in silence, then came and sat down.

'You know, my dear, at first I had an ulterior motive in getting to know you. I wanted to form connections in society. But then, when I came to know you, how trivial that was in comparison with you! This does not make you angry?'

She made no answer, but merely touched his hand with hers. He understood its meaning: 'No, I am not angry.'

'You said just now . . .,' he broke off, feeling it was too much of a liberty. 'You said that you love me, but – forgive me – I believe there is something else, too, which troubles you and stands in your way. What is it?'

It's now or never, she thought. He is bound to find out anyway. And he will not cry off now. Oh, but how terrible if he did!

She looked lovingly at his large, noble, powerful figure. She loved him more than Nicholas now and, but for Nicholas being emperor, she would not have preferred him to Kasatsky.

'Listen. I cannot be untruthful and must tell you everything. You ask me what is the matter. It is that I have loved someone before.'

She pleadingly put her hand on his. He did not speak.

'You want to know who it was? It was him, the emperor.'

'But we all love him. When you were at school, I suppose . . .'

'No, it was after. It was an infatuation, then I got over it. But I must tell you . . .'

'Well, what?'

'That there was more to it.'

She covered her face with her hands.

'What? You gave yourself to him?'

She said nothing.

'You were his mistress?'

She said nothing.

He leapt to his feet and stood before her pale as death, his face quivering. He remembered now the kindly greeting Nicholas had given him when he met him on the Nevsky.

'My God! What have I done, Steve?'

'Don't touch me, don't touch me! Oh, how insufferable!'

He turned and went to the house. There he met her mother.

'What is it, Prince? I . . .' Seeing his face, she stopped. Suddenly he flushed with rage.

'You knew about this and were going to use me as a cover. If you were not both women . . .,' he cried, raising his enormous fist over her – then he turned and fled.

If the man who had been his fiancée's lover had been a private citizen he would have killed him. But it was his adored tsar.

The next day he took leave from his duties and resigned his commission. To avoid seeing anyone he said that he was ill, and went to the country.

He spent the summer on his estate putting his affairs in order. At the end of the summer he did not return to St Petersburg, but went to the monastery which he entered as a monk.

His mother wrote trying to dissuade him from such a decisive step. He replied that the call of God was more important than any other consideration, and that he felt this call. Only his sister, who was as proud and ambitious as her brother, understood him.

She understood that he had become a monk in order to be superior to those who wanted to demonstrate their superiority over him. And she understood him correctly. By becoming a monk he was showing his scorn for all those things which seemed so important to others and which had seemed so important to him when he was an officer; he was placing himself on a new eminence from which he could look down on the people he had previously envied. But he was swayed not by this feeling alone, as his sister thought. Within him there was another, truly religious feeling of which she knew nothing, a feeling which, mingled with his pride and desire for supremacy, now governed him. His disillusionment with Mary (his fiancée), whom he had supposed so angelic, and his sense of injury were so strong that he was brought to despair, and despair brought him – to what? To God and to the faith of his childhood which had remained intact within him.

3

ON the Feast of the Intercession Kasatsky entered the monastery.

The abbot was of gentle birth, he wrote scholarly works and was an elder – that is he belonged to that succession of monks which stemmed from Wallachia, monks who submit without murmur to a chosen preceptor. The abbot was a pupil of the famous elder Amvrosii, who had been the pupil of Makarii, the pupil of Paisii Velichkovsky. And to the abbot Kasatsky subjected himself as pupil.

In the monastery, enjoying the sense of his own superiority, Kasatsky took the same pleasure as elsewhere in attaining the highest perfection in both inward and outward things. Just as in his regiment he had been not merely an impeccable officer but one who did more than was necessary and set new standards of perfection, so too as a monk he strove to be perfect: constantly working, abstemious, meek, gentle, pure in thought as in deed, and obedient. This last quality (or attainment) in particular made life easier for him. Many of the demands made on him by living in a much visited monastery close to the capital he disliked and found corrupting, but all such feelings were dispelled by the obedient fulfilment of his duties. It was not his business to think, but to carry out his appointed task, which might be to keep vigil over the relics, to sing in the choir or to keep the accounts of the hospice. All possibility of doubt on any conceivable matter was removed by this obedience to his elder. It was only obedience that stopped him feeling oppressed by the length and monotony of the church services, by the triviality of the visitors, and by the negative features of the brethren; but all these things he not only joyfully endured, but found in them a source of consolation and support. 'I do not see the point of hearing the same prayers several times a day, but I know that it has to be done, and

knowing that it has to be done I take pleasure in the prayers.'
The elder told him that just as one needs material food to
sustain life, so, too, one needs spiritual food – praying in
church – to sustain the life of the spirit. Kasatsky believed this,
and indeed the church services for which he sometimes found
it hard to get up in the morning undoubtedly brought him
comfort and happiness. He was made happy by the consciousness of his own humility and of the absolute rightness of his
actions, all of which were determined by the elder. His concern
in life was not only to work for the fuller subjugation of his
own will and for greater humility; he wished also to attain all
the Christian virtues which seemed to him at first so easy to
attain. He gave all his property to the monastery and felt no
regret. Sloth was unknown to him. Demeaning himself before
lesser men was not only easy for him, but even a source of joy.
He even found it easy to overcome the sin of lust – both glut-
tony and concupiscence. The elder warned him particularly
against this sin, and Kasatsky rejoiced in the knowledge that he
was free from it.

Only the memory of his fiancée tormented him. It was not
just the memory, it was also the vivid picture he had of what
might have been. He kept thinking of one of the emperor's
favourites whom he knew. She had subsequently married and
become a fine wife and mother; her husband occupied an important position, had power, honour, and a good wife who
repented of her past.

In his better moments Kasatsky was not troubled by these
thoughts. At such times his recollections simply made him glad
that he was freed from these temptations. But there were other
times when that by which he now lived suddenly faded, and
though he never ceased to believe in that by which he lived, he
lost sight of it, was unable to summon it up within him, and he
was overwhelmed by his memories and – a terrible thing – by
remorse for his conversion.

His only salvation in this situation was obedience – work and

the whole day occupied in prayer. He said his prayers and performed his devotions as usual; he prayed even more than usual,
but he prayed in body alone and his spirit was not in it. This
state would last for a day, sometimes two, and then pass of
itself. But these one or two days were terrible. Kasatsky felt he
was in the power not of himself or of God but of some other
being. And all that he could do – and did – at such times was to
follow his elder's counsel: hold on, attempt nothing for the
present, and wait. In general, the whole of this time Kasatsky
lived not by his own will, but by the will of his elder, and he
felt a curious sense of tranquillity in this submission.

In this way Kasatsky spent seven years in the monastery
which he first entered. At the end of the third year he took his
vows and was ordained, adopting the monastic name of
Sergius. Taking his vows was inwardly an important event for
Sergius. He had always in the past felt much comfort and
spiritual uplift when he took communion, and now, when he
himself was the celebrant, the act of preparing the bread and
wine filled him with ecstasy and spiritual joy. But this feeling
in the course of time became gradually less intense, and once
when he was celebrating in the depressed mood that came on
him from time to time he sensed that this feeling, too, would
one day pass. And indeed it did lose its force, though the habit
remained.

By the seventh year of his life in the monastery Sergius was
generally bored. He had learnt all there was to learn and
achieved all there was to achieve, and there was nothing left to
do.

His apathy on the other hand grew steadily worse. During
this time he had learnt of his mother's death and Mary's
marriage. Both pieces of news he received with indifference.
All his attention and interest were focussed on his own inner
life.

In his fourth year as a monk the bishop showed him special
favour and the elder told Sergius that if an appointment to

some higher sphere were offered him he should not refuse it. At this the monastic ambition which Sergius in other monks had found so repellent was sparked in him. He was appointed to a monastery near the capital. He wished to refuse, but the elder ordered him to take the appointment. He accepted it, took leave of the elder and moved to the new monastery.

This move to a monastery near the capital was an important event in Sergius's life. There were many temptations of every kind and he devoted his entire strength to withstanding them.

In his previous monastery Sergius had been little troubled by the temptations of women, but here this temptation presented itself with terrifying force and even took specific form. A certain lady well known for her wayward conduct began making advances to Sergius. She spoke to him and asked if he would visit her. Sergius sternly refused, but was horrified at the distinctness of his desire. Such was his alarm that he wrote to the elder; and in addition, to keep himself in check he sent for his young novice and, overcoming his shame, confessed to him his weakness and begged him to follow him and make sure that he went nowhere except to the services and about his appointed tasks.

It was also a great trial to Sergius that the abbot of the monastery was a clever, worldly man making his career in the church, for whom he felt the deepest aversion. However he struggled against it, Sergius could not overcome this aversion. He made himself submit, but at the bottom of his heart he never ceased to condemn him. And in the end this evil feeling burst out.

It was in his second year at the monastery and it happened as follows. On the Feast of the Intercession the night service was conducted in the main church of the monastery. There were many visitors, and the abbot himself was the celebrant. Father Sergius was in his usual place, praying – that is, he was in that state of conflict which regularly came on him during services, especially in the main church, when he himself was not celebrating. This conflict came from the annoyance caused him by the visitors, the gentlemen and especially the ladies. He tried not to see them, to pay no attention to all that went on: the soldier who showed them to their places, pushing aside the ordinary people, the ladies pointing out the monks to each other – often himself and another monk who was known for his good looks. He tried to blinker himself, to see nothing but the shining candles by the icon-screen, the icons and the clergy conducting the service, to hear nothing but the words of the prayers as they were sung and spoken, and to have no other feeling but that sense of self-abandon in the consciousness of fulfilling an obligation, which he always experienced as he listened and anticipated the words of the prayers he had heard so many times before.

As he stood, bowing and crossing himself when necessary, in conflict with himself, one moment coldly censorious, the next deliberately suspending all thought and feeling, he was approached by the sacristan, Father Nicodemus (he was another great trial for Father Sergius, who could not avoid reproaching him for the way he flattered and toadied to the abbot). Father Nicodemus bowed, bending to the ground, and said that the abbot wished to see him in the sanctuary. Father Sergius straightened his robe, put on his monk's cap and carefully made his way through the throng.

'Lise, look there to the right, it's him,' he heard a woman's voice say [in French].*

'Where, where? He's not all that good-looking.'

He knew they were speaking of him. Hearing them, he repeated as he always did in moments of temptation: 'And lead us not into temptation,' then with head and eyes lowered he passed by the ambo, stepped round the precentors in their vestments who were crossing in front of the icon-screen, and

---

*French dialogue in Tolstoy's text has been translated. Indication of the use of French in the original is generally given, as here, by a note in square brackets. *Translator.*

went through the north door into the sanctuary. On entering
he bowed to the ground and crossed himself as usual before
the icon; he then raised his head and, without turning,
glanced from the corner of his eye at the abbot. He saw
him standing with another person wearing something that
glittered.

The abbot in his vestments was standing by the wall; his
short podgy hands were thrust from under the chasuble that
covered his portly body and stomach and he rubbed the gold
lace on it as he spoke, smiling, to an officer in the uniform of a
general of the imperial suite with royal ciphers and aiguillettes,
which Father Sergius noted at once with his practised military
eye. The general had been the commander of his own regiment. He evidently now held an important post and Father
Sergius saw at once that the abbot knew it and took pleasure
in it and that was why he was beaming all over his fat red face
with the receding hair. Father Sergius felt grieved and offended
and this feeling was increased when he discovered from the
abbot that he had been summoned for no other purpose than
to satisfy the curiosity of this general who had wanted to see, as
he put it, his 'former comrade in arms'.

'Very glad to see you have taken your vows,' said the
general, extending his hand. 'I hope you have not forgotten an
old comrade.'

The abbot's face, red amidst the whiteness of his hair,
smiling as if in approval of the general's words, the well-
groomed face of the general with its complacent smile, the
reek of wine on his breath and of cigars from the whiskers on
his cheeks were too much for Father Sergius. He bowed once
more to the abbot and said:

'Did your reverence wish to see me?'

He stopped. The whole expression of his face and posture
asked the question: Why?

The abbot said:

'Yes, I wanted you to meet the general.'

'Your reverence,' said Father Sergius, turning pale, his lips quivering, 'I abandoned the world in order to save myself from temptations. Why do you put temptations in my way here in God's house and at a time of prayer?'

'Go then, go!' said the abbot, angry and frowning.

The next day Father Sergius asked forgiveness of the abbot and the brethren for his pride, but after spending the night in prayer he also decided that he must leave this monastery. He wrote to his elder telling him this and begging to be allowed to return to the elder's monastery. He wrote that he was conscious of his weakness and of his inability to maintain the struggle against temptation on his own without the elder's help. And he repented of his sinful pride. By the next post a letter came from the elder in which he wrote that the cause of all the trouble was Sergius's pride. He explained to him that his outburst of anger came about because he had humbled himself by refusing religious honours not for the sake of God, but to satisfy his own pride, as if to say: 'See the sort of man I am: I want nothing.' That was why he had found the abbot's action intolerable – that *he* who had scorned everything for God should be displayed like a wild animal! 'If you scorned fame for God,' he wrote, 'you would have borne this. Worldly pride is still not extinguished in you. I have thought and prayed about you, Sergius my son, and this is what God has spoken to me concerning you: that you should live as before and submit. It has recently become known that the saintly hermit Hilarion has died in the hermitage. He lived there eighteen years. The abbot of Tambino asked if there is any brother who would like to live there, and just then your letter arrived. Go to Father Paisii in the monastery at Tambino. I will write to him. Ask if you may occupy Hilarion's cell. You cannot replace him, but you need solitude in which to subdue your pride. God bless you.'

Sergius did as the elder said. He showed his letter to the abbot and with his permission gave up his cell, left all his belongings to the monastery, and went to the hermitage at Tambino.

The prior there, who was of merchant stock and ran things extremely well, received Sergius simply and calmly; at first he gave him a lay brother, but then, at Sergius's request, left him to himself. The cell was a cave hollowed in the hill. There Hilarion was buried. His burial-place was in the rear chamber of the cave; in the front chamber there was a recess where Sergius could sleep on a straw mattress, a small table and a shelf with icons and books on it. By the outside door which could be locked there was another shelf on which was placed the food brought daily from the monastery by one of the monks.

And Father Sergius became a hermit.

4

AT Shrovetide in the sixth year of Sergius's life of seclusion a merry party of well-to-do men and women, after their pancakes and wine, set off on a *troika* ride. The party was made up of a couple of lawyers, a wealthy landowner, an officer and four women – the wives of the officer and the landowner, the landowner's unmarried sister, and an attractive divorcée, a wealthy eccentric whose escapades were a continual source of surprise and consternation in the town.

The weather was splendid and the road as smooth as a ballroom floor. When they had gone eight or nine miles from the town they stopped to consider whether they should go back or carry on.

'Well, where does this road lead?' asked Makovkina, the attractive divorcée.

'It goes to Tambino – that's another eight miles,' said one of the lawyers, who was making advances to Makovkina.

'Where does it go then?'

'It goes on to L—— by way of the monastery.'

'You mean the place where that Father Sergius lives?'

'That's it.'

'You mean Kasatsky? The handsome hermit?'

'Yes.'

'Mesdames! Gentlemen! Let's go and see Kasatsky. We can have a breather in Tambino and get a bite to eat there.'

'But we would never get back tonight.'

'That doesn't matter. We can spend the night at Kasatsky's.'

'We could do. The monastery has a guest-house which is very good. I stayed there when I was defending Makhin.'

'That's not for me. I'm going to spend the night at Kasatsky's.'

'That you'll never do, not even the great almighty you.'

'Won't I? Do you want to bet?'

'All right. You spend the night in Kasatsky's cell and I'll pay you what you like.'

'The winner decides.'

'Yes. And the same for you.'

'Very well. Let's go then.'

They gave the drivers some wine and themselves fetched a hamper containing pies, wine and bonbons. The ladies wrapped themselves up in their white dog-fur coats. The drivers had an argument about who should lead; one of them, a young fellow, turned half about in devil-may-care style, brandished his long whip and gave a shout, then with harness-bells jingling and sledge-runners screeching they were off.

The sledge slightly shook and swayed; the trace-horse galloped evenly and merrily along, its tightly lashed tail lifting over the brass-studded breeching; the level, slippery road sped away behind; the driver drove in dashing style, giving an occasional flick of the reins. One of the lawyers and the officer opposite him bantered with the lady sitting by Makovkina. Makovkina herself sat still, wrapped tight in her fur coat. She was thinking: It's the same revolting thing all the time: shiny red faces smelling of wine and tobacco, saying the same thing, thinking the same thing, and all the time for the same revolting purpose. And they are all quite happy and convinced that that is the way it must be, and they can go on living like that until they die. But I can't. I'm tired of it all. I want something that would shatter all this, turn it upside down. Perhaps like those people – in Saratov, wasn't it – who went for a drive and got frozen to death. What would our lot do? How would they react? Despicably, I suppose. Everyone for himself. Yes, and I would be as bad as the rest. At least I am good-looking, though. They know it too. But what about this monk? Does he really no longer have any idea of these things? Of course he does. It's the one thing they do understand. Like that cadet last autumn, and what a fool he was . . .

'Ivan Nikolaich,' she said.

'Yes, what can I do for you?'

'How old is he?'

'Who?'

'Kasatsky, of course.'

'He's in his forties, I think.'

'And does he receive everybody?'

'Yes, he does, though not all the time.'

'Cover my legs for me. Not like that, clumsy! A bit more, more – that's right. But you don't have to squeeze them.'

And so they came to the forest where Kasatsky's cell was.

Makovkina got out and told the others to drive on. They tried to talk her out of it, but she became cross and insisted on their going. The sledge moved on and she in her white dog-fur coat set off along the track. The lawyer got out and stayed to watch.

5

IT was the sixth year of Father Sergius's life as a hermit. He was forty-nine. It was a hard life, though the hardship lay not in the fasting and prayer (these were no hardship), but in an inner conflict which he had never expected. There were two causes of this conflict: doubt and carnal desire. And these two adversaries always raised their heads together. He saw them as two different adversaries, but in fact they were one. When he banished doubt he also banished desire. But he thought of them as two separate devils and struggled separately against them.

'Oh, God, why dost thou not give me faith?' he thought. 'Lust is one thing. St Antony struggled against it, and others, too. But they had faith, and there are times – minutes, hours, days – when I have none. What is the point of the whole world and its delights, if it is sinful and has to be renounced? Why didst thou create temptations to sin? Sin? But is it not sinful fancy for me to leave the pleasures of the world and prepare for myself a reward in a place where there may after all be nothing?' At his words he was seized with horror and self-loathing, and castigated himself: 'Vile creature – you, who would be a saint!' And he knelt to pray. But no sooner had he begun than he pictured himself vividly as he had been in the monastery and how grand he had looked in his monk's cap and robe. And he shook his head. 'No, this is no good. It is a deception. But it is others I deceive, not myself or God. There is nothing grand about me. I am just pitiful and absurd.' He drew back the sides of his cassock, looked at his pathetic legs clad in underdrawers, and smiled.

He let the cassock fall back into place and began to say his prayers, crossing himself and bowing. 'And shall this bed be unto me a coffin?' he prayed. And a devil seemed to whisper: 'A solitary bed is a coffin, anyway. It's all a lie.' And in his mind he saw the shoulders of the widow with whom he had lived. He shook himself and went on with his prayers. When he had finished the set prayers, he took the Gospels, opened them and lighted on a passage which he often repeated and which he knew by heart: 'Lord, I believe: help thou mine unbelief.' He suppressed all his rising doubts. As one stands an unstable object, so he propped his faith on its tottering leg and backed carefully away in order not to knock it and cause it to collapse. Once more the blinkers were on, and he was calm again. He repeated his childhood prayer: 'Lord, take me, take me,' and he felt not only easy in mind, but joyfully content. He crossed himself and lay down on the narrow bench on his thin mattress, his summer cassock under his head. He fell asleep. Sleeping lightly, he fancied he heard harness-bells. He did not know if it was real or a dream. But then he was woken from his sleep by a knocking at the door. He got up, thinking he must be mistaken. But the knocking came again. Yes, it was a knock near by, at his door, and there was a woman's voice.

'Lord! Is it then true what I read in the Saints that the devil takes on woman's form? ... Yes, it is a woman's voice. A tender, shy, sweet voice. Pshah!' He spat. 'No, it is just my imagination,' he said and walking over to the corner where there was a small lectern, he knelt down with that accustomed regular movement which was in itself a comfort and pleasure to him. He bent forward, his hair falling over his face, and pressed his now sparsely covered forehead on the cold, damp mat. (There was a draught through the floor.)

... he read the psalm which old Father Pimen had told him gave help against manifestations of the devil. Effortlessly he raised his light, wasted body on his powerful, restless legs, and was going to go on reading, but instead of reading he involuntarily strained his ears to see if he could hear anything. He wanted to hear. It was perfectly still. Water went on dripping from the roof into the butt at the corner. There was a fine drizzling mist outside eating away the snow. It was very, very still. Then suddenly by the window there was a rustling and the distinct sound of a voice – a tender, shy voice which could only belong to an attractive woman. It was saying:

'Let me in. For the Lord's sake . . .'

Every drop of blood seemed to rush to his heart and stop. He could not breathe. 'Let God arise; and let his enemies be scattered . . .'

'I'm no devil . . .' he could hear the lips smiling as they spoke. 'I'm no devil. I'm just a sinful woman who has gone astray – not metaphorically, literally.' (She laughed.) 'I'm frozen through and want to shelter . . .'

He put his face to the pane. The glass shone from the reflection of the icon-lamp. He put his hands to the sides of his face and peered out. He saw mist and drizzle, a tree. Yes, there to the right, yes, she was there. A woman in a white long-haired fur coat and hat, with a very sweet, kind, frightened face: she was there two inches from his own face, leaning towards him. Their eyes met and there was a moment of recognition. Not that they had ever seen each other, for they had never met, but in the look that passed between them they (he in particular) felt that they knew one another, understood one another. After this look all doubt was dispelled: this was no devil, but a woman, simple, kind, sweet and shy.

'Who are you? What do you want?' he asked.

'Come on, open up,' she said, skittishly peremptory. 'I'm frozen stiff. I've lost my way, I tell you.'

'But I am a monk, a hermit.'

'Well, open up then. Or do you want me to freeze to death on your doorstep while you go on praying?'

'But what will you . . .'

'I shan't eat you. For God's sake, let me in. I'm chilled to the bone.'

She was beginning to feel scared herself, and there was a catch in her voice as she spoke.

He stepped back from the window and looked at the icon of Christ in his crown of thorns. 'Help me, oh Lord. Help me, oh Lord,' he said, crossing himself and bowing to the ground. Then he went to the door leading into the porch and opened it. In the porch he felt for the latch and began unfastening it. He heard footsteps outside as she walked from the window round to the door. There was a sudden cry of 'Ah!' and he realized that she had stepped into the puddle that had formed outside the door. His hands trembled and he was quite unable to lift the latch against the pressure of the door.

'What are you up to? Let me in. I'm soaked through and absolutely frozen. There are you worrying about saving your soul while I freeze to death.'

He pulled the door towards him, lifted the latch and without thinking jerked the door outwards so that it bumped against her.

'I beg your pardon,' he said, suddenly slipping back into his old accustomed way of addressing a lady.

Hearing his apology, she smiled. 'He's not so frightening after all,' she thought.

'Oh, it's all right,' she said, stepping past him. 'It's for you to pardon me. I would never have dreamt of it if there had not been a special reason.'

'Please come in,' he said, allowing her to pass. He was struck by the powerful scent of fine perfume, something not experienced by him for a long time. She went through the porch into the inner room. He closed the outer door without replacing the latch, crossed the porch and went inside.

'Lord Jesus Christ, Son of God, have mercy upon me, a sinner, have mercy upon me, a sinner,' he prayed incessantly, not just inwardly but outwardly, too, involuntarily shaping his lips to the words.

'What can I do for you?' he said.

With water dripping off her on to the floor she stood in the middle of the room. There was laughter in her eyes.

'Pardon me for disturbing your seclusion, but you see the fix I am in. It was all because we went for a drive out of town and I bet that I could walk back on my own from Vorobevka. But then I lost my way and if I hadn't come across your cell . . .' she lied. But she was so disconcerted by his face that she could not go on. She had expected him to be quite different. He was not as handsome as she had imagined him, but she thought him a fine-looking man. His curling grey-streaked hair and beard, his thin straight nose, and his eyes which burned like coals when he looked at you straight made a deep impression on her. He saw that she was lying.

'Yes, well . . .' he said, looking at her and again lowering his eyes. 'I shall go in here and you can make yourself at home.'

Taking down the lamp, he lit a candle, bowed low to her and went into the tiny room behind the partition. She heard him moving things about. 'Probably barricading himself in,' she thought, smiling. She then threw off her white dog-fur cloak and began taking off her hat, which was caught in her hair, and the knitted scarf she wore underneath it. When she stood at the window she had not been soaked at all and had only said she was as a pretext to make Kasatsky let her in. But she had stepped in the puddle by the door and the water had gone over her left ankle, filling her bootee and overshoe. She sat down on his bed – a mere board with a rug over it – and began taking off her shoes. She thought the tiny cell charming. The narrow inner room, some eight feet by ten, was absolutely spotless. There was nothing in it but the bed on which she sat, a shelf over it containing books, a small lectern in the corner, and nails by the door with a top-coat and cassock, above the lectern an icon of Christ in his crown of thorns and an icon-lamp. There was a curious smell of oil, sweat and earth. She liked it all, even the smell.

She was worried about her wet feet, particularly the left one, and she hurried to take off her shoes, smiling all the time, pleased not so much at having achieved her aim as at seeing how she had disturbed this charming, striking, strange and attractive man. 'He didn't respond, well that's no great matter,' she told herself.

'Father Sergius,' she called. 'Father Sergius, that's your name, isn't it?'

'What do you want?' came his quiet voice.

'You will forgive me, won't you, for disturbing your solitude? There really was nothing else I could do. I would have been ill and I can't be sure that I'm not as it is. I'm all wet and my feet are like ice.'

'I'm sorry,' said the quiet voice, 'but there is nothing I can do.'

'I wouldn't disturb you for the world. I shall just stay till it's light.'

He did not reply. She heard him whispering something – he was obviously praying.

'You won't be coming in here?' she asked, smiling. 'I ought to take my things off to dry out.'

He did not reply and went on praying in even tones on the other side of the partition.

'He is a man all right,' she thought, struggling to pull off her squelching overshoe. She tugged at it, but it would not come off and she thought how funny it was. She laughed quietly but, aware that he could hear her and that her laughter would affect him in the way she wished, she laughed more loudly, and this gay, natural, good-natured laughter did indeed affect him, and precisely in the way she wished.

'Yes, you could fall in love with a man like him. Those eyes. And that straightforward, noble and – pray as he will – that passionate face!' she thought. 'It's no good pretending to us women. As soon as he put his face to the window and saw me, he knew, he realized. There was a glint in his eyes, then down came the shutters again. He was in love with me, wanted me. Yes, wanted me,' she said, at last succeeding in removing her overshoe and bootee, and now trying to take off her long gartered stockings. In order to get them off she had to lift her skirts. She had a qualm of conscience and said: 'Don't come in.' But there was no answer from behind the partition. The steady murmuring continued and there were also sounds of movement. 'He will be bowing to the ground,' she thought, 'but bowing won't help him. He is thinking about me, just as I am about him. He has got the same feeling as he thinks about these legs,' she said, as she pulled off the wet stockings, treading her bare feet on the bed and drawing them up beneath her. She sat for a moment like that, hugging her knees and gazing pensively into space. 'This remote and quiet place, and no one would ever know . . .'

She got up, took her stockings to the stove and hung them over the damper. It was an unusual kind of damper: she turned it, then stepping lightly on her bare feet went back and again sat with her feet up on the bed. Behind the partition all was quiet. She looked at the tiny watch hanging from her neck. It was two o'clock. They should be here about three, she thought. There was only an hour to go.

'Am I just to sit here on my own then? Nonsense!' she thought. 'I'm not going to do that. I'll call him.'

'Father Sergius, Father Sergius! Sergei Dmitrievich! Prince Kasatsky!'

There was no sound through the door.

'Really, it's too bad of you. I wouldn't call you if I didn't need something. I'm ill. I don't know what it is,' she said in a suffering voice. 'Ah! Ah!' she groaned, falling on to the bed. And oddly enough, she did feel genuinely weak and faint, full of aches and pains and seized with feverish shivering.

'Listen. You must help me. I don't know what it is. Oh, oh!' She unhooked her dress, baring her breast, and threw out her arms which were uncovered to the elbow. 'Oh, oh!'

All this time he stood praying in the store-room. He had finished the evening prayers and was now standing motionless, his eyes fixed on the end of his nose as he prayed mentally, repeating in spirit: 'Lord Jesus Christ, Son of God, have mercy on me.'

But he heard everything. He heard the rustle of silk as she took off her clothes, the tread of her bare feet across the floor; he heard her as she rubbed her feet with her hand. He felt his own weakness and how close he was to perdition; and for that reason went on praying without cease. He felt rather like the hero in the fairy-tale must have felt when he had to walk on and never look round. In the same way Sergius heard and sensed danger and disaster above him and all around and the only way he could escape was by not for a moment turning to look at it. But suddenly the desire to look overwhelmed him. Just at that moment she said:

'Look, you're being inhuman. I could die.'

All right, he thought, I'll go to her. But I will do as that holy father who laid one hand on the harlot and put the other in the fire. I have no fire though. He looked around. The lamp. He put his finger over the flame and knit his brows in readiness to withstand the pain. For some time he seemed not to feel it, but suddenly, before he could decide whether or not it hurt and how much, he winced and pulled away his hand, shaking it. 'No, I can't do it.'

'For God's sake come! I'm dying. Oh!'

Am I then lost? No, I am not.

'I'll come in a moment,' he said. Then he opened the door and without looking at her walked past and went through the door into the porch where he chopped his firewood. There he felt for the chopping-block and for the axe which stood against the wall.

'Just a moment,' he said, and taking the axe in his right hand, he laid his left forefinger on the block and with a swinging blow of the axe struck it below the second joint. More lightly than a piece of wood of its thickness the finger flew off, turned and with a thud dropped first on the edge of the block, then to the floor.

He heard the sound before he was aware of any pain. But before he could be surprised that it did not hurt he felt a fiery pain and the warm flow of blood. He quickly pulled the hem of his cassock round the stump of his finger and pressing it to his thigh went back through the door. He stopped before the woman with eyes lowered.

Quietly he asked: 'What is it you want?'

She saw the pallor of his face and his quivering left cheek, and was suddenly ashamed. She leapt to her feet, snatched up her fur coat and wrapped it round her.

'Oh yes, I felt ill ... It's a chill ... I ... Father Sergius ... I ...'

He raised his eyes, which shone with tranquil joy, and looked at her.

'My dear sister,' he said, 'why did you wish to destroy your immortal soul? Temptations must come into the world, but woe betide that person by whom temptation comes ... Pray that God may forgive you.'

She listened, looking at him. Then suddenly she heard a dripping sound. She looked and saw blood running from his hand down his cassock.

'What have you done to your hand?' She remembered the noise she had heard and, seizing the icon lamp, ran into the porch. She saw the bloodstained finger on the floor. She came back, paler than he, and was going to speak, but he quietly went into the store-room and fastened the door.

'Forgive me,' she said. 'How can I redeem my sin?'

'Go away.'

'Let me bandage your hand.'

'Go away from here.'

Without speaking she hurriedly dressed. When she was ready with her fur coat on she sat and waited. There was a jingle of bells outside.

'Father Sergius, forgive me!'

'Go. God will forgive.'

'Father Sergius, I'll lead a different life. Don't abandon me.'

'Go.'

'Forgive me. Give me your blessing.'

'In the name of the Father, Son, and Holy Ghost,' came the words from behind the partition. 'Go.'

She went sobbing from the cell. The lawyer was coming towards her.

'Well, I've lost and that's that. Where will you sit?'

'It doesn't matter.'

She got into the sledge and never spoke the whole way home.

A year later she took her first vows as a nun and in the nunnery lived strictly under the direction of the hermit Arsenii, who wrote to her from time to time.

6

FATHER SERGIUS spent seven more years as a hermit. At first he accepted many of the things people brought him – tea, sugar, white bread, milk, clothing and firewood. But as time went on he regulated his life with increasing strictness and in the end took nothing for himself except some black bread once a week. Everything else that he was brought he distributed to the poor who visited him.

Father Sergius spent all his time in his cell praying or talking to his visitors, who came in ever greater numbers. He only left his cell when he went – two or three times a year – to church and when he needed to fetch water or firewood.

It was after he had lived five years in this way that the Makovkina episode took place – the nocturnal visit, the change which then came over her, her entry into the nunnery, all of which soon became common knowledge. After this Father Sergius's renown began to grow. More and more visitors arrived, monks came and settled round his cell, and a church and a guest-house were built. Father Sergius's fame – with, as always, exaggerated accounts of his achievements – spread further and further afield; people thronged to him from distant parts and brought the sick to him, declaring that he would cure them.

The first cure he worked was towards the end of the seventh year of his life as a hermit. A fourteen-year-old boy had been brought to Father Sergius by his mother, who asked him to lay his hands on him. It had never entered Father Sergius's head that he might be able to cure the sick; such an idea would have seemed to him a great sin of pride. But the boy's mother kept pleading with him; she fell at his feet and asked why, if he healed others, he would not help her son, and she begged him in the name of Christ to do so. Father Sergius told her that only God heals, but she replied that all she asked was that he should lay his hands on the boy and say a prayer. Father Sergius refused and went back to his cell. But the next day (it was autumn and the nights already cold) when he came out of his cell to fetch water, he again saw the mother and her son, a pale, wasted boy of fourteen, and heard the same entreaties. And he recalled the parable of the unjust judge and though before he had had no doubts about the need to refuse he was now less certain. With this doubt in his mind he knelt and prayed until some resolution came to him. The answer that came was that he must do what the woman wanted, that her faith might save her son; if that happened, he, Father Sergius, would be no more than the insignificant instrument chosen by God.

And Father Sergius went out and did as she wished: he laid his hand on the boy's head and prayed.

The mother and son left. A month later the boy recovered and the fame of the sacred healing powers of Sergius the Elder (as they now called him) spread through the whole district. After this never a week went by without sick people coming on foot or by conveyance to visit Father Sergius. And not having refused some, he could not refuse others and he laid his hand on them and prayed, and many were healed, and Father Sergius's fame spread further and further.

Thus he passed nine years in the monastery and thirteen as a hermit. Father Sergius now looked like an elder: his beard was long and white, but his hair, though sparse, was still black and curling.

7

FOR some weeks past Father Sergius had been preoccupied with the nagging doubt as to whether he had been right to accept the situation which had not so much arisen as been forced on him by the archimandrite and the abbot. It had started with the recovery of the fourteen-year-old boy. Since then every month, week, and day Sergius had felt that his inner life was being destroyed and supplanted by an outward life. It was like being turned inside out.

Sergius saw that he was a means of attracting visitors and donations to the monastery and that consequently the monastery authorities were ordering the pattern of his life so as to take full advantage of him. For instance, he was no longer allowed any opportunity to work. His every need was provided for and all that was asked of him was that he should not fail to give his blessing to the visitors who came to see him. For his convenience they arranged days when he might receive visitors. They provided a room for receiving men visitors and a place where he could give his blessing to others who came – it was enclosed by a rail to protect him from being knocked over by the rush of his women visitors. If he was told that these people needed him, that it would be contrary to Christ's law of love to deny these people their wish to see him, and that it would be cruel to remove himself from them, he could only agree. But as he surrendered himself to this way of living, so he felt his inner life turn outwards and the fount of living water in him fail, and he felt that what he did was more and more done for people and not for God.

In all he did – exhorting people or simply blessing them, praying for the sick, advising people on the way to live, receiving thanks from those he had aided by healing (as they claimed) or by instruction – he could not help taking pleasure and being concerned about the results of his actions and the influence they had on people. He thought of himself as a burning light, and the more he thought this the more he felt the divine light of truth inside him fade and die. How much is what I do done for God, how much for people? – this was the question which tormented him all the time and which he not so much could not as would not answer to himself. In the depths of his heart he felt that the devil had turned all his service for God into service for people. He felt this because whereas before it had distressed him to be forced from his seclusion, it was now seclusion that he found distressing. His visitors were a burden to him, but in his heart of hearts he was pleased that they came and was pleased to be surrounded by their praises.

There was even a time when he decided to go away and hide. He even worked out how he would do it. He provided himself with peasant clothes – a smock, cloth leggings, a caftan and cap, explaining that he needed them to give to those who came to him for help. And he kept these clothes in his cell, planning one day to put them on, cut his hair and go away. He would first take a train, then after 200 miles get off and go about the villages. He asked an old pilgrim, a former soldier, how he travelled and how readily people gave alms and shelter. The old soldier explained, telling him the best places to get alms and shelter, and Father Sergius proposed to follow his example. One night he even got dressed, intending to leave, but he did not know which was more right: to stay or to run away. He could not decide, but his indecision passed – he again settled down and succumbed to the devil, and his peasant clothing served merely to remind him of what he had thought and felt.

Every day more and more people came to him, and he was left with less and less time for spiritual fortification and prayer. He had lucid moments when he likened himself to a place where once had been a spring. 'There was a weak spring of living water which poured from me and through me. That was the true life when "she" had tempted him (he always remembered with rapture that night and "she", who was now the Reverend Mother Agniya). She had tasted of that pure water, but since then, before ever any water can gather people come to drink it, jostling and pushing each other. And the spring has been trampled in and nothing is left but mud.' Thus he thought in his rare moments of lucidity, but his usual state was one of weariness and a pleasant sense of self-righteousness for the weariness he felt.

It was spring. On the eve of the Feast of Mid-Pentecost Father Sergius was celebrating the night service in his own church which was built in a cave. There were as many people as the church would hold – about twenty. They were all wealthy people – gentry or merchants. Father Sergius allowed anyone to come, but the choice of congregation was made by the monk appointed to assist him and by the attendant who was sent to his cell each day from the monastery. A throng of people, eighty or so pilgrims (mostly peasant women), crowded outside, waiting for his blessing when he came out. Father Sergius celebrated the office and when he came out to process to the tomb of his predecessor, singing *Glory to God*, he staggered and would have fallen had he not been supported by a merchant standing behind him and by the monk acting as deacon who was behind the merchant.

There was a chorus of women's voices: 'What is it? Master! Father Sergius! Dear soul! Lord almighty! He's gone white as a sheet.'

But Father Sergius at once recovered and, though very pale, pushed aside the merchant and the deacon and went on with the singing. Father Serapion, the deacon, and the sub-deacons, as well as Sofiya Ivanovna (a lady who resided permanently near Father Sergius's cell and tended to his needs), all begged him to bring the service to an end.

'I'm all right. It's nothing,' said Father Sergius with a smile that was barely perceptible through his whiskers. 'Don't interrupt the service.'

Yes, he thought, this is the way of the saints. And immediately he heard behind him the voices of Sofiya Ivanovna and the merchant who had supported him: 'He's a saint, an angel of God!' Not heeding their entreaties, he went on with the service.

Everyone crowded back through the narrow passages into the tiny church and there he completed the service, shortening it only slightly.

When the service was over Father Sergius blessed those present and went out to the bench that stood beneath the elm tree by the entrance to the cave. He felt the need of rest and fresh air, but as soon as he went outside a crowd of people rushed forward wanting his blessing and asking his advice and help. Among them were women pilgrims who spent their lives visiting holy places and elders and being moved to ecstasy by every sacred place and elder that they saw. Father Sergius knew well this common type of pilgrim, the most irreligious, unfeeling and conventional of all. There were men, too, mostly discharged soldiers, old men who had lost the habit of a settled life; living in poverty, drunkards for the most part, they drifted from monastery to monastery just to keep themselves fed. And there were common peasants, men and women, who came with their selfish requests for cures and for help in deciding some purely practical question – marrying off a daughter, renting a store, buying land or getting absolution for a child accidentally smothered or begotten out of wedlock.

For Father Sergius it was all long familiar and of no interest. He knew that he would learn nothing from these people, that they would stir in him no religious feeling, but he liked to see them: they were people to whom he, his blessing and his words were precious and necessary, so although seeing them was irksome, he found it also gratifying. Father Serapion wanted to tell them that he was tired and send them away, but Father Sergius, recalling the words of the Gospel 'Forbid them (the little children) not to come unto me' and feeling touched at the thought of his own goodness, said they should be allowed to stay.

He got up, went over to the crowded rail and began to bless them and answer their questions. Even he was moved by the faintness of his voice. But, despite his wishes, he could not receive them all: once again everything went black, he staggered and grasped the rail. Once again he felt a congestion in his head. He turned pale, then suddenly flushed.

'We must wait until tomorrow,' he said. 'I cannot go on today.' He gave them his blessing and moved towards the bench. Again he was supported by the merchant who, taking his arm, helped him to the seat.

There were cries from the crowd: 'Father! Father! Good master! Don't leave us. We are lost without you.'

The merchant seated Father Sergius on the bench beneath the elm, then, acting in the role of policeman, took vigorous steps to get rid of the crowd. True, he spoke quietly so that Father Sergius could not hear, but his tone was firm and sharp:

'Clear off now, clear off. He's given you his blessing – what more do you want? Hop it now or you'll catch it from me. Go on, off! You there, granny, you in the black socks, get away! Where do you think you're going? You heard – it's all finished. There's another day tomorrow, but that's it for to-day.'

'Master, I only want to peep at his dear face,' said the crone.

'I'll give you a peep! Where do you think you're going?'

Father Sergius saw that the merchant was being rather hard and in his faint voice told the lay brother to stop him driving the people away. Father Sergius knew he would do so anyway and he was anxious to be left alone to rest, but he sent the lay brother with the message in order to make a good impression.

'It's all right,' replied the merchant. 'I'm not chasing them, I'm just appealing to them. I mean, they'll cheerfully do a chap to death. They've no pity, these people. They only ever think of themselves. No, you can't come through, I've told you! Go away. Tomorrow.'

And the merchant dispatched them all.

The merchant's zeal stemmed partly from his fondness for order and for chivvying and telling people what to do, but it was mainly prompted by the fact that he had need of Father Sergius. He was a widower with an only daughter, a sickly girl who was still single, and he had brought her a thousand miles to be healed by Father Sergius. In the two years she had been ill he had taken her to various places for treatment. First he took her to the clinic in the provincial capital (which had a university), but to no effect; then he took her to a peasant healer in Samara province, which made her slightly better; after that, at great expense, he took her to a Moscow doctor, but again to no effect. He had been told that Father Sergius performed cures and had now brought her to him. So after getting rid of all the people, the merchant went up to Father Sergius and came straight to the point: falling on his knees he said in a loud voice:

'Holy father, have mercy on my ailing child. Deliver her from the pain of her infirmity. I make bold to supplicate at thy holy feet.'

And he placed one hand cupped on the other. All this he did and said as if it was something clearly and firmly established by law and custom, as if there was no other right and proper way to ask for his daughter to be cured. He acted with such assurance that Father Sergius also felt it was right that he should act and speak in this particular way. However, he told him to rise and explain what was the matter. The merchant told him that his daughter, a single girl of twenty-two, had fallen ill two years before, following the sudden death of her mother. It came on 'just like that', as he put it, and she had never been the same since. So now he had brought her a thousand miles and she was waiting in the guest-house until Father Sergius sent for her. She did not go anywhere in the daytime because she was afraid of the light and could only come out after sunset.

'Is she very weak?' asked Father Sergius.

'No, she's not specially weak. She's a well-made girl. It's just the neurastheny, like the doctor said. Father Sergius, if you told me I could bring her today, I would have her here straight away. Holy father, bring life to a father's heart; restore his offspring – by your prayers save his ailing child!'

And the merchant again fell on his knees and remained motionless, his head turned to one side above his two cupped hands. Again Father Sergius told him to rise. He reflected on the hardships of his work and how he nonetheless humbly carried on; he gave a deep sigh, then after a few seconds' pause said:

'Very well. Bring her this evening. I will pray for her, but I am tired now.' He closed his eyes. 'I will send for you later.'

The merchant withdrew, tiptoeing over the sand (which only made his boots squeak louder), and Father Sergius remained alone.

Father Sergius's whole life was taken up with services and visitors, but this had been a particularly trying day. In the morning an important dignitary had called and talked to him for a long time; after that there was a lady and her son. The son was a young university teacher, an atheist; his mother, who was a fervent believer and devoted to Father Sergius, had brought him along and persuaded Father Sergius to have a talk with him. It had been very hard going. The young man, evidently not wishing to argue with a monk, had condescendingly agreed with everything he said, but Father Sergius could tell that the young man did not believe and despite that was perfectly happy, untroubled and at ease. Father Sergius looked back on their conversation with displeasure.

'Will you have something to eat, master?' enquired the lay brother.

'Yes, you can bring me something.'

The lay brother disappeared into the tiny cell, which stood ten yards from the entrance to the cave, and Father Sergius was left on his own.

The time had long passed when Father Sergius lived alone, fending for himself and living on nothing but communion loaves and bread. It had long been demonstrated to him that he had no right to neglect his health, and he was now given lenten food of the more nourishing kinds. He did not eat much, but he ate a great deal more than previously and often took pleasure in his food, unlike earlier when he had eaten with loathing in the consciousness of sin. So it was on this occasion: he ate some millet porridge, and had a cup of tea and half a white loaf.

The lay brother went away and he was left alone on the bench beneath the elm.

It was a glorious May evening. The birches, aspens, elms, cherry-trees, and oaks had just come into leaf. The cherry-bushes behind the elm were in full blossom, their petals still unshed. Nightingales, one near by and two or three more in the bushes by the river, trilled and warbled. From the river came the distant sound of workmen singing, evidently on their way home from work. The sun had sunk behind the wood and its broken rays burst patchily through the greenery. On this side everything was light green, on the other side, where the elm was, it was dark. There were beetles in the air, flying into things and dropping.

After supper Father Sergius began his mental prayers: 'Lord

Jesus Christ, Son of God, have mercy upon us.' He then began reading the psalm, but while he was doing so a sparrow suddenly flew down from one of the bushes on to the ground. It came up to him, chirping and hopping, but then, frightened by something, it flew away. He said the prayer in which he spoke of the renunciation of the world and hastened to finish it so that he could send for the merchant and his sick daughter. She interested him. She interested him because she was a diversion, a new face, and because she and her father regarded him as a holy man, a person whose prayers were answered. He repudiated such ideas, but at the bottom of his heart he too saw himself in that way.

He often wondered how he, Stepan Kasatsky, had come to be such an extraordinary holy man, indeed a miracle-worker; but that he was these things he never had any doubt: he could not fail to believe in miracles which he himself had witnessed, from the sickly boy up to the old woman who through his prayers had recently had her sight restored.

Strange though it was, it was fact. And so it was that the merchant's daughter interested him – because she was someone new, because she had faith in him, and because she presented him with an opportunity to give further proof of his powers of healing and to bolster his reputation. 'They come from hundreds of miles away,' he thought. 'I am written about in the papers, the emperor knows of me, and so do people in Europe, in unbelieving Europe.' And he felt suddenly ashamed at his vanity and again he prayed to God: 'Lord, heavenly king, comforter, the spirit of truth, come unto us and dwell in us, and cleanse us from all impurity, and save, good Lord, our souls. Cleanse me from the corruption of worldly fame by which I am afflicted,' he repeated. And he remembered, too, how many times he had prayed in this way and how fruitless these prayers had been: his prayers performed miracles for others, but for himself he could not obtain God's release from this trivial passion.

He recalled his prayers when he first lived as a hermit, when he prayed to be given purity, humility, and love, and how it had seemed then that God had heeded his prayers; he had been pure and had cut off his finger – and he raised the wrinkled stump and kissed it. It seemed to him that then, when he was always loathing himself for his sinfulness, he had been humble; and as he recalled the tender joy he had felt at that time on meeting a drunken old soldier who came to him and asked for money, and on meeting 'her', it seemed that he had been capable of love too. But now? He asked himself: did he love anyone? did he care for Sofiya Ivanovna or Father Serapion? did he have any feeling of love for those people who had visited him today? for the learned youth he had talked to so didactically, concerned only with showing how clever he was and how abreast of the times in education? He liked and needed their love, but for them he felt none. He had now neither love, humility, nor purity.

He had been pleased to discover that the merchant's daughter was twenty-two, and was interested to know if she was good-looking. When he asked if she was weak, he had actually wanted to know whether or not she was attractive as a woman.

'Have I sunk so low?' he thought. 'Lord, help me and raise me up, oh Lord, my God.' He put his hands together and prayed. The nightingales warbled. A beetle flew into him and crawled across the back of his head. He brushed it off. 'But does He exist? I might be knocking at a house locked on the outside . . . The lock is on the door and I might see it. The lock is the nightingales, the beetles, nature. Perhaps that young man is right.' He began praying aloud; he prayed a long time, until these thoughts had vanished and once again he was calm and assured. He rang the bell, and when the lay brother came, told him that the merchant and his daughter might be fetched.

The merchant arrived with his daughter on his arm. He brought her into the cell and left straight away.

The daughter was a fair-haired girl, extremely white and pale and plump, extremely short, with the frightened face of a child and the full rounded body of a woman. Father Sergius remained on the bench at the entrance. The girl stopped as she passed him and he blessed her. He was horrified at the way he studied her body. She went on into the cell and he felt as if he had been stung. He could tell by her face that she was sensuous and feeble-minded. He got up and went inside. She sat on the stool, waiting for him.

When he came in she stood up.

'I want to go to Daddy,' she said.

'Don't be afraid,' he said. 'Where is the pain?'

'It's all over,' she said, and a smile suddenly lit her face.

'You will get well,' he said. 'Pray.'

'What's the point of praying? I have prayed and it doesn't do any good.' She was still smiling. 'But you say a prayer and lay your hands on me. I've dreamt about you.'

'What was your dream?'

'I dreamt that you put your hand on my heart like this.' She took his hand and pressed it to her breast. 'Just here.'

He gave her his right hand.

'What is your name?' he asked, trembling all over and feeling that he was vanquished, incapable now of controlling his lust.

'Mary. Why?'

She took his hand and kissed it, then she put her arm round his waist and hugged him.

'What are you doing?' he said. 'Mary. You are a devil.'

'Well, what does it matter?'

And holding him in her arms she sat down with him on his bed.

At daybreak he went out on to the steps.

'Did all this really happen? Her father will come. She will tell him. She is a devil. And what shall I do? There it is, the axe

I used to chop off my finger.' He seized it and turned to go into the cell.

He was met by the lay brother.

'Do you want me to chop some wood? Let me have the axe, then.'

He gave him the axe and went into the cell. She lay there asleep. He looked at her in horror. He went through, got down his peasant's clothes and put them on. He took some scissors and cut his hair, then set off down the path to the river where he had not been for four years.

A road went along the river. He took this road and walked until dinner-time, when he turned off into a rye-field and lay down. Towards evening he came to a village by the river. He did not go into the village but kept along the steep bank of the river.

It was early morning, half an hour or so before sunrise. Everything was grey and gloomy and there was a cold dawn wind blowing from the west. 'Yes, I must make an end of it. God does not exist. How shall I do it? Throw myself into the river? I can swim, so I would not drown. Hang myself? Yes, there is my girdle, just put it over a branch.' It seemed so simple and so close that he was horrified. As usual in moments of despair he wanted to pray. But there was no one to pray to. God did not exist. He lay with his head propped on one elbow. Suddenly such a desire to sleep overcame him that his arm could no longer support his head; he straightened his arm, laid his head on it and at once fell asleep. But he slept only for a moment and immediately woke again and lay half-dreaming, half-reminiscing.

He dreamt of himself when he was little more than a child at his mother's house in the country. A carriage drove up and out of it got his uncle Nikolai with his enormous black spade beard. He had with him a little wispy girl – Pasha; she had large, gentle eyes and a pathetic, timid face. They were all boys together and she was being brought to join them. And they

had to play with her, and it was boring. She was silly. In the
end they teased her and made her show them how she could
swim. She lay on the floor and went through the motions and
they laughed and made fun of her. She saw them mocking her
and blushed in patches. She looked so pathetic that he had been
ashamed and he could never forget that crooked, kindly, sub-
missive smile. And Sergius remembered seeing her again. It
was long afterwards. She was married to a landowner who had
squandered all her money and used to beat her. She had a
couple of children, a son and daughter, but the son had died
as a boy.

Sergius remembered seeing how unhappy she was. He saw
her later in the monastery, by then a widow. She was just the
same – not exactly stupid, but insipid, insignificant, pathetic.
She came with her daughter and the girl's fiancé. They were
poor now. Then he heard that she lived in some district town
in real poverty. 'Why am I thinking about her?' he wondered.
But he could not get her out of his mind. 'Where is she? How
is she getting on? Is she still as unhappy as when she showed us
how to swim on the floor? But why am I thinking about her?
What am I doing? I have to put an end to myself.'

The thought again struck horror into him and to escape it
he again turned his mind to Pashenka.

He lay a long time thus, thinking of the need to end his life
and of Pashenka. Pashenka seemed to him a means of salvation. Finally he went to sleep. He dreamt that an angel came
to him and said: 'Go to Pashenka and learn from her what you
must do, how you have sinned and how you can be saved.'

He woke up and having decided that his dream was a vision
sent by God, joyfully resolved to do as he had been told. He
knew the town where she lived – it was 200 miles away – and
he set off towards it.

8

PASHENKA had long since ceased to be 'Pashenka': she was now Praskovya Mikhailovna, old, withered and wrinkled, and mother-in-law to Mavrikiev, a government clerk – who was a failure in life and given to drink. She lived in the district town where her son-in-law's last appointment had been; there she kept the family – her daughter, her sickly, neurasthenic son-in-law and five grandchildren. She provided for them by giving piano lessons to merchants' daughters at fifty kopeks an hour. Some days she would have four hours, other days five, and this brought in about sixty roubles a month. That is how they lived for the time being while they waited for some new opening for Mavrikiev. Praskovya Mikhailovna had sent off letters to all her friends and relations asking for help in finding him a situation and she had also written to Father Sergius, but her letter did not arrive in time to reach him.

It was Saturday and Praskovya Mikhailovna was mixing some currant bread which long ago her father's serf cook used to make so well. She intended it as a Sunday treat for her grandchildren.

Masha, her daughter, was fussing with the youngest child; the older children were at school. Her son-in-law had had a wakeful night and was now asleep. Praskovya Mikhailovna had also slept little the night before, trying to mollify her daughter who was angry with her husband. She knew her son-in-law was a weakling incapable of talking or acting in any other way, and she knew it was a waste of time for his wife to reproach him, so she did what she could to appease them, to put a stop to the reproaches and ill-feeling. It was almost physically too much for her when people were at odds with each other. She saw so clearly that behaving like this could only make things worse, not better. It was not even something she thought; the sight of malice simply upset her, just as she would be upset by a bad smell, a harsh voice, or someone striking her.

She was just telling Lukerya how to mix the leavened dough and feeling rather pleased with herself, when Misha, her six-year-old grandson, wearing his apron and darned stockings came running into the kitchen on his little bent legs. He looked frightened.

'Granny, there's a terrible old man looking for you!'

Lukerya glanced outside.

'That's right. It looks like a pilgrim, m'am.'

Praskovya Mikhailovna rubbed her thin arms together to clean them, wiped her hands on her apron and was on the point of going into the living-room to fetch five kopeks from her purse when she remembered that ten kopeks was the smallest she had. She decided instead to give him some bread and went to the larder, but then suddenly blushed at the thought of grudging him the money. She told Lukerya to cut him a piece of bread while she went for the ten-kopek piece. 'It's a punishment to you,' she told herself. 'Now you give twice over.'

She apologetically handed the bread and money to the pilgrim, feeling no pride in her generosity as she did so but rather shame that she was giving so little. The pilgrim had such an impressive look about him.

Sergius had begged his way for 200 miles. He was now tattered, thin, swarthy in face; his hair was cut short and he wore a peasant cap and boots; yet despite this and despite the humble way he bowed, he retained that impressive look which was so attractive. But Praskovya Mikhailovna did not recognize him. It was impossible that she should, not having seen him for nearly thirty years.

'I'm afraid it's all we can manage,' she said. 'Perhaps you would like a bite to eat.'

He took the bread and money. Praskovya Mikhailovna was surprised that instead of going away he looked at her.

'Pashenka. I have come to you. Please take me in.'

His fine black eyes, glistening with rising tears, looked at her intently, imploringly. His lips quivered piteously beneath his now almost white whiskers.

Praskovya Mikhailovna caught at her shrivelled breast, her jaw dropped and she stared goggle-eyed at the face of the pilgrim.

'It can't be! Why, it's Stepan! Sergius! Father Sergius!'

'Yes, it's him,' said Sergius quietly. 'It's not Sergius, though, nor Father Sergius, but the great sinner Stepan Kasatsky, the great lost sinner. Take me in and help me.'

'It's never possible! But how do you come to be so lowly? Come along in.'

She stretched out her hand, but he did not take it and followed her in.

But where should she take him? It was only a small apartment. At first she had a tiny room, little more than a box-room, for herself, but she had let her daughter have it and she was there now getting the baby to sleep.

'Just sit down here. I'll only be a minute,' she said to Sergius, pointing to the bench in the kitchen.

Sergius at once sat down and with an obviously accustomed movement slid the straps of his knapsack first from one shoulder, then from the other.

'My goodness, how lowly you've become! You were so famous, and now suddenly . . .'

Sergius made no reply and just smiled gently as he put his bag by his side.

'Masha, do you know who this is?'

In a whisper Praskovya Mikhailovna told her daughter who Sergius was, then between them they carried the bed and cradle out of the box-room so that Sergius could use it.

Praskovya Mikhailovna took him into this tiny room.

'Have a rest in here. It's not much, I'm afraid. But now I must be off.'

'Where are you going?'

'I give lessons here. I'm ashamed to admit it – I teach music.'

'Music – that's fine. There's one thing though, Praskovya Mikhailovna. I have come to see you about something. When could we have a talk?'

'Perhaps this evening? It would be a pleasure.'

'Yes, all right. But one more request: tell no one who I am. You are the only one I have confided in. Nobody knows where I have gone. That is how it must be.'

'Oh, but I have told my daughter.'

'Then tell her not to mention it.'

Sergius took off his boots, lay down, and having had no sleep the night before and having walked twenty-five miles, he at once fell asleep.

When Praskovya Mikhailovna came back Sergius was sitting in his room, waiting for her. He had not come out for dinner, but ate some soup and millet porridge that Lukerya brought him in his room.

'You are back sooner than you said?' asked Sergius. 'Can we talk now?'

'That I should be blessed with such a visit! I missed a lesson. I can make it up ... I always dreamt about going to see you, I wrote to you, and then I am blessed in this way.'

'Pashenka, I want you to take what I am about to say as a confession, as what I would say before God in the hour of my death. Pashenka, I am no saint. I am not even a simple, ordinary person. I am a sinner, a puffed-up, foul, loathsome, lost sinner, whether the worst in the world I do not know, but I am the lowest of the low.'

Pashenka at first looked at him wide-eyed: she believed what he said. Then, when the truth had fully sunk in, she touched his hand and with a smile of compassion said:

'Steve, might you not be making too much of it?'

'No, Pashenka. I am a fornicator, a murderer, a blasphemer and a fraud.'

'Gracious heavens, what are you saying?' said Praskovya Mikhailovna.

'But I have to live. I who thought I knew everything, I who taught others how to live – I know nothing and would like you to teach me.'

'What do you mean, Steve? You are joking. Why do you make fun of me?'

'All right then, I am joking. But you – tell me about yourself. What sort of life have you had?'

'Me? My life has been vile, bad, it couldn't have been worse, and now God is punishing me, and rightly. There is so much wrong in the way I live.'

'What about your marriage? How did that go?'

'It was all wrong. I got married, fell in love – it was sheer depravity. Father was against it, but I took no notice and married him. And after I was married I never helped my husband, but only tormented him with my jealousy which I could never get the better of.'

'I heard he drank.'

'He did, but it was I who failed to comfort him. I used to reproach him. But it was a sickness really. He couldn't stop himself, and I remember now how I refused him anything to drink. We had terrible scenes.'

And she looked at Kasatsky with suffering in her fine eyes evoked by the memory.

Kasatsky remembered hearing that Pashenka's husband used to beat her. And now, looking at her thin, shrivelled neck with the prominent veins behind her ears and the sparse hair, half-brown, half-grey, gathered into a bun, he seemed to see it happening.

'Then I was left on my own with the two children and nothing to live on.'

'But you had some property?'

'Oh, we sold that when Vasya was alive, and we . . . spent it all. I had to live somehow and like all of us – young ladies – I had no skill of any kind. Though I was worse, more useless than most. So we used up the last of what we had, I taught the children and learnt a little myself too. Then Mitya fell ill – he was in his fourth year at school – and the Lord took him. And Masha fell in love with Vanya – that's my son-in-law. He's really a good fellow, but just unlucky. He's not well.'

She was interrupted by her daughter calling: 'Mother, do take Misha. I can't be everywhere at once.'

Praskovya Mikhailovna started, got up, and with quick steps went through the door in her well-worn shoes and came back at once with a little boy of two who sprawled back in her arms and grasped her kerchief with his little hands.

'Where was I? Oh yes . . . he had a good position here, the head of the office was very nice, but Vanya couldn't cope and resigned.'

'What is the trouble with him?'

'Neurasthenia. It's a terrible thing to have. We've seen doctors about it, but they say he would have to go away and we can't afford it. I'm still hoping he will just get over it. He has no special pain, but . . .'

'Lukerya!' they heard him call in his cross, feeble voice. 'They keep sending her away just when she's wanted. Mother!'

'I'll just be a minute,' said Praskovya Mikhailovna, breaking off her story again. 'He hasn't had his dinner yet. He can't eat with us.'

She went out, attended to something in the other room and came back wiping her thin hands.

'So that's how it is. We keep complaining and are never satisfied but, thank God, the grandchildren are fine and well, and life is not too bad. But what need is there to talk about me?'

'What do you live on then?'

'There's the little bit I earn. I used to find music so boring, but it really has come in useful now.'

Her small hand rested on the chest of drawers by which she was sitting and she worked her thin fingers as if playing an exercise.

'What do you get paid for your lessons?'

'Some pay a rouble, others fifty or thirty kopeks. They are very good to me.'

'And do your pupils make good progress?' asked Kasatsky with a hint of a smile in his eyes.

At first Praskovya Mikhailovna thought he was not being serious and looked inquiringly in his eyes.

'Yes, some get on well. There's one splendid girl, the butcher's daughter. She is a nice, good girl. Of course, if I were a respectable woman I would have been able to use Father's connections to get Vanya a post. But there it was, I could not do a thing, and this is the state I have brought them all to.'

'Yes, of course,' said Kasatsky, bending his head forward. 'And tell me, Pashenka, do you go to church at all?'

'Oh, don't mention it. It's terrible how slack I have got. I keep the fasts with the children and sometimes go to church, but I might not go for months at a time. I send the children.'

'And why don't you go yourself?'

She blushed.

'To tell the truth, I don't feel it fair on my daughter and the grandchildren if I go to church in rags. And I have nothing new to wear. And then I'm just too lazy.'

'And do you pray at home?'

'Yes, I pray. But it is just automatic, not real praying. I know that isn't the way, but I don't have any proper feeling. I have nothing, only the knowledge of how thoroughly bad I am...'

'Yes, yes, that's right,' said Kasatsky, as if in approval.

'All right, I'm just coming,' she said in answer to her son-in-law who called, and straightening her thin braid of hair, she went out of the room.

This time she was gone for some time. When she returned, Kasatsky was sitting as before with his elbows on his knees and his head bent forward. But his knapsack was now on his back.

As she came in carrying a small tin lamp without a globe, he raised his fine, weary eyes to look at her and heaved an enormous sigh.

'I didn't tell them who you are,' she began diffidently. 'I just said that you were a pilgrim and came of good family and that I used to know you. Let's go into the dining-room and have some tea.'

'No ...'

'All right, I'll bring it in here.'

'No, I don't want anything. God save you, Pashenka. I am going. If you pity me, tell no one that you have seen me. By the living God I beg you to tell no one. Thank you. I would bow at your feet, but I know it would upset you. Good-bye, in the name of Christ.'

'Give me your blessing.'

'God will bless you. In Christ's name, good-bye.'

He was about to go, but she made him wait while she brought him bread, cracknels and butter. He took them and went outside.

It was dark and before he was past the second house Praskovya Mikhailovna had lost sight of him and could only tell where he was because the priest's dog barked as he passed.

'So that was the meaning of my dream. Pashenka is all that I should have been and was not. I lived for people, pretending it was for God, while she lives for God and thinks she is living for people. Yes, one good deed, one cup of water given without thought of reward is worth more than all the benefits I ever worked for men. But surely in some part I genuinely wished to serve God?' he thought. And the answer came to him: 'Yes, but that was defiled and choked by human glory. And God does not exist for one such as I, who lived for human glory. I will seek Him now.'

He set off, travelling from village to village as he had done on his way to Pashenka, now in company with other pilgrims, now going on his own, begging for his bread and a lodging overnight. Occasionally he was scolded by a bad-tempered housewife or cursed by a drunken peasant, but in the main people gave him food and drink and now and then something for the journey. The upper-class look about him disposed some people in his favour. But there were others who appeared to take pleasure in seeing one of the gentry also reduced to beggary. All, however, were won over by his gentle manner.

If he found a copy of the Gospels in a house he often read out of it, and wherever it was those who listened were always moved and astonished, as if what he read was something completely new and at the same time long familiar.

If he managed to help anyone – by giving advice, writing a letter, or settling a quarrel – he saw nothing of their gratitude because he would go away. And gradually God began to manifest Himself in him.

Once he was walking along with two old women and an old soldier when they were stopped by a lady and gentleman in a chaise drawn by a trotter and another couple on horseback. The two on horseback were the husband and daughter of the lady in the chaise, whose companion was evidently a visiting Frenchman.

They stopped them so that the Frenchman could see *les pélérins*, these people who were driven by the superstition characteristic of the Russian common people to do no work and wander from place to place.

They spoke in French, supposing that they would not be understood.

'Ask them,' said the Frenchman, 'if they really believe that their pilgrimage is pleasing to God.'

The question was translated and the old women answered:

'As God sees fit. Our feet have found us favour, may our hearts not do the same?'

The soldier was asked and replied that he was all alone and had nowhere to go. They asked Kasatsky who he was.

'I am a servant of God.'

'What does he say? He is not telling us,' said the Frenchman.

'He says he is a servant of God.'

'He must be a priest's son. He has some breeding. Have you got any change?'

The Frenchman had some small change and he gave them each twenty kopeks.

'But tell them it is not for buying candles with, but to treat themselves to some tea. Tea, tea,' he said smiling. 'For you, old chap,' he said, patting Kasatsky's shoulder with his gloved hand.

'Christ save you,' answered Kasatsky, not replacing his cap and bowing his bald head.

Kasatsky was specially gladdened by this encounter, for he had scorned worldly opinion and had done a very paltry, easy thing: he had humbly accepted twenty kopeks and passed them on to a fellow pilgrim, a blind beggar. The less he cared for the opinion of men, the more he felt the presence of God.

Kasatsky travelled about in this way for eight months. In the ninth month he was detained in one of the provincial capitals, where he was passing the night in a refuge with other pilgrims. Having no papers, he was taken to the police-station. When questioned about his identity-card he answered that he had no card, that he was a servant of God. He was classed as a vagrant, taken to court, and exiled to Siberia.

In Siberia he settled on the holding of a wealthy peasant. He still lives there, working in the owner's vegetable garden, teaching the children and tending the sick.

MASTER AND MAN

1

It happened in the 1870s on the day after the December feast of St Nicholas. This was a festival day in the parish and for Vasilii Andreich Brekhunov, the proprietor of the local inn and a merchant of the Second Guild, it was impossible to get away: he had to be at church – he was a churchwarden – and then there were relations and friends to be received and entertained at home. But finally the last guest departed, and Vasilii Andreich made ready to leave at once in order to call on a neighbouring landowner about the purchase of a coppice he had long been negotiating for. Vasilii Andreich was in a hurry to get there so as not to be forestalled in this advantageous deal by any of the town merchants. The young landowner was asking 10,000 for the coppice only because Vasilii Andreich offered 7,000. And 7,000, after all, was only a third of its actual value. Vasilii Andreich might have got an even better deal, since the wood was in his own district and there was a long-standing arrangement between him and the village-based merchants of the locality that no merchant would make a higher bid in another's district, but Vasilii Andreich had discovered that timber-merchants from the provincial capital were planning to come and bid for the coppice at Goryach-kino, so he decided to go at once and settle the deal with the landowner. Consequently, as soon as the festivities were over he took from his chest 700 roubles of his own money and added 2,300 roubles of the church money held by him to make it up to 3,000. He carefully counted the money, put it in his wallet, and made ready to leave.

Nikita, the only one of Vasilii Andreich's men who was not drunk that day, ran off to harness the horse. Nikita was not drunk that day because he was a heavy drinker and after the final fling he had before the fast, when he sold his coat and leather boots to buy liquor, he had sworn to give it up. He had not drunk for over a month and refrained even now, despite the temptation of seeing vodka being consumed on every hand these first two days of the festival.

Nikita was a peasant of fifty from a near-by village. He was no manager, as people said, and most of his life he had not lived at home but in other people's service. He was generally esteemed for his industry, skill and strength as a worker, but above all for his good-natured, pleasant character; however, he never settled down anywhere because twice a year, and sometimes more often, he had a heavy bout of drinking and then he not only drank every last thing he possessed, but also got disorderly and quarrelsome. Vasilii Andreich himself had sacked him several times, but took him back again because he was honest, fond of animals and, above all, cheap. Vasilii Andreich did not pay Nikita the eighty roubles a workman such as he was worth, but about forty, which he paid without any proper reckoning a bit at a time, and then for the most part not in money but in goods from his shop charged at a high price.

Nikita's wife Marfa, once a lusty good-looking woman, kept things going with their lad and a couple of girls. She did not ask Nikita to live at home – first because for twenty years or so she had been living with a cooper, a peasant from another village who lodged with them, and secondly because although she could rule Nikita when he was sober, she was scared to death of him when he had been drinking. Once he had got drunk at home and probably in order to pay his wife back for all his meekness while sober he had broken open her clothes chest, taken out all her best finery and with an axe had chopped all her sarafans and dresses into shreds on the chopping-block. All Nikita's wages were given to his wife, and Nikita made no objection. It had been the same now: two days before the festival Marfa had gone to Vasilii Andreich and got from him white flour, tea, sugar and a gill of vodka, which came to two or three roubles; she also took five roubles in cash and thanked him as if he was doing some special favour, while in fact even by the lowest reckoning Vasilii Andreich owed Nikita something like twenty roubles.

'We don't have any fixed agreement, do we?' Vasilii Andreich would say to Nikita. 'You take what you need and work it off later. I'm not like other people who would make you wait and reckon it all up and make deductions. With us it's all fair and square: you work for me and I see you are looked after.'

In saying this Vasilii Andreich honestly believed that he was benefiting Nikita: such was the conviction he could put into his words and such was the support given by Nikita and everyone else dependent on his money to his belief that he was not cheating, but benefiting, them.

'Yes, I know, Vasilii Andreich. I'd say I work and do my best for you as I would for my own father. I know it very well,' answered Nikita, very well knowing that Vasilii Andreich was cheating him, but also feeling there was no point in trying to sort out with him what he was owed: as long as he had no other job he had to live and must take what he was given.

Now, on receiving his master's order to harness up, Nikita, cheery and willing as ever, went to the outhouse with his light, brisk, waddling step, took from its nail the heavy tasselled leather bridle and, jingling the bit-rings, went to the closed shed where the horse he had to harness was kept on its own.

'Lonesome are you, you silly old thing?' said Nikita in reply to the faint whinny of welcome given him by the lone horse in the shed – a well-made dappled dark-bay stallion of middling height and rather low in the rump. 'There, there, there's plenty of time for that. Let's get you watered first,' said Nikita, talking to the horse as if he could understand just what he was saying. With the flap of his coat he flicked over the stallion's sleek, grooved back which was chafed and covered with dust and put the bridle over his fine young head, straightened his ears and forelock and after taking off the halter led him off to be watered.

Carefully picking his way out of the shed, which was deep in manure, Dapple played up and lashed out a hind leg, making as if to kick Nikita who was trotting by his side to the well.

'Now then, now then, you rascal!' said Nikita, knowing well how careful Dapple was to kick out his leg just far enough to touch his greasy sheepskin jerkin but not actually hit him. Nikita particularly enjoyed this trick of the horse's.

Dapple drank his fill of the chill water and gave a sigh, shuddering his thick, wet, hairy lips from which drops of clear water dripped into the trough; he was suddenly still, as if sunk in thought, then all at once gave a loud snort.

'All right, don't if you don't want to. We'll know where we are then, only don't you go asking for more,' said Nikita, in all seriousness explaining his actions to Dapple; he then ran back to the outhouse tugging the spirited young horse by the rein as it kicked with its hind legs, filling the yard with the clatter of hoofs.

None of the other hired men were about. There was only the cook's husband, who did not work for Vasilii Andreich and was only there because of the holiday.

'Be a good chap and go and ask what sledge he wants harnessed,' Nikita said to him. 'Is it the big one or the little one?'

The cook's husband went off into the high-standing, metal-roofed house and was soon back to say that it was the small sledge that was ordered. Nikita had meanwhile put on the horse's collar and strapped on the studded saddle; carrying the light painted shaft-bow in one hand and leading the horse with the other he went to the two sledges which stood in the out-house.

'Right then, the little one it is,' he said. He then led the intelligent horse – which all the time made out to be trying to bite him – between the shafts and with the help of the cook's husband began putting on the harness.

When everything was about ready and it only remained to fix the reins Nikita sent the cook's husband to get some straw from the shed and a piece of sacking from the barn.

'There we are then. Now, now, don't you stick out!' said Nikita, pressing well down into the sledge the newly threshed oat-straw brought by the cook's husband. 'Now we'll lay this bit of canvas on the bottom and the sacking can go on top. Like so and like so, and there's a nice comfortable seat,' he said, suiting the action to the word and tucking the sacking down over the straw right round the seat.

'There's a good fellow, many thanks,' said Nikita to the cook's husband. 'Many hands make light work.' Then, after sorting out the leather reins which had a ring at the joined end, Nikita perched himself on the driver's seat, touched the good horse, which was impatient to be off, and they crossed the frozen midden of the yard to the gate.

'Uncle Nikita, uncle, uncle!' cried a shrill voice after him. A boy of seven wearing a black sheepskin coat, new white felt boots and a warm cap came running out from the porch into the yard. 'Let me have a ride,' he begged, buttoning his coat as he ran along.

'Come on then, run, sweetheart,' said Nikita and stopped to let the boy get on – it was his master's son, a pale, thin little fellow who was now beaming with joy. He then drove out on to the road.

It was after two o'clock. It was freezing – about minus 10 – and it was dull and windy. Half the sky was covered with low dark cloud. It was quite still in the yard, but out in the street you noticed the wind more: snow was blowing from the roof of the shed next door and there was a swirl of spiralling snow at the corner by the bath-house. No sooner had Nikita driven out of the gate and headed the horse towards the front steps, than Vasilii Andreich, wearing a long cloth-covered sheep-skin coat tightly belted with a sash low on his waist and with a cigarette in his mouth, stepped from the porch on to the tall steps which were covered with trodden snow and which creaked beneath his leather-cased felt boots. He stopped, took a last draw at his cigarette, threw down the stub and trod on it; then breathing the smoke out through his moustache and giving a sidelong glance at the horse as it came through the gate, he began tucking down the points of his fur-lined collar on either side of his ruddy face – clean-shaven but for the moustache – to prevent the fur catching the moisture from his breath.

'So you're there already, you scamp, are you,' he said, seeing his son in the sledge. Roused by the vodka he had drunk with his guests, Vasilii Andreich was feeling more than usually pleased with all that he possessed and all that he did. Seeing his son, 'the son and heir' as he always called him in his mind, gave him now a great deal of pleasure; he looked at him, screwing up his eyes and showing his long teeth as he smiled.

Vasilii Andreich's wife, a pale, thin woman who was expecting a baby, stood behind him in the porch waiting to see him off, her head and shoulders swathed in a woollen shawl through which only her eyes were visible.

'Honestly, you ought to take Nikita,' she said, coming diffidently out of the doorway.

Vasilii Andreich did not answer, but what she said was evidently disagreeable to him for he frowned angrily and spat.

'You've got all that money with you,' his wife went on in the same plaintive voice. 'And what if there's a storm? You really ought to take him.'

'The way you keep on you'd think I needed a guide to show me the road,' said Vasilii Andreich in the unnatural tight-lipped manner he customarily adopted when discussing a business deal, enunciating each syllable with the utmost precision.

'No, really, you ought to take him. Do as I ask for the Lord's sake,' repeated his wife, tucking her shawl the other way.

'The way you keep on! What's the point of taking him?'

'I'm ready if you like, Vasilii Andreich,' said Nikita cheerfully. 'Only if I go somebody will have to feed the horses,' he added, speaking to the mistress.

'I'll see about it, Nikita. I'll get Semen to do it,' she said.

'Shall I come then, Vasilii Andreich?' asked Nikita, waiting.

'I suppose we'd better humour the old woman. But if you're going to come, go and put on a warmer coat,' said Vasilii Andreich smiling again and giving a wink at Nikita's superannuated, greasy sheepskin jacket which was falling apart, with tears under the arms and down the back and a tattered fringe around the skirt.

'Here, old chap. Come and hold the horse a minute,' Nikita called to the cook's husband in the yard.

'No, let me, let me,' piped the boy, taking his chilled red little hands from his pockets and grabbing the cold leather reins.

'Only don't go fussing too much with that coat of yours. Be quick about it!' Vasilii Andreich shouted, grinning at Nikita.

'I'll be back in a jiffy, master,' said Nikita, and trotting pigeon-toed in his felt boots with patched soles he ran back to the yard and into the hired men's quarters.

'Arina, quick, let's have my long coat off the stove. I'm going with the master,' said Nikita, running into the hut and taking down his sash from the nail.

The cleaning-woman who had had a nap after dinner and was just putting on the samovar for her husband greeted Nikita cheerily and, infected by his haste, she too bustled herself and took down the threadbare cloth caftan, worn through in places, which was drying on the stove. She hurriedly began shaking it to remove the creases.

'You can have a nice time with your husband now and no one to bother you,' Nikita said to the cook, it being for him a matter of good-natured politeness to say something if ever he found himself alone with anybody.

He put the narrow tangled sash round his waist, drew in his stomach, which was lean enough anyway, and pulled the sash in as tight as he could over his sheepskin jacket.

'There we are then,' he said when he had done this, addressing now not the cook but the sash as he tucked its ends into his belt. 'You won't come undone now.' Then raising and lowering his shoulders to give freedom to his arms, he put on his long coat, flexed his back again to make room for his arms, gave a tuck under each armpit and took his gauntlets off the shelf.

'Right, that's fine,' he said.

'Nikita, you should put something else on your feet,' the cook said. 'Those boots are no good.'

Nikita stopped as if reminded of something.

'Yes, I should . . . But no, this will do. It's not far.'

And he ran off into the yard.

'Won't you be cold, Nikita?' asked the mistress when he reached the sledge.

'Cold? No. I'll be nice and warm,' answered Nikita, arranging the straw at the front of the sledge to cover his feet and tucking his whip – not needed for the willing horse – beneath the straw.

Vasilii Andreich was already seated, his back with its covering of two fur coats practically filling the whole of the curved rear of the sledge. He immediately took the reins and started the horse. As the sledge moved Nikita perched himself on the left at the front, with one leg hanging over the side.

2

THE willing stallion got the sledge going with a gentle screech of the runners and moved off at a brisk pace over the packed snow of the frosty village street.

'What are you tagging on for? Let's have the whip, Nikita!' cried Vasilii Andreich, evidently delighted with his son and heir who was attempting to perch himself on the back of the runners. 'I'll give it to you! Off you run to your mother, you rapscallion!'

The boy jumped off. Dapple quickened his ambling pace and with a snort moved into a trot. Kresty, where Vasilii Andreich's house was, consisted of six houses. They were no sooner past the blacksmith's house at the end of the row than it was at once apparent that the wind was much stronger than they had thought. Already the road was hardly visible. The sledge tracks were immediately covered over and you could only tell where the road was because it was higher than the rest. Snow whipped up from the fields on either side and there was no telling where earth and sky began and ended. Telyatino wood which you could always see clearly was just a dark shape vaguely discernible now and then through the clouds of powdery snow. The wind came from the left, driving Dapple's mane persistently to the right of his steep plump neck and blowing sideways his full tail which was tied in a simple knot.

Nikita was sitting on the windward side and his long collar was pressed flat against his face and nose.

'He can't really get going. Too much snow,' said Vasilii Andreich, taking pride in his good horse. 'I went to Pashutino with him once and he did it in half an hour.'

'You what?' asked Nikita, not catching what he said because of his collar.

'I said I once got to Pashutino in half an hour,' shouted Vasilii Andreich.

'Not surprising. He's a good horse,' said Nikita.

They were silent for a while. Vasilii Andreich felt like talk-ing.

'I suppose you've told your missus not to give liquor to the cooper?' he asked in the same loud voice. Vasilii Andreich was so convinced that Nikita must be flattered to converse with an important, intelligent man like him and so pleased was he with his banter that it never occurred to him that Nikita might find the subject disagreeable.

Again Nikita failed to catch his master's words which were borne away on the wind.

In his loud, distinct voice Vasilii Andreich repeated his joking remark about the cooper.

'They can go their own way, Vasilii Andreich. I don't go into their affairs. As long as she doesn't harm the boy, she can do what she likes.'

'Quite right,' said Vasilii Andreich. 'Well then, are you going to buy a horse come the spring?' he asked, changing the subject.

'I'll have to,' Nikita answered, turning down the collar of his caftan and leaning over towards his master.

Now Nikita was interested in the conversation and did not want to miss anything.

'The boy's grown up now and must plough for himself. We've always hired help otherwise.'

'Why don't you have my docked horse? I wouldn't ask much!' cried Vasilii Andreich, who because of his excited state had now got round to his favourite, all-absorbing interest – making money.

'If you'll let me have fifteen roubles or so, I'll get one at the fair,' said Nikita, knowing that a good price for the docked horse Vasilii Andreich wanted to pass off on him was seven or eight roubles and that, if he took the horse, Vasilii Andreich would reckon it worth twenty-five roubles and then not pay him a penny for six months.

'It's a good horse. I'd as soon see you benefit as I would my-self. Brekhunov will never do you down, that's the truth. I don't mind if I lose on it, not like other people. Honestly,' he shouted in the tone of voice he always used when talking round clients, 'It's a right good horse!'

'True enough,' said Nikita with a sigh, and convinced that there was nothing more worth hearing he let go of his collar, which at once flew up over his ear and face.

For some half an hour they travelled in silence. The wind blew through into Nikita's side and arm where his sheepskin coat was torn.

He huddled himself up and blew into his collar which covered his mouth. He was not cold all over.

'What do you think – shall we go through Karamyshevo or take the straight road?' asked Vasilii Andreich.

The road through Karamyshevo was a faster one staked out with a good line of posts on each side, but it was farther. The direct way was shorter, but the road was little used and where it was marked at all the posts were poor and likely to be covered over with snow.

Nikita thought for a while.

'It's a bit further through Karamyshevo, but it's a better road.'

'But the straight way . . . if we can keep to the road through the gully there is a good stretch after that through the wood,' said Vasilii Andreich, who was keen to take the shorter road.

'Please yourself,' said Nikita, and again released the flap of his collar.

Vasilii Andreich did so, and half a mile further on, where the tall branch of an oak-tree with a few dry, still unfallen leaves swung in the wind, he turned off to the left.

On turning, they had the wind almost head-on. Light snow began to fall. Vasilii Andreich drove, puffing out his cheeks and blowing out his breath upwards into his moustache. Nikita dozed.

They travelled like this in silence for some ten minutes. Suddenly Vasilii Andreich spoke.

'You what?' asked Nikita, opening his eyes.

Vasilii Andreich made no reply, twisting himself as he looked back and then forward, ahead of the horse. The horse, his coat curled and matted with sweat on the neck and groins, went at a walk.

'You what?' repeated Nikita.

'You what, you what!' Vasilii Andreich mimicked him angrily. 'Can't see any posts. We must be off the road.'

'Stop then. I'll see if I can find it,' said Nikita and jumping lightly from the sledge and taking his whip out from under the straw, he went off to the left, away from the side on which he had been sitting.

There was no great depth of snow that year so there was no difficulty in moving about, but still in some places the snow was knee-deep and got in over the top of one of Nikita's boots. Nikita went to and fro, feeling for the road with his feet and the whip, but it was nowhere to be found.

'Any good?' asked Vasilii Andreich when Nikita got back to the sledge.

'It's not over here. We'll have to try the other side.'

'Look, there's something dark ahead. Go and take a look,' said Vasilii Andreich.

Nikita once more went off and came up to the dark patch – it was earth which had blown off the bared fields of winter wheat and blackened the snow where it settled. Nikita walked to and fro on the right as well and came back to the sledge. He brushed the snow off himself, shook it out of his boot and got on to the sledge.

'We must go to the right,' he said firmly. 'I had the wind on my left before and now it's straight in my face. Go right!' he firmly repeated.

Vasilii Andreich did as he said and turned to the right. And there was still no road. They travelled like this for some time.

The wind was as strong as ever and snow started falling again.

'We're completely lost by the looks of it,' said Nikita suddenly, as if he was pleased. 'What's that?' he said, pointing to black potato haulms sticking through the snow.

Vasilii Andreich stopped the horse which was now sweating and heaving its steep flanks.

'What is it then?' he asked.

'It's the Zakharovka fields, that's where we are. We've gone right out of our way.'

'Nonsense!' responded Vasilii Andreich.

'It isn't nonsense, Vasilii Andreich. It's just as I say.' said Nikita. 'You can tell by the sound of the sledge – it's potato fields we're on. Look, those heaps there – where they've gathered the haulms. It's the Zakharovka factory fields.'

'Heavens, how did we land up here?' said Vasilii Andreich. 'And what do we do now?'

'We just need to keep straight on,' said Nikita, 'and we're bound to come out somewhere, either Zakharovka or else the manor farm.'

Vasilii Andreich did as Nikita said and started the horse going in the direction he indicated. They drove on like this for quite a long time. Sometimes they came on to winter wheat fields blown clear of snow and the sledge grated over the bumpy frozen earth. Sometimes they drove across old fields of spring and winter corn where stalks of wormwood and stubble showed above the snow, bending to the wind. Sometimes they drove into deep, even snow, uniformly white, its surface unmarked by anything at all.

The snow came down, sometimes too it rose upwards. The horse, its sweating coat matted and frosted, was clearly tired out and went at a walk. All of a sudden he lost his footing and plumped into a gully or ditch. Vasilii Andreich was going to stop, but Nikita shouted at him:

'What are you stopping for? Now we're in we've got to get out. Come on there, boy! Gee up! Gee up! Come on, boy!' he shouted cheerily at the horse, jumping out of the sledge and sinking deep in the ditch himself.

The horse gave a lunge and at once got clear on to the hard frozen bank.

It was evidently a man-made ditch.

'Where are we then?' said Vasilii Andreich.

'We'll soon see,' answered Nikita. 'Keep moving and we'll come out somewhere.'

'Surely that's Goryachkino wood there,' said Vasilii Andreich, pointing to a dark shape that loomed out of the snow ahead.

'We'll see what wood it is when we get closer,' said Nikita.

Nikita saw that long dry willow leaves were blowing from the direction of this dark shape ahead, so knew that it was not a wood, but some kind of settlement, though he preferred to say nothing. And true enough, they had hardly gone twenty yards from the ditch when they saw the shapes of trees ahead of them and heard a new dismal sound. Nikita had guessed right: it was not a wood, but a row of tall willows which still bore a few sparse, wind-tossed leaves. The willows were evidently planted along the ditch of a threshing-floor. As they came up to the trees, which soughed dismally in the wind, the horse suddenly rose up on its forelegs, higher than the sledge, got its hind legs too on to this higher level and turned to the left, no longer sinking knee-deep in the snow. It was the road.

'We've made it,' said Nikita. 'But I don't know where to.'

The horse went unerringly along the road that lay hidden beneath the snow and they had gone less than a hundred yards when a long straight shape loomed before them – the wattle wall of a threshing-barn, the roof of which was thick with snow, which constantly showered to the ground. Past the threshing-barn the road turned, putting the wind behind them, and they drove into drifted snow. But ahead they could see a gap between two houses, so the drift had evidently formed across the road and they had to go on through it. And indeed when they had made their way through the drift they came into a street. At the end house there was some frozen washing on the clothes-line flapping furiously in the wind: two shirts – one red, one white, a pair of trousers, legging cloths, and a skirt. The white shirt tugged at the line with special fury, waving its arms.

'The woman there must be lazy or mortal sick, leaving her washing out over the holiday,' said Nikita as he eyed the blowing shirts.

3

AT the beginning of the street it was still windy and the snow lay thick on the road, but in the middle of the village it was calm, warm and cheering. A dog barked outside one of the houses, a woman with her jerkin pulled up over her head ran up to one of the others and, after pausing on the threshold to look at the travellers, went in at the door. From the middle of the village came the sound of girls singing.

The wind, snow and frost seemed less in the village.

'But this is Grishkino,' said Vasilii Andreich.

'Right you are,' replied Nikita.

It actually was Grishkino. It turned out that they had gone off the road to the left and travelled four or five miles out of their way, though still in the general direction of where they were going. From Grishkino to Goryachkino was about three miles.

In the middle of the village they came upon a tall man walking down the centre of the road.

'Who's that?' the man shouted, stopping the horse. Immediately he recognized Vasilii Andreich and catching hold of the shaft worked his hands along it till he came to the sledge and sat himself on the driving-seat.

It was Isai, a peasant Vasilii Andreich knew, who was famed in the district as the leading horse-thief.

'Why, Vasilii Andreich! Where on earth are you off to?'

said Isai, breathing over Nikita the smell of the vodka he had been drinking.

'We were trying to get to Goryachkino.'

'Then you're well out of your way! You should have gone the Malakhovo way.'

'It's all very well what we should have done, but we didn't,' said Vasilii Andreich, pulling up the horse.

'A good horse,' said Isai, looking it over and with an accustomed movement pulling the loosened knot on its thick tail up to the dock.

'Will you be stopping overnight then?'

'No, my friend. We've got to go on.'

'Must be important. Who's this then? Ah – Nikita Stepanych!'

'Who else would it be?' answered Nikita. 'I hope we won't miss the road again, old friend.'

'How can you miss the road! Turn back, go straight up the street, then keep on straight at the end. Don't go to the left. You'll come out on the main road, and then you turn off to the right.'

'Where is the turning off the main road?' asked Nikita. 'Is that the summer road or the winter one?'

'The winter one. As soon as you leave the village there are some bushes, opposite the bushes there's a big oak marker with a bushy top – that's it.'

Vasilii Andreich turned the horse back and set off through the village.

'You could stop overnight!' Isai shouted after them.

But Vasilii Andreich made no answer and urged the horse on: three miles of level road, one of them through forest, seemed easy enough, especially since the wind appeared to have dropped and the snow was easing off.

After going along the street over the smooth-run snow, marked here and there by fresh droppings of manure, and after passing the house with the clothes hung out (the white shirt had come off and hung now by one frozen sleeve), they came again to the fearful soughing willows and found themselves once more in open country. The storm had not merely not abated, but seemed to have increased. The road was completely snowed over and you could only tell you were still on it by the marker posts. But ahead even the posts were hard to make out because of the wind in their faces.

Vasilii Andreich screwed up his eyes and bent his head forward, straining to make out the posts, but for the most part he gave the horse his head and left it to him. And in fact the horse kept to the road and went on, turning right and left with the bends in the road which he could sense beneath his feet, with the result that although the snow fell thicker and the wind blew stronger, the posts were still to be seen, now on the right, now on the left.

They travelled like this for ten minutes or so when suddenly just ahead of the horse a dark moving shape appeared in the slanting curtain of driving snow. It was some people going the same way. Dapple came right up to them and his hoofs banged against the seat of the sledge in front.

There were cries from the sledge: 'Go round – Hi! – Get on ahead!'

Vasilii Andreich started overtaking. There were three peasants and a woman in the sledge. They had obviously been out visiting and were returning after celebrating the holiday. One of the peasants was lashing the snow-covered rump of the jade with a switch. The two who were riding at the front shouted something and waved their arms; the woman, well wrapped up and covered with snow, huddled motionless in the back of the sledge.

'Where are you from?' cried Vasilii Andreich.

'A – a – a . . .' was all he could hear.

'I said: where are you from?'

'A – a – a . . .' shouted one of the peasants at the top of his voice, but it was still impossible to hear who they were.

'Come on! Don't give way!' cried the other, beating away at the horse with his switch.

'Been out celebrating?'

'Come on! come on! Semka, get a move on! Overtake them! Faster!'

The side members of the sledges bumped, the sledges almost locked together, then separated and the peasants' sledge began to fall back.

The shaggy, full-bellied jade, which was covered in snow and panting under the low shaft-bow as it clearly expended its last strength in its vain effort to escape the flicking switch, struggled through the deep snow, drawing its short legs high up under its body. Its muzzle, obviously that of a young horse, with its lower lip drawn in like a fish's, flared nostrils, and ears flattened back in terror, held level with Nikita's shoulder for a few seconds, then began to fall back.

'That's what drink does,' said Nikita. 'They've driven that horse to a standstill. Nothing but heathen!'

For some minutes they could hear the exhausted horse breathing heavily through its nostrils and the drunken shouts of the peasants; then the sound of the breathing faded and the cries too were lost. Once more there was nothing to be heard but the wind whistling in their ears and now and then the faint scraping of the runners on the road where it was blown free of snow.

This encounter cheered and reassured Vasilii Andreich and he boldly urged the horse on, relying on its judgement and not heeding the posts.

Nikita had nothing to do and as always when the opportunity offered he dozed, catching up with lost sleep of which there was always plenty. All at once the horse stopped and Nikita pitched forward and nearly fell.

'We're wrong again,' said Vasilii Andreich.

'What's the trouble?'

'Can't see any posts. We must be off the road again.'

'If we're off the road, then we'd better find it,' said Nikita tersely. He stood up and once more, stepping lightly on his pigeon-toed feet, set off to walk through the snow.

He walked about for a long time, being lost from sight, then reappearing and disappearing once more. At last he came back.

'There's no road here. It might be ahead somewhere,' he said, sitting down on the sledge.

It was getting noticeably dark. The storm was no worse, but it was not diminishing either.

'If we could only get a sound of those peasants,' said Vasilii Andreich.

'They've not caught up with us, so we must be well off the road. Who knows – they might be lost too,' said Nikita.

'Which way do we go then?' asked Vasilii Andreich.

'We must give the horse his head,' said Nikita. 'He'll take us. Let's have the reins.'

Vasilii Andreich gave him the reins, the more pleased to do so because his hands were starting to freeze inside his warm gloves.

Nikita took the reins and just held them, trying to keep them quite still and taking pleasure in the intelligence of his favourite horse. And indeed the intelligent animal, cocking one ear, then the other each way in turn, moved off at an angle.

'Just keep quiet,' said Nikita. 'He knows what he's doing. Go on, go on, then! That's it, that's it!'

The wind now blew from behind and it felt warmer.

'He's got sense, he has,' Nikita said, still taking pleasure in the horse. 'Now your Kirghiz horse is strong all right, but he's stupid. But this one, see how he's using his ears. No need for the telegraph, he can tell a mile away.'

And, indeed, in less than half an hour something dark loomed up ahead – either a wood or a village, and posts appeared again on the right-hand side. They were evidently back on the road.

'But this is Grishkino again,' Nikita said suddenly.

And indeed to the left of them was the same threshing-barn with the snow driving from the roof, and further along the same clothes-line with the frozen washing, the shirts and trousers still flapping as furiously as ever in the wind.

Again they drove into the street, again it was calm and warm and cheery, again they saw the dung-marked roadway, again heard voices and singing, again the dog barked. It was now so dark there were lights in some of the windows.

Half-way down the street Vasilii Andreich turned the horse towards a large double-fronted brick house and pulled him up at the front steps.

Nikita went to a snowed-up window where there was a light that shone on the darting snowflakes outside. He tapped it with the handle of his whip.

'Who's there?' came a voice in answer to Nikita's summons.

'It's Mr Brekhunov from Kresty, good heart,' replied Nikita. 'Come out for a minute, will you?'

The person inside moved away from the window and in a minute or two there was the sound of the inner door unsticking, then the clicking of the latch on the outside door and an old peasant, tall and white-bearded, with a sheepskin jacket thrown over his best white shirt, poked his head out of the door which he held pushed against the wind. Behind him was a young man in a red shirt and leather knee-boots.

'Vasilii Andreich. Is that you?' said the old man.

'We've gone adrift, friend,' said Vasilii Andreich. 'We were making for Goryachkino and landed up here. Then we went on and got lost again.'

'My word, you're well out of your way,' said the old man. 'Petrukha, go and open the gate,' he said to the young man in the red shirt.

'Right you are,' replied the other cheerily and ran into the porch.

'But we aren't stopping the night,' said Vasilii Andreich.

''Tis no time for travelling. It's night now – you should stop over till morning.'

'I'd be glad to, but I've got to get on. I'm on business, so can't stop.'

'Well, at least have a warm up,' said the old man. 'The samovar's going, come along inside.'

'Yes, we can have a warm up,' said Vasilii Andreich. 'It won't get any darker and when the moon's up there will be more light. What about it, Nikita, shall we go in for a warm?'

'Well, yes, I wouldn't mind a warm up,' said Nikita, who was chilled to the bone and wanted very much to get into the warm and thaw out his frozen limbs.

Vasilii Andreich went into the house with the old man while Nikita drove through the gate opened by Petrukha and, following his directions, put the horse into a shed. The shed was deep in mire and the tall shaft-bow caught on the cross-beam. Some hens and a cock which had settled on the beam cackled in displeasure and scratched at the beam with their claws. Startled sheep, their feet rattling on the frozen mire, scurried to one side. A dog, seeing the stranger, gave a frenzied yelp and, in a state of fright and malice, set up a continuous yapping bark like a puppy.

Nikita had a word with them all: as he tethered the horse he apologized to the hens, assured them that he would not disturb them any more, reproached the sheep for getting frightened about nothing, and all the time tried to reason with the dog.

'There, that'll do nicely,' he said, beating the snow off himself. 'Goodness, what a carry-on!' he added, addressing the dog. 'Now, that'll do. That's enough, silly dog, that's enough. You're just getting yourself worked up,' he said. 'We're not robbers, we're friends...'

'It's like they say – the three home advisers,' said the young man, with a shove of his powerful arm pushing the sledge which was still outside under shelter.

'How's that – advisers?' said Nikita.

'Like it says in Paulson's book:* if a robber comes up to the house, the dog barks – it means look out; when the cock crows it means get up; and when the cat has a wash it means you've got a visitor, so be ready to welcome him,' said the lad smiling.

Petrukha could read and write. The only book he possessed was that of Paulson, which he practically knew by heart, and he was fond of quoting from it whenever it seemed apposite, especially when, as now, he was a bit tipsy.

'That's very true,' said Nikita.

'You must be frozen,' Petrukha added.

'That I am,' said Nikita, and they went across the yard and through the porch into the house.

4

THE homestead to which Vasilii Andreich had come was one of the most prosperous in the village. The family owned five plots of land and rented other land besides. The farm had six horses, three cows, two year-old heifers, and a couple of dozen sheep. There were twenty-two in the family which worked it: four married sons, six grandchildren (of whom Petrukha alone was married), two great-grandchildren, three orphaned children, and four daughters-in-law with their children. It was one of those rare households where the property had not been divided; but here too a latent inner discord was at work (started, as always, among the womenfolk), which would inevitably soon lead to a division. Two of the sons lived in Moscow working as water-carriers, another was in the army. At home just now were the old father and mother, the second

---

*I. I. Paulson (1825–98) was a well known author of educational books. The book in question is his very popular *Reading Book*, a compilation of stories, poems, etc. – *Translator.*

son, who ran the farm, the eldest son who had come back from Moscow for the holiday, and all the women and children. Besides the family there was a neighbour visiting who was godfather to one of the sons.

In the main room a lamp with a shade over the top hung above the table, throwing a bright light on the tea things, vodka bottle and food below and on the brick walls which were hung with icons in the corner opposite the door and with pictures on either side. Vasilii Andreich sat at the table in the place of honour wearing just his black sheepskin jacket. He was sucking his frosted whiskers and surveying the people and the room with his bulging hawk-like eyes. At the table with Vasilii Andreich sat the bald, white-bearded old master of the house in his white homespun shirt; next to him in a fine printed cotton shirt the son home from Moscow for the holiday, who had brawny shoulders and back, then the other son, a broad-shouldered fellow, the one who now ran the farm, and the neighbour – a lean peasant with red hair.

The peasants had already had some vodka and food. They were now about to drink tea and the samovar was already humming on the raised floor by the stove. On the boarded shelf which served as their bed and on top of the clay stove there were children. A woman sat on the wooden bunk, leaning over a cradle. The old mistress of the house, whose face was a mass of tiny wrinkles which ran in all directions and covered even her lips, was looking after Vasilii Andreich.

As Nikita entered the room she was just serving her visitor with vodka, which she had poured for him in a small thick glass tumbler.

'No offence, Vasilii Andreich, but you must join in the celebration,' she said. 'Drink up now, my dear.'

The sight and smell of the vodka deeply disturbed Nikita, especially just now when he was frozen through and exhausted. He frowned and, after shaking the snow from his cap and caftan, he stood in front of the icons and three times bowed to them, making the sign of the cross, seemingly unaware of those present; he then turned to the old master of the house and bowed first to him, then to all those at the table, and then to the womenfolk standing by the stove, wishing them good cheer on the feast-day. Keeping his eyes off the table he began to take off his caftan.

'You're frosted up good and proper,' said the elder brother, looking at Nikita's face, eyes and beard which were powdered with snow.

Nikita removed his caftan and, after shaking it out again, hung it against the stove and went up to the table. He was also offered some vodka. There was a moment's anguished struggle: he was on the point of taking the glass and downing the clear fragrant liquid, but a glance at Vasilii Andreich reminded him of his pledge – he remembered the boots sold for drink, he remembered the cooper, he remembered his son and the horse he had promised to buy him for the spring, and with a sigh he refused.

'I'm much obliged, but I don't drink,' he said, frowning, and sat down on the bench by the second window.

'How's that?' said the elder brother.

'I just don't drink, that's all,' said Nikita, not looking up and squinting down at his straggly moustache and beard as he thawed the icicles from them.

'It's not good for him,' said Vasilii Andreich, eating a cracknel to follow up the vodka he had drunk.

'Well, have some tea then,' said the kindly old woman. 'You must be frozen, poor soul. You womenfolk there, get a move on with the samovar.'

'It's all ready,' answered one of the son's wives and wiping with her apron the covered samovar, which was boiling over, she brought it with difficulty to the table, lifted it and set it down with a bump.

Meanwhile Vasilii Andreich was telling how they had lost their way and twice come back to the same village, how they

MASTER AND MAN 93

had wandered aimlessly and met the drunken peasants. His hosts listened with surprise, explained where and why they had missed the road, who the drunken peasants were, and told them the way they should go.

'Why, a little child would get to Molchanovka from here!' said the neighbour. 'You've just got to take the right turning off the main road – there's a bush there. And you didn't make it!'

'You ought to stop the night,' urged the old woman. 'The women can make you up a bed!'

'You could go in the morning. It'd be just the thing,' her husband chimed in.

'Can't do it, my friend. I've got business,' said Vasilii Andreich. 'What you lose in an hour takes a year to make up,' he added, remembering the coppice and the dealers who might forestall him. 'We'll get there, won't we?' he said, turning to Nikita.

Nikita took a long time to answer, as if still preoccupied with thawing out his beard and moustache.

'As long as we don't get lost,' he said gloomily.

Nikita was gloomy because he felt a desperate need for vodka and the only thing which might kill this desire was tea, which he had not yet been given.

'It's only a matter of getting to the turning. We shan't get lost after that: it's forest all the way,' said Vasilii Andreich.

'It's up to you, Vasilii Andreich. If you say we go, we go,' said Nikita, taking the glass of tea which was handed to him.

'We'll have a good drink of tea, then be away.'

Nikita said nothing. He merely shook his head, and carefully pouring some tea into the saucer began warming his hands and permanently swollen toil-worn fingers in the steam. Then he bit off a tiny morsel of sugar, bowed to his hosts and said:

'Your very good health' – and gulped down the warming liquid.

'Somebody would maybe see us as far as the turning,' said Vasilii Andreich.

'Why yes, certainly,' said the elder son. 'Petrukha can harness up and take you as far as that.'

'Right then, Petrukha,' said Vasilii Andreich. 'Get harnessed up. I'll make it worth your while.'

'There's no need for that, my dear,' said the kindly old woman. 'It's a pleasure.'

'Go and harness the mare, Petrukha,' said the elder brother.

'Right you are,' said Petrukha with a smile, and, grabbing his cap from the nail, at once ran off to harness the horse.

While he was doing this the conversation returned to where it had broken off when Vasilii Andreich had come to the window. The old man was complaining to his neighbour (who was the village headman) about his third son, who had not sent him a present for the festival, though he had sent his wife a French kerchief.

'Young folk today are getting out of hand,' said the old man.

'That they are. You just can't cope with them,' said his neighbour. 'Too clever by half they are these days. Look at Demochkin – broke his father's arm. All through being too clever.'

Nikita listened to them and studied their faces. He evidently would have liked to join in the conversation, but being fully occupied with his tea, he merely nodded approvingly. He drank glass after glass and felt a growing sensation of warmth and well-being. The conversation continued for a long time on the same topic – what a bad thing it was to divide a property, and the conversation was evidently not concerned with the general question, but with a division in this particular family, which was wanted by the second son who sat by keeping grimly silent. It was evidently a sore point and the whole family was concerned about it, but out of propriety they did not discuss their private affairs before outsiders. In the end, however, the old man could contain himself no longer and in a tearful voice declared that as long as he lived there would be no division, that his family was well provided for, but if they divided they would all be beggared.

'Just like the Matveevs,' said the neighbour. 'They were prosperous till they divided, then they all went empty-handed.'

'And that's what *you* want,' said the old man to his son.

The son made no answer and there was an awkward silence. It was broken by Petrukha who had already harnessed the horse and come back inside. He had been in the room for a few minutes, smiling all the time.

'Paulson's got a fable like that,' he said. 'A father gave his sons a broom and told them to break it. They couldn't do it whole, but twig by twig it was easy. It's the same as this,' he said, smiling broadly. 'We're all ready,' he added.

'If we're ready, then we'll go,' said Vasilii Andreich. 'As for dividing, granfer, you stick to your guns. You built it up and you're the master. Take it to the justice. He'll tell you what's right.'

'He's got that stubborn and full of himself,' the old man went on tearfully, 'that there's never a moment's peace. It's as though the devil's got into him.'

Nikita, meanwhile, having finished his fifth glass of tea still did not tip his glass upside down, but laid it on its side in the hope that he might get a sixth. But the samovar was now empty and the mistress did not give him any more, and anyway Vasilii Andreich began getting his coats on. There was nothing for it: Nikita rose too, replaced his well nibbled piece of loaf-sugar in the sugar-bowl, wiped his perspiring face with the hem of his jacket and went to put on his caftan.

When he was dressed he gave a deep sigh, and, thanking his hosts and bidding them good-bye, went out of the warm, light room into the dark, cold porch, where the wind howled in and snow lay driven through the crack in the shaking doors. From the porch he went out into the dark yard.

Petrukha in a fur top-coat stood with his horse in the middle of the yard. With a broad smile he was reciting a verse he had read in Paulson:

> 'The storm be darkling o'er the sky,
> It spins the whirling snow,
> Now like a beast it roars out wild,
> Now like a babe sobs low.'

Nikita nodded his head in approval as he straightened out the reins.

The old man came out to see Vasilii Andreich off. He brought a lantern into the porch to light the way for him, but the wind immediately blew it out, and even in the yard one could tell that the storm had got up stronger than ever.

Quite a storm, thought Vasilii Andreich. Perhaps we shan't make it after all. But it's no good – there's business to do! Anyway I'm all set now and they've got their horse ready harnessed. We'll get there, God willing!

The old man also thought they should not go, but he had tried once to persuade them to stay and had not been heeded. There was no point in asking again. Perhaps I'm just getting faint-hearted in my old age and they'll get there all right, he thought. At any rate we'll get to bed betimes and shan't be put out.

The idea of danger never as much as occurred to Petrukha: he knew the road and the whole district perfectly; besides that, he was much cheered by that line of verse 'it spins the whirling snow', because it expressed so exactly what was happening in the yard. Nikita did not want to go at all, but he was long accustomed to having no will of his own and doing as others bid, so there was no one to hinder their departure.

5

VASILII ANDREICH went over to the sledge, having difficulty in finding it in the darkness. He got in and took the reins.

'You lead the way!' he shouted.

Petrukha, kneeling in the wide seatless sledge, started his horse. Dapple, who had long been whinnying as he sensed the mare in front, charged after her and they drove out into the street. Once more they went through the village, along the same road, past the house with the frozen washing which it was now too dark to see, past the barn, now snowed up almost to the eaves with snow still dropping endlessly from the roof, past the dismally soughing willows that whistled and bent in the wind, and then once more they were out in the snowy sea that raged above and below. The wind was so strong that when it blew from the side and its full force caught the occupants of the sledge, the sledge heeled over and the horse was pushed sideways off its course. Petrukha led, driving his good mare at a jogging trot and giving an occasional cheerful shout. Dapple followed eagerly after the mare.

When they had travelled thus for some ten minutes Petrukha turned and shouted something. In the wind neither Vasilii Andreich nor Nikita could catch his words, but they guessed they had come to the turning. And indeed Petrukha turned off to the right and the wind which had been from the side now blew head-on. Over on the right a dark object loomed in the snow: it was the bush by the turning.

'Well, God speed you!'

'Many thanks, Petrukha.'

'The storm be darkling o'er the sky,' cried Petrukha, and was lost from sight.

'A regular poet,' said Vasilii Andreich, flicking the reins.

'He's a nice fellow, a real good sort,' said Nikita.

They drove on.

Nikita, well wrapped up, his head pressed down into his shoulders so that his modest beard lay along his neck, sat in silence, trying to lose none of the warmth he had got from the tea at the peasant's house. In front of him he saw the straight lines of the shafts, which continually played tricks on him by looking like the edges of a regular road; he saw the rising and falling rump of the horse with the knotted tail streaming sideways, and further ahead the high shaft-bow and the horse's bobbing head and neck with flying mane. Now and then he glimpsed a marker post, by which he knew that so far they were still on the road and that nothing was required of him.

Vasilii Andreich drove, leaving it to the horse to keep to the way. But though Dapple had recovered his wind in the village there was no zest in his running and he seemed to keep straying off the road, so that Vasilii Andreich had several times to correct him.

'There's a post on the right, and another, and another,' Vasilii Andreich counted. And there's the forest, he thought, peering at something dark ahead. But what he took for the forest was merely a bush. They went past it and on for another fifty yards or so – there was no fourth post and no forest either. We'll be up to the forest any moment, thought Vasilii Andreich, and feeling in high spirits after the vodka and tea, he did not bother to stop, but continued shaking the reins, and the good obedient animal responded and ambled and trotted on in the direction it was made to go, though knowing full well that it was quite the wrong way. Ten minutes passed and there was still no forest.

'We're off the road again,' said Vasilii Andreich, pulling up the horse.

Without a word Nikita got out of the sledge and holding his caftan tight in the wind, which first made it cling to him and then nearly blew it off his shoulders, he began plodding about in the snow. First he went one way, then the other. Two or three times he disappeared from view completely. Finally he came back and took the reins out of Vasilii Andreich's hands.

'We've got to go right,' he said firmly and decisively, turning the horse.

'Very well, go right if that's the way,' said Vasilii Andreich, handing over the reins and pushing his frozen hands into his sleeves.

Nikita did not answer.

'Come on, old boy, put your back in it!' he shouted to the horse, but the horse, despite the shaking of the reins, only went at a walk.

The snow was knee-deep in places and the sledge jolted forward to the movements of the horse.

Nikita took the whip which hung at the front of the sledge and gave the horse a lash. The good beast, unused to the whip, plunged forward and broke into a trot, but immediately slowed again to an amble, then to a walk. They went on like this for another five minutes. It was so dark and snow swirled so thickly in the air and off the ground that sometimes even the shaft-bow could not be seen. It sometimes seemed that the sledge was standing still and that the countryside was rolling away behind them. All of a sudden the horse stopped abruptly, evidently sensing something amiss ahead. Nikita once more jumped lightly off the sledge, tossing aside the reins, and went to the front of the horse to see why it had stopped. But at the first step he tried to take further his feet slipped from under him and he went rolling down a sharp drop.

'Hold up, there! Hold up!' he said to himself, falling and trying to stop himself, but he could not get a grip and came to a halt only when his feet dug deep into the thick layer of snow he had brought down with him to the bottom of the gully. Disturbed by Nikita's fall, a drift of snow overhanging the drop showered down on top of him and filled his collar.

'You beast,' Nikita said reproachfully, addressing the snowdrift and the gully and shaking the snow from his collar.

'Nikita! Hi, Nikita!' Vasilii Andreich shouted down to him. But Nikita made no response.

He was too busy: he shook himself free of snow, then looked for the whip which he had dropped as he slid down the slope. When he had found it he made to climb straight up at the point where he had come down, but this proved impossible: he kept sliding back down again and so had to move along the gully bottom to find a way up. Six or seven yards from the place where he slid down he managed to clamber up on all fours, then followed the edge of the gully back to where the horse should be. He could see neither the horse nor the sledge, and being to the leeward got sight of them only after hearing the shouts of Vasilii Andreich and the neighing of Dapple calling him.

'All right, I'm coming. What's all that noise about?' he said to Dapple.

Only when he came right up to the sledge did he see the horse and Vasilii Andreich standing by it, looking enormous.

'Where the devil did you get to? We'll have to go back. At least to Grishkino,' Nikita's master berated him angrily.

'I'd be glad enough to go back, Vasilii Andreich, but which way do we go? This gully here is that deep that if you fell in you'd never get out. I was fair shook by it and had a job to get back up.'

'Well, we can't stay here, can we? We've got to go somewhere,' said Vasilii Andreich.

Nikita did not reply. He sat on the sledge with his back to the wind, took off his boots and shook out the snow that had packed inside them, after which he took some straw and carefully pushed it into his left boot to stop up a hole.

Vasilii Andreich said nothing, as though he was now leaving everything to Nikita. When he had got his boots on again Nikita tucked his feet into the sledge, once more drew on his gauntlets, then picked up the reins and turned the horse along the edge of the gully. But they had not gone a hundred yards when the horse again stopped and refused to budge. Before it lay another gully.

Once more Nikita got out and began plodding through the snow. He walked about for some time, and when at last he reappeared it was from the opposite direction to the way he had gone.

'Vasilii Andreich, you there?' he called.

'Over here!' Vasilii Andreich called back. 'Well, what did you find?'

'Can't fathom it at all. It's too dark. We're in among some gullies, can't tell which. We'd better head into the wind again.'

Once more they set off, once more Nikita plodded about through the snow, got back into the sledge, then again plodded in the snow till finally he stopped, panting, by the sledge.

'What now?' asked Vasilii Andreich.

'I'm dead beat, that's what!' said Nikita. 'And the horse is nearly done in too.'

'What do we do then?'

'Just hang on a minute.'

Nikita walked off again, but soon returned.

'Keep after me,' he said, going on ahead of the horse.

Vasilii Andreich had stopped giving orders and obediently did as Nikita told him.

'This way, after me,' shouted Nikita and went off quickly to the right, grasping Dapple's reins and leading him down a slope into a drift of snow.

At first the horse refused, but then plunged forward in hopes of leaping across to the other side of the drift. He failed to do so, however, and sank up to his collar in the snow.

'Get out!' Nikita shouted to Vasilii Andreich, who had remained sitting in the sledge. Then, grasping one of the shafts from underneath, Nikita began pushing the sledge on to the horse. 'It's tough going, old chap,' he said to Dapple. 'But there's nothing for it – so heave! Come on, come on, a bit more!' he cried.

The horse plunged forward – once, then again, but still failed to extricate himself and sank back as if pondering something.

'This won't do now, will it, old boy,' Nikita gently chided Dapple. 'Once more now!'

Again Nikita tugged at the shaft on his side; Vasilii Andreich did the same on the other side. The horse jerked his head, then made a sudden lunge forward.

'Come on now! That's it! You won't sink in!' shouted Nikita.

One leap, then another and another, and finally the horse was free of the drift. He stopped, breathing heavily and shaking himself. Nikita was going to lead him on, but Vasilii Andreich with his double layer of fur coats had got so out of breath that he could walk no further and collapsed into the sledge.

'Let's get my breath back,' he said, loosening the kerchief which he had tied round the collar of his top-coat in the village.

'It's not so bad here,' said Nikita. 'You lie there and I'll lead the horse.' And with Vasilii Andreich in the sledge he took the horse by the bridle and led him on for a dozen yards downhill, then up a little and stopped.

The place where Nikita had stopped was not right in the hollow where snow driven from the bank above could settle and cover them completely, but it was still fairly sheltered from the wind by the rim of the gully. There were moments when the wind seemed to be dropping, but they were only brief and as if to make up for this respite the storm then blew ten times harder, the wind gusting and swirling more viciously than ever. One such gust struck as Vasilii Andreich, having recovered his breath, got out of the sledge and went over to Nikita to consider what they should do. Both involuntarily bent forward and delayed speaking until the gust had spent its fury. Dapple also flattened his ears in displeasure and shook his head. When the gust had dropped a little, Nikita took off his gauntlets, shoved them into his girdle and after blowing on his hands began to untie the reins from the shaft-bow.

'What's that you're doing?' asked Vasilii Andreich.

'Unharnessing. What else can we do? I'm all in,' Nikita answered, as if apologizing.

'But we'll get somewhere surely?'

'We shan't get anywhere. We'll only wear the horse out. Poor thing, he's done in anyway,' said Nikita, pointing to the horse which stood obediently ready, his steep wet flanks heaving. 'We'll have to stay here the night,' Nikita repeated casually, as if he was going to spend the night at an inn, and began undoing the hamestrap. The points of the hames sprang apart.

'Might we not freeze to death?' said Vasilii Andreich.

'Maybe so, but you can't help that,' answered Nikita.

6

VASILII ANDREICH felt quite warm in his two fur coats, especially after his exertions in the snow-drift, but a chill ran down his spine when he realized that he actually had to spend the night here. To steady his nerves he sat in the sledge and reached for his cigarettes and matches.

Nikita meanwhile unharnessed the horse. He undid the girth and back-strap, unthreaded the reins, and after releasing the tugs pulled off the shaft-bow. All the time he was talking to the horse to cheer it.

'Come on then, out you come,' he said as he led him from the shafts. 'Now we'll just hitch you up here. I'll put you some straw down and take off your bridle,' he went on, performing the actions as he said them. 'You have a bite to eat, then you'll feel better.'

But Dapple was evidently not comforted by Nikita's talk. He was restless, shifting from foot to foot, huddling against the sledge with his rump to the wind and rubbing his head on Nikita's sleeve.

As if only to please Nikita by not refusing the offered straw which he pushed under his muzzle Dapple snatched a wisp of straw from the sledge, but at once decided that this was no time for eating and let it go. It was immediately scattered and borne away by the wind, then covered with snow.

'Now let's rig up a signal,' said Nikita. He turned the sledge into the wind and using the back-strap he tied the shafts together, then lifted them up and pulled them in against the front of the sledge. 'There, now if we get snowed over good people will see from the shafts where we are and dig us out,' said Nikita, beating his gauntlets together and then putting them on. 'That's something I learnt from the old folk.'

Meanwhile Vasilii Andreich had loosened his top-coat and under cover of its flaps was striking sulphur matches on his steel box, but his hands were shaking and one after the other the matches flared and before they were properly alight or else the moment he put them to his cigarette they were blown out by the wind. In the end one match did light properly. It momentarily lit up the fur of his coat, his hand with the gold ring on his crooked index-finger, and the snow-covered straw that showed from under the sacking, and his cigarette was alight. He avidly drew on it a couple of times, inhaling the smoke and breathing it out through his moustache; he was going to inhale again, but the burning end of tobacco was whisked off by the wind and carried away in the same direction as the straw.

But even these few draws of tobacco smoke raised Vasilii Andreich's spirits.

'If we've got to stay here the night, then that's that!' he said with decision.

'Half a minute, I'll make a flag too,' he said, picking up the kerchief which he had taken from his collar and dropped in the sledge. He removed his gloves, stood up at the front of the sledge and, stretching up to reach the back-strap, tightly tied the kerchief to it alongside one of the shafts.

The kerchief at once began furiously flapping, clinging one moment to the shaft, then blowing free, pulling and cracking.

'A handy job,' said Vasilii Andreich, admiring his work and sinking back into the sledge. 'It would be warmer together, but there's not room for the two of us,' he said.

'I'll find myself a spot,' answered Nikita. 'But we must put something over the horse, poor thing he's all of a sweat as it is. Let's have this,' he said, coming up to the sledge and pulling the sacking from under Vasilii Andreich.

He took the sacking and folded it in two and put it over Dapple, after removing the saddle and breeching.

'It'll help to keep you warm, you silly old thing,' he said, putting the breeching and saddle back on over the sacking.

With this task completed, Nikita returned to the sledge.

'Would you be wanting that bit of canvas?' he said. 'And then if you let me have some straw.'

He took the canvas and straw from under Vasilii Andreich and went round the back of the sledge. He dug out a hollow for himself in the snow and laid the straw inside; he then pulled his cap well down, wrapped himself in his caftan, and sat himself on the straw with the canvas over him, leaning against the back of the sledge to protect himself from the wind and snow.

Vasilii Andreich shook his head at what Nikita was doing, disapproving as he did in general of the uneducated, stupid ways of the peasants. He began to settle down for the night.

He spread the remaining straw more evenly over the sledge, built it up a little under his side and with his hands thrust up his sleeves he tucked his head into the angle at the front of the sledge to get some shelter from the wind.

He did not feel like sleep and lay thinking. He thought of only one thing – that which constituted for him the sole purpose, sense, pride and joy in life: how much money he had made and how much he might still make; how much money people he knew had made and what they were now worth, the means by which this money was made, and how much more money they and he could make together. The purchase of the wood at Goryachkino was of immense importance to him. With this wood he hoped to make an immediate profit of maybe 10,000 roubles. And he began a mental calculation of the value of the coppice – he had seen it in the autumn and counted every tree in its five acres.

'The oak will go for sledge-runners. Then of course timber for building. And there should be around 400 cubic yards of firewood a *desyatina*★,' he said to himself. 'At the very least that'll give me 225 roubles a *desyatina*. There are fifty-six *desyatinas* – that's fifty-six times a hundred twice, fifty-six times ten twice and fifty-six times five.' He could see that this came to over 12,000 roubles, but without his abacus he could not work it out exactly. I shan't give 10,000 just the same. I'll give 8,000, and that can be not counting the clearings. I'll slip the surveyor a hundred or a hundred and fifty and he'll see I get four or five *desyatinas* of clearing. He'll let it go for 8,000. He can have 3,000 down straight away. That ought to bring him round, he thought, pressing the wallet in his pocket with his forearm. Heaven knows how we came to miss the way! There should be forest here and the keeper's hut. Should be able to hear the dogs. Damned creatures never bark when you want them to. He eased his collar away from his ear and listened: all he could hear was the wind whistling as before, the kerchief flapping and cracking between the shafts and the falling snow whipping against the bast front of the sledge. He pulled his collar to again.

If we had only known, we could have stayed overnight. Well, it doesn't matter. We'll be there tomorrow. It's only an extra day. And the others won't be travelling in this weather either. And he remembered that by the ninth of the month he

★ 1 *desyatina* = 2·7 acres. – *Translator*.

should be getting paid by the butcher for the wethers he had sold him. He was going to come himself; he'll find me away and the wife won't know about taking the money. No education at all she's got. No idea how to behave in company, his thoughts went on, as he recalled her awkwardness with the police-superintendent who had been among his guests only that day. But what can you expect from a woman? Where has she ever been to see anything? What was it like at home in my parents' time? Nothing special – father was just a well-off peasant with a hulling-mill and an inn – that was all he had. And in fifteen years what have I achieved? A shop, two taverns, a flour-mill, a granary, two estates on lease, a house and barn with a good metal roof, he remembered with pride. Not like in father's time. Who's the big man in the district now? Brekhunov.

And why is that? Because I keep my mind on my business, exert myself – not like others who idle around or fritter their time away. I'll miss a night's sleep. Blizzard or not I go out just the same. And that's how I get things done. They think you can whistle and money comes to you. No, you've got to work for it and use your brains. Like this – spending the night out of doors and going without sleep. Even at night your mind never at rest, he reflected with pride. They think you get on in the world through luck. Look at the Mironovs, they're in the millionaire bracket now. And why is that? You've got to work for it; God will provide. Just as long as you keep healthy.

And the idea that he, too, might be a millionaire like Mironov who had started from nothing so excited Vasilii Andreich that he felt a sudden need to talk to someone. But there was nobody to talk to . . . If they had got to Goryach-kino he could have had his talk with the owner and outsmarted him.

My word, it doesn't half blow! We'll be that snowed up we shall never get out in the morning, he thought as he listened to the gust of wind which blew into the front of the sledge, bending it over and whipping the snow against the sheet of bast. He raised himself slightly and looked around. In the shifting white darkness he could only see Dapple's dark head and his back covered by the wind-blown sacking, and his thick knotted tail; and all around on every side, ahead and behind, there was the same monotonous shifting white gloom, which seemed at moments to grow a fraction lighter, at others to thicken still more.

I should never have listened to Nikita, he thought. We ought to have gone on – we would have come out somewhere. We could even have gone back to Grishkino and spent the night at Taras's. And now we are stuck here all night. What was so good then? Oh yes, that God rewards hard work and gives nothing to loafers, idlers, and fools. Yes, and we must have a smoke! He sat back and got out his cigarette-case. He then turned over on to his stomach, using the flap of his coat to protect the flame from the wind, but the wind found its way through and one after the other blew out the matches he lit. In the end he contrived to get one alight and lit his cigarette. He was enormously pleased with this achievement. Although the wind consumed more of the cigarette than he did, he still inhaled two or three times and his spirits rose again. Once more he huddled against the back of the sledge, wrapped himself up, and began again going over past events and day-dreaming, when without realizing it he suddenly slipped from consciousness and fell into a doze.

But all of a sudden he came to, as if jolted awake by something. Perhaps it was Dapple tugging straw from under him, perhaps some sudden twinge inside him: whatever it was, he woke up with his heart pounding so fast and strong that the sledge seemed to be shaking under him. He opened his eyes. Round about it was just the same, except that it seemed lighter. It's getting light, he thought. So it can't be long till morning. But he remembered at once that it was only lighter because the moon had risen. He raised himself up and looked first at the horse. Dapple still stood with his back to the wind, shaking all over. The snow-covered sacking had blown up on one side, the breeching had slipped over, and the horse's head, covered with snow, with the mane and forelock streaming in the wind was now better visible. Vasilii Andreich twisted round towards the back of the sledge and looked over it. Nikita was still in the same position, just as he had sat down. The canvas, which he had put on top of him, and his legs too were deep in snow. I hope the fellow doesn't freeze to death; it's shoddy stuff he's wearing. The next thing I'll be held responsible for him. What a useless lot they are. No education at all, thought Vasilii Andreich, and he was going to take the sacking off the horse to put over Nikita, but it was too cold to get up and move about and anyway he was afraid that the horse might freeze. What did I bring him along for anyway? It was all because of her stupidity! thought Vasilii Andreich, remembering his unloved wife. And once more he sprawled over and got into his old position towards the front of the sledge. Well, my uncle once spent a whole night out in the snow and was none the worse for it, he recalled. But then, he thought as another instance came to mind, when they dug Sevastian out he was dead, all stiff like a lump of frozen meat.

If I'd stopped for the night in Grishkino there would be nothing to worry about. Then, pulling his coat tight about him to make sure that the warmth of the fur was nowhere wasted and kept the cold from his neck, his knees and his feet, he shut his eyes and tried to go back to sleep. But now, however much he tried, he could not fall asleep. On the contrary he felt wide awake and active. He began once again reckoning up his profits and what people owed him, again he boasted inwardly, delighted with himself and the position he had reached in life, but his thoughts were now constantly interrupted by a creeping fear and his irritation at not having stopped overnight in Grishkino. How much better I would be stretched out on a bench in the warm. He turned over several times and tried to settle himself in a position that was more comfortable and sheltered from the wind, but every position seemed uncomfortable. He would once more sit up, get into a new position, tuck his coat round his legs, close his eyes and lie still. But each time his cramped legs in their thick felt boots started aching or else there was a draught somewhere, and he would lie for a while, annoyed by the thought that he might now be lying comfortably in a warm house in Grishkino, and then again sit up, turn about, tuck himself in and once more settle down.

Once Vasilii Andreich fancied he heard cocks crowing in the distance. Overjoyed, he turned down his coat and listened intently, but however much he strained his ears he could hear nothing but the sound of the wind whistling in the shafts and flapping the kerchief, and the snow whipping against the bast front of the sledge.

All this time Nikita was sitting just as he had from the outset, without stirring and not even replying to Vasilii Andreich when he called to him a couple of times. A fat lot he cares. He must be asleep, Vasilii Andreich thought in annoyance, looking over the back of the sledge at Nikita who was covered thick with snow.

Vasilii Andreich got up and lay down a couple of dozen times. The night seemed it would never end. It must be getting on for morning now, he thought once as he raised himself and looked around. Let's have a look at my watch. If I undo my coat I'll get frozen. But if I can see it's getting towards morning I'll feel much better. We can start getting harnessed up. In his heart of hearts Vasilii Andreich knew that it could not yet be morning, but he was becoming increasingly nervous and wanted both to check his instinct about the time and also to deceive himself. He carefully undid the hooks of his inner fur jacket and thrust his hand into his breast where he fumbled for some time before getting to his waistcoat. With the utmost difficulty he extracted his silver watch painted with enamel flowers. He looked at it, but could see nothing without a light. He again lay face downwards, supporting himself on his elbows and knees as he had when lighting his cigarette, got out his matches and tried to light one. He set about it more systematically than before and having felt out the match with the biggest phosphorus head he lit it first go. He moved the dial into the light and glanced at it. He could not believe his eyes . . . It was only ten past twelve. The whole night still lay ahead.

Ah, it's a long night! thought Vasilii Andreich and a chill ran down his spine. Then, fastening his coats again and covering himself over, he huddled into the angle of the sledge to wait patiently. Suddenly through the monotonous noise of the wind he distinctly heard a new, living sound. It got steadily louder until it was fully distinct, then just as steadily it grew fainter. There was no doubt what it was: it was a wolf. And this wolf was howling somewhere so close that you could hear the modulations of its cry as it moved its jaws. Vasilii Andreich threw back his collar and listened carefully. Dapple also listened intently, twitching his ears and, when the wolf's cry was completed, shifted his feet and gave a warning snort. After that Vasilii Andreich was totally unable to calm down, much less get to sleep. Try as he would to concentrate on his calculations and business affairs, on his good name, his merits and his wealth, he was gripped by a growing fear, which dominated all his thoughts, and to all else was added the question: why had he not stopped for the night in Grishkino?

Hang the wood! I'm doing well enough without that. Ah, if only there was somewhere we could spend the night! he said to himself. They say that drunk people are the ones who freeze to death, he thought. And I've been drinking. And, as he thought how he felt, he found he was beginning to tremble, whether from cold or fear he could not tell. He tried to cover himself up and lie as he had before, but this was now impossible. He could not keep still, he felt he had to get up and do something in order to repress the fear that rose within him and which he felt powerless to resist. He again got out his cigarettes and matches, but there were only three matches left now and they the poorest ones. All three struck without catching light.

'Damn you, go to hell then!' he swore – at what he did not know – and flung the crumpled cigarette away. He was going to throw the matchbox away too, but restrained himself and thrust it into his pocket. He was now in such a state of agitation that he could no longer keep still. He got out of the sledge, and, turning his back to the wind, began pulling his belt in tight and low round his waist.

What's the point of lying here waiting to die? Why not get on the horse and clear out of here? the thought suddenly struck him. The horse can go all right with someone on his back. And as for him, he thought concerning Nikita, dead or alive it's all the same. What sort of life has he got? Life means nothing to him, but – praise be to God – I've got something to live for . . .

He unhitched the horse, slipped the reins over his neck, and tried to jump on to his back, but his coats and boots were too heavy and he slid off. Then he tried to mount standing on the sledge, but the sledge rocked beneath his weight and again he came off. At the third attempt by drawing the horse close into the sledge and standing carefully on its side he at last succeeded in sprawling himself across the horse's back. He lay like that for a little, then edged himself forward a couple of times and finally put a leg over the horse's back and got himself seated, with his feet resting on the horizontal strap of the breeching. The jerk of the sledge as it swayed woke Nikita. He half rose, and Vasilii Andreich had an impression that he said something.

'You and your stupid ideas! You don't expect me to die for nothing, do you?' shouted Vasilii Andreich and tucking the flying tails of his coat under his knees he turned the horse and set him going away from the sledge in the direction where he supposed the forest and the keeper's hut to be.

7

SINCE settling himself behind the sledge with the canvas over him Nikita had sat perfectly still. Like anyone who lives close to nature and knows the meaning of want he had plenty of patience and could wait for hours or even days with an easy mind and temper. He heard his master call him, but did not answer because he did not want to disturb himself to reply. He still felt warm after the tea and from all the movement of struggling through the drifted snow, but he knew that this warmth would not last long and that he would not have the energy to keep warm by moving about, because he felt the same weariness that a horse does when it stops and, regardless of the whip, just cannot go on and its master sees that he must feed it to make it work any more. One of Nikita's feet – the one in the holed boot – was chilled through and the feeling had already gone from his big toe. And apart from that he was getting steadily colder all over. It occurred to him that before morning he might and most probably would die, but the prospect did not strike him as all that unpleasant or terrifying. To him the thought of death was not particularly unpleasant because his whole life had not been one long holiday, far from it – it had been a life of unending service to others of which he was now growing weary. And the thought was not all that terrifying because apart from the various masters such as Vasilii Andreich whom he had served in this life, he had always felt himself dependent on that greatest of all masters who had sent him into this world and he knew that even in death he would still be in the power of this great master, who would not treat him amiss. Sorry to leave all the old familiar things? Well, that's the way it is, you'll just have to get used to the new ways.

What of my sins? he thought and recalled his drunkenness, the money he had squandered on drink, the terrible way he had treated his wife, his swearing, not going to church, not keeping the fasts and all the other things which the priest rebuked him for at confession. I've sinned all right. But did I bring it on myself? It's how God made me. Oh, how I've sinned! But what can you do about it?

It was only at first that he thought in this way about what might befall him that night, after that he gave it no further thought and became lost in various memories which came to mind. He remembered the arrival of Marfa, the drunkenness of the workmen, and the times he had given up drink, then he recalled the present journey, Taras's house, the talk about dividing property, and he thought of his own boy, and of Dapple, who would be warmer now under the horse-cloth, and then of his master who was making the sledge creak as he tossed and turned in it. Poor chap, he thought, he must be wishing he'd never come, I reckon. Living like he does you don't want to die. It's different for the likes of me. And all these memories began to grow confused and intermingled in his mind, and he fell asleep.

When Vasilii Andreich rocked the sledge as he got on the horse, the back of the sledge, against which Nikita was leaning, jerked away from him and he was struck in the back by one of the runners. This caused Nikita to wake up and change his position whether he liked it or not. Straightening his legs with difficulty and causing the snow to fall off them, he stood up – and at once his whole body was pierced by an excruciating coldness. Realizing what Vasilii Andreich was doing, he wanted him to leave the piece of sacking which the horse did not need so that he could use it as a cover himself, and he called out to him about it.

But Vasilii Andreich did not stop and vanished in the curtain of powdery snow.

Left on his own Nikita thought for a moment what he should do. He felt he had not the strength to go in search of some dwelling. He could not go back to where he was sitting

since it was now covered with snow. Nor did he feel there
was any prospect of getting warm in the sledge, because he
had nothing to put over him, and there was no longer any
warmth in this caftan and top-coat. He was so cold he might
have had only his shirt on. A feeling of dread came over him.
'Lord, our Father in Heaven!' he said, and was relieved
by the consciousness that he was not alone and that there was
someone who heard him and would not abandon him. He
gave a deep sigh and, leaving the sacking over his head, he got
into the sledge and lay down in the place where his master had
lain.

But he could not get warm in the sledge either. At first he
shivered all over; after that the shivering passed and he began
to lose consciousness. He did not know if he was dying or falling asleep, whichever it was he felt equally prepared.

8

MEANWHILE Vasilii Andreich was driving the horse on with
feet and reins towards where for some reason he supposed the
forest and the keeper's hut to be. He was blinded by the snow,
the wind seemed anxious to hold him back, but relentlessly he
drove the horse on, crouching forward and continually drawing his coat across him and tucking it between himself and the
small cold saddle which stopped him sitting properly. Though
with difficulty, the horse obediently went at an ambling pace
along the way he was made to go.

For some five minutes Vasilii Andreich rode as he thought in
a straight line, seeing nothing but the horse's head and the
white wilderness, hearing nothing but the wind whistling past
the horse's ears and the collar of his fur top-coat.

There was suddenly something dark ahead. His heart
thumped with joy and he headed towards this dark something,
already seeing it as the walls of houses in the village. But the

dark shape did not keep still, it kept moving, and it was not the village but a tall patch of wormwood that had grown up along the edge of a field and stood up clear of the snow, frantically tossing in the wind, which bent it over and whistled through it. For some reason the sight of this wormwood tormented by the merciless wind made Vasilii Andreich shudder and he hastily urged the horse on, not noticing that in going towards the wormwood he had completely changed course and was now pointing the horse in a quite different direction, though he still supposed he was heading for where the keeper's hut should be. But the horse kept pulling to the right and Vasilii Andreich continually had to make him go left.

Once more there was something dark ahead. He was overjoyed, certain that this really must now be the village. But again it was a field-boundary with wormwood growing along it. The tall dry weeds tossed and swayed as frantically as ever and unaccountably terrified Vasilii Andreich. But it was not only that the weeds were the same – alongside ran hoof-prints partly covered with blown snow. Vasilii Andreich stopped and bent to take a closer look: it was the lightly covered tracks of a horse and it could be no one else's but his own. He had evidently been going in a circle and in quite a small compass. This way I'm done for! he thought, but so as not to give way to his fear he drove the horse on more urgently than before, peering ahead into the snowy white gloom in which shining dots seemed to appear, only to vanish the moment he tried to focus on them. Once he thought he heard the bark of a dog or the howl of a wolf, but the sound was so faint and indistinct that he could not tell if he had actually heard it or if it was just his fancy, so he stopped to listen.

All at once there was a terrible deafening cry right in his ears and everything shuddered and shook beneath him. Vasilii Andreich grabbed the horse's neck, but that too was shuddering and the terrible cry was more terrifying than before. For some seconds Vasilii Andreich could not collect himself and realize what it was. In fact all that had happened was that Dapple – for good cheer or as a cry for help – had let out a loud, well-tuned neigh. 'Damned horse! Proper put the wind up me!' said Vasilii Andreich to himself. But even though he now knew what had caused his fear he could not shake it off.

I've got to come to and get a grip on myself, he thought, but still he could not help himself and pressed the horse on, without noticing that he now had the wind behind him and not in his face. His body, especially in the crutch, where it was exposed and touched the saddle, was chilled through and aching, his arms and legs trembled, his breath came in gasps. He could see that he would perish in this awful waste of snow and saw no way of escape.

Suddenly the horse collapsed under him. It was deep in a drift and began to struggle, falling over on its side. Vasilii Andreich sprang off. In doing so he pulled over the breeching which supported his foot and twisted askew the saddle to which he held while jumping off. No sooner had Vasilii Andreich sprung clear than the horse found its feet again and plunged ahead. It gave a couple of leaps, let out another neigh and disappeared from sight, trailing the sackcloth and breeching behind and leaving Vasilii Andreich alone in the snowdrift. Vasilii Andreich dashed after it, but the snow was so deep and his fur coats so heavy that with every step he sank in over his knees and after running some twenty yards he was out of breath and stopped. What will become of it all? he thought. The coppice, the wethers, the leasehold, my shop and taverns, my metal-roofed house and barn, my son and heir? What's going on? It just can't be true! And for some reason he remembered the wormwood tossing in the wind which he had twice passed and experienced such a feeling of terror that he did not believe that this was actually happening to him. He thought it must all be a dream and tried to wake up, but there was no other, waking world. It was real snow which lashed his face and settled on him and numbed his right hand whose glove he had lost; and this was a real wilderness, this place where he was now alone, like the wormwood, waiting for death, inevitable, swift and pointless.

Mother of Heaven, Holy Father Nicholas, thou who teachest the way of abstinence . . . he recalled the prayers said the day before, and the icon with the black face framed in the golden riza, and the candles he sold for lighting to this icon which were then promptly returned to him and stored away in a bin, scarcely used. And he begged this same Nicholas the miracle-worker to save him, and promised to offer prayers and candles to him. But at the same time he realized clearly and certainly that the face on the icon, the frame, the candles, the priest and the prayers were all very important and necessary *there*, in church, but that where he was they could do nothing for him, and that there was not and could not be any possible connection between these candles and prayers and his present desperate plight. I must not despair, he thought. And he had an idea. I must follow the tracks of the horse before they get covered. The horse will lead me aright. I might even catch him. The great thing is not to hurry or I'll get tired out and be worse off still. But despite his intention to go slowly, he hurried on and ran, continually falling and getting up and falling again. The horse tracks were already hard to see where there was no depth of snow. I'm done for, thought Vasilii Andreich. I can't follow the tracks and I'll never catch up with the horse. But at that very moment as he looked ahead he saw something black. It was Dapple – and not only Dapple, but also the sledge and the upright shafts with his kerchief. With the breeching and sackcloth pulled over to one side Dapple now stood where he had been before, only nearer the shafts; he was shaking his head, which was held down by the reins caught up in his leg. It turned out that Vasilii Andreich had got stuck in the same gully where he and Nikita had got stuck earlier; the horse was taking him back to the sledge and where he had jumped off was no more than fifty yards away from it.

9

VASILII ANDREICH struggled to the sledge and caught hold of it. For some time he stood motionless, trying to calm down and recover his breath. Nikita was not where he had left him, but there was something in the sledge covered with snow and Vasilii Andreich guessed it was Nikita. He felt no fear now: if he was afraid of anything it was only of that awful state of fear that had come over him on the horse and especially when he was left alone in the snowdrift. At all costs he must keep this fear at bay and to do this he had to have some task, something to occupy him. He made a start by turning away from the wind and loosening his top-coat. Then as soon as he had got his breath a little he shook the snow out of his boots and his left-hand glove (the other was lost beyond recall and was probably under a foot of snow by now), pulled in his girdle again tight and low round his waist – the way he did when he stepped from his store to deal with the peasants who came with their wagons of corn for sale – and prepared for action. The first task that occurred to him was to free the horse's leg. This Vasilii Andreich did and having got the rein clear he tethered Dapple to the iron bracket on the front of the sledge where he had been before. He then started to go slowly round the back of the horse to straighten the saddle, breeching, and sackcloth. But as he did so he noticed a stirring in the sledge and Nikita's head lifted itself from beneath its covering of snow. Evidently with great effort Nikita, already far gone with cold, raised his body and sat up, waving his hand strangely in front of his face as though brushing away flies. He waved his hand and said something and to Vasilii Andreich it seemed that he was calling him. He left the sacking as it was and went to the sledge.

'What is it?' he asked. 'What's that you say?'

'I'm dying, I am.' Nikita spoke with difficulty, his voice faltering. 'What I've earned – let the boy have it, or the wife, doesn't matter which.'

'The frost's got you, has it?' said Vasilii Andreich.

'I'm dying, I can feel it . . . forgive me, for Christ's sake,' said Nikita plaintively, still waving his hands across his face as though brushing away flies.

Vasilii Andreich stood some half a minute without speaking or moving, then suddenly, with the same decisiveness as when he shook hands to clinch some advantageous deal, he moved back a step, turned up the sleeves of his top-coat and with both hands began digging the snow off Nikita and out of the sledge. When he had got it clear, Vasilii Andreich hastily undid his belt, opened out his coat and, giving Nikita a shove, lay on top of him, covering him not only with the coat, but also with his body which was warm and heated from moving about. He secured the coat, using his hands to tuck in the sides between Nikita and the sledge and his knees to hold down the bottom edge, and lay face down, resting his head against the bast front of the sledge. He now no longer heard the movements of the horse or the whistling of the wind – he listened only to Nikita's breathing. For a long time Nikita lay quite still, but then gave a loud sigh and stirred.

'There now – and you talk about dying! You just lie there and get warm, that's the way . . .' began Vasilii Andreich.

But much to his surprise he found he could not go on because tears came to his eyes and his chin began quivering. He stopped speaking and tried to swallow the lump that rose in his throat. I've really got the wind up, I can see. I'm failing, he thought. But this failing was not disagreeable to him, on the contrary it gave him a special feeling of happiness such as he had never had before.

'That's the way,' he said to himself, feeling a curious solemn state of bliss. He lay for quite a long time, wiping his eyes on

the fur of his coat and tucking under his knees the right side
of his coat which kept blowing up in the wind.

But he desperately wanted to tell someone about the joy he
felt.

'Nikita,' he said.

'I'm all right. Warm,' the answer came from under him.

'I nearly came to grief, old chap. And you would have died
of cold, and I would have . . .'

But at this point his cheeks again began quivering, his eyes
brimmed with tears and he could not go on.

Never mind, he thought. I know what it is I know.

He lay for a long time in silence.

He was warmed underneath by Nikita and on top from his
fur coat, but his hands, which held down his coat on either side
of Nikita, and his legs, from which the coat was constantly
being blown by the wind, began to freeze. The right hand on
which he had no glove was particularly bad. But he gave no
thought to his legs and hands and considered only how he
might warm back to life the peasant who lay beneath him.

Several times he looked at the horse. He saw that its back
was uncovered and that the sackcloth and breeching were lying
in the snow; he saw that he should get up and cover the horse,
but he could not bring himself to leave Nikita and disturb his
state of bliss even for a moment. He felt not the slightest fear
now.

He'll be all right, he told himself, speaking of his warming
Nikita back to life in the same boastful way as he talked about
his purchases and sales.

Vasilii Andreich lay like this for an hour, two hours, three
hours, but he did not notice the passage of time. Impressions of
the blizzard, the shafts, the horse under the shaft-bow floated
through his mind, all jogging before his eyes; then he remembered Nikita who was lying underneath him; other memories
mingled with these impressions – the feast-day, his wife, the
police-superintendent, the candle-bin, and he thought of Nikita

again lying under this bin, and of the peasants who came to buy and sell, and he saw white walls, and houses roofed with metal and Nikita lying underneath them; then everything jumbled together, one thing merged with another, and just as the colours of the rainbow combine to form a single white light, so all these different impressions merged into a single nothingness, and he fell asleep. He slept long and dreamlessly, but as dawn approached his dreams returned. He dreamed he was standing by the candle-bin; Tikhon's wife wanted a five-kopek candle for a holy day and he tried to get one for her, but his hands were pushed tight in his pockets and he could not lift them. He wanted to go round the bin, but his legs would not move: his new, freshly cleaned overshoes were fixed to the stone floor and it was impossible to lift them or to step out of them. And suddenly the candle-bin was no longer a candle-bin but a bed, and Vasilii Andreich dreamed he was lying on his stomach on the candle-bin – his bed, that is – at home. He lay on the bed and was unable to get up, though he had to because Ivan Matveich, the police-superintendent, would be collecting him at any moment and he had to go with him to see about buying a coppice or else to put Dapple's breeching straight. And he asked his wife: 'Has he not come yet, Nikolaevna?' and she said: 'No, not yet.' And he heard someone drive up to the front steps. That must be him. No, they have gone past. 'Hi, Nikolaevna, has he still not come?' 'There's no sign of him.' And he lay on the bed, still unable to rise, waiting, and the waiting filled him with dread and also with bliss. And then suddenly his bliss was complete: the person he was waiting for came, and it was not Ivan Matveich, the superintendent, but someone else, though still the person he was expecting. This person came and summoned him and he who summoned him was the same as he who had called him and commanded him to lie on top of Nikita. And Vasilii Andreich was glad that this someone had come for him. He cried joyfully: 'I'm coming,' and his own shout roused him. And he woke up, but on waking he was no longer as when he fell asleep. He attempted to get up but could not, he tried moving his arm, but could not. His leg too would not move. He tried to turn his head, but could not do that either. He was surprised, but not at all worried by this. He realized that this was death, but this too did not in the least concern him. He remembered that Nikita was lying underneath him and that Nikita was now warm again and alive, and he felt that he was Nikita and Nikita him and that his own life was not in him but in Nikita. And he listened carefully and could hear Nikita breathing, even faintly snoring. Nikita is alive, so I am alive, too, he told himself in triumph.

And he remembered about his money, his shop, his house, his purchases and sales and the Mironovs' millions; it was hard for him to understand why this man they had called Vasilii Brekhunov had concerned himself with the things he had. He never knew what life was about, he thought concerning Vasilii Brekhunov. He never knew, but I do. I know now for sure. *Now I know.* And once more he heard the call of the one who summoned him. 'Coming, coming,' his whole being answered in joy and ecstasy. And he felt that he was free and that nothing held him any more.

And indeed Vasilii Andreich neither saw, nor heard, nor felt any more in this world.

All around the air was thick with swirling snow, which settled over the fur top-coat of the dead Vasilii Andreich, over Dapple who shook in every limb, over the now scarcely visible sledge, and over Nikita who lay, warmed back to life, in the bottom of the sledge beneath the body of his now dead master.

10

JUST before morning Nikita awoke. It was the cold striking into his back again that woke him. He dreamed he was driving back from the miller's with a load of flour for the master and, as he crossed the stream, he missed the bridge and got the cart stuck. And he dreamed that he got under the cart and tried to raise it on his arched back. It was odd, though, because the cart refused to budge and clung to his back and he could neither raise it nor get out from underneath it. It crushed the small of his back. And the cart was very cold! He obviously had to get out. 'Hey, that'll do,' he said to whoever it was pressing the cart down on his back. 'Unload the sacks!' But the cart pressed down on him and got colder and colder, then suddenly there was a curious knocking and he woke up properly. It all came back to him. The cold cart was his master frozen to death and lying on top of him. The knocking was Dapple, who had kicked the sledge a couple of times with his hoof.

'Andreich, hey there, Andreich!' Nikita called warily to his master, already sensing the truth and flexing his back.

But Andreich made no reply and his stomach and legs were firm and cold and heavy like weights.

He must be dead. God rest his soul, thought Nikita.

He twisted his head, dug a hole through the snow in front of him with his hand and opened his eyes. It was light. The wind still whistled through the shafts and the snow still fell, only now it no longer lashed against the bast sides of the sledge but was silently drifting ever deeper over the sledge and the horse. There was now no sound of movement or breathing from the horse. He'll have frozen to death too, thought Nikita. And indeed the kicking on the sledge which had woken Nikita was the dying effort made by Dapple, already frozen stiff, to keep on his feet.

'Oh Lord, our Father, you're calling me as well,' said Nikita to himself. 'Well, thy will be done. It's a fearsome thing though. But then, you only die once and it comes to all of us. Let it only be soon . . .' And he slipped his hand under cover again, shut his eyes and lapsed into oblivion, fully convinced that now he was dying for sure.

It was dinner-time the following day when Vasilii Andreich and Nikita were eventually dug out by some peasants – seventy yards from the road and less than half a mile from the village.

The snow had drifted right over the sledge, but the shafts and kerchief were still visible. Dapple was standing waist-deep in snow with the breeching and sackcloth slipped to one side. He was white all over; his dead head was drawn low into his hard frozen neck; icicles hung from his nostrils; his eyes were frosted over, and they too were crusted with icicles, like tears. This one night had so wasted him that all that was left of him was skin and bones. Vasilii Andreich was stiff, like a frozen carcase of meat, and when he was pulled off Nikita his legs were stuck awkwardly apart just as he had placed them. His bulging hawk-like eyes were iced over and under the trimmed moustache his open mouth was packed with snow. Nikita, however, was still alive, though frost-bitten all over. When they woke him up Nikita was convinced that he was dead and that what was happening to him now was not in this world but in the next. When he heard the shouts of the peasants who were digging him out after heaving aside the stiffened body of Vasilii Andreich he was at first surprised that in the next world peasants shouted just as on earth, and that Vasilii Andreich's body was there too; but when he realized that he was still here in this world he was more sorry than pleased, especially when he became aware that the toes of both his feet were frost-bitten.

Nikita was in hospital for two months. Three of his toes were amputated, but the others got better, so that he was able to work, and he lived another twenty years, first working as a general hand and then, as he got on in years, as a watchman. He died only this year – at home, as was his wish, lying below the icons with a wax candle in his hands. Before he died he asked forgiveness of his wife and forgave her her affair with the cooper. He also took leave of his son and his grandchildren and died genuinely glad that with his death there would be one less mouth for his son and daughter-in-law to feed and that now he really was passing from this wearisome life into that other life which with each passing year and hour had become for him more comprehensible and appealing. Is he better or worse off in that place where he awoke after this, his actual death? Was he disappointed, or did he there find what he had expected? That we shall all soon know.

HADJI MURAT

Translator's Note

FROM the beginning of the eighteenth century wars with Turkey and Persia had drawn Russia into the Caucasus. Gradually a line of forts and Cossack outposts was established along the northern boundary of the Caucasus to act as a shield against invasion and a base for expansion southwards. The absorption of Georgia (which lies south of the main Caucasus range) into the Russian Empire in 1800 created both the opportunity and the need to undertake the conquest of the remainder of the Caucasian isthmus. It was no easy task: the terrain was mountainous, cleft with deep valleys, and in many areas thickly forested; the local tribes were fiercely independent, warlike, and highly skilled in the raiding and harassing tactics suited to the country. In the event the conquest of the Caucasus involved a long and bitter struggle which lasted into the second half of the nineteenth century.

The policy of subjugation was first vigorously pursued under General Ermolov, who was commander-in-chief in the Caucasus from 1816 to 1826. The destructive campaigns conducted by Ermolov extended Russia's control of territory, but had also the effect of uniting the otherwise factious tribes in opposition to the invader. This union was reinforced by their common Muslim faith which at the time was undergoing a revival as a result of the spread of Muridism. Muridism was essentially a movement directed towards personal spiritual perfection, in which a murid ('one who desires [the path]') subjected himself to the discipline and instruction of a murshid ('one who shows'). However, the movement readily took on political significance when conducted in the context of an infidel invasion of Muslim lands. The call for Muslim purity and for holy war (*ghazavat*) against the Russians was given in the 1820s by the Imam Kazi-Mullah (killed fighting the Russians in 1832), and then by his successors as Imam – Hamzad (killed by Hadji Murat in 1834), and Shamil, the most formidable and skilful of all Caucasian leaders. The Murid War lasted for thirty years and only with its end in 1859 was the Russian conquest of the Caucasus complete.

The base for Russian operations in the Caucasus was the so-called 'Line', a chain of forts and Cossack stations stretching from the Black Sea to the Caspian along the River Kuban in the west and the River Terek in the east. The Line was divided into two commands, the western 'Right Flank' and the eastern 'Left Flank': it was on the Left Flank, facing Chechnia and Daghestan that the events described in *Hadji Murat* took place. As the Russians extended their control deeper into the Caucasus they established similar chains of forts on east-west parallels further south. Progress for the Russians was inevitably slow. There was no question of defeating the tribesmen in decisive pitched battles, and costly heroic assaults on the mountaineers' strongholds achieved only temporary gain, since it was usually impossible to maintain and supply the position won. Of greater effect in the long run was the Russian policy of making life insupportable for the natives by raiding villages, destroying crops and slaughtering stock. (A typical raid is described in chapter 16 of *Hadji Murat*.) Russian operations depended on freedom of movement and this was long denied them. Wherever Russian troops moved they were harried by the mountaineers, who took full advantage of the terrain, where lines of march lay along narrow valleys or ridges in the mountains and, especially in Chechnia, through forest. An important contribution to the eventual success of the Russians was the policy of forest clearing, by which paths were cut through the forest of sufficient width to allow a column to pass with a musket shot's distance of clear space on side. A column on the march was protected on each flank by a line of sharpshooters who moved along the edge of the clearing (where the going was usually particularly hard because of the transverse spurs and gullies which lined the valley tracks).*

Most of Tolstoy's story is factual or based on fact. Hadji Murat, the most daring and successful of Shamil's lieutenants, defected to the Russians in December 1851, his reception and movements while in Russian hands were as described by Tolstoy, his flight and death took place in April 1852. The portraits of the major Russian participants in these events (Nicholas I, Vorontsov, the younger Vorontsov and his family, Chernyshev, Loris-Melikov, Kozlovsky, etc.) are also factually based, even if coloured in some cases by the author's prejudices. It is only among the subordinates on either side that Tolstoy had recourse to his own invention, and even these lesser characters are not all fictional – an important exception being Poltoratsky, the company commander who appears in chapters 3–5: the character is based on a real officer of that name whose memoirs of his service in the Caucasus supplied Tolstoy with important material for the account of Hadji Murat's reception at Vozdvizhenskoe.

Tolstoy uses a number of native words in *Hadji Murat*. Where their meaning can be deduced from the context I have generally retained them without translation. Where the meaning is not obvious I have incorporated the English rendering in the text alongside the native words. Native terms relating to status, dress, dwellings, etc. I have preferred to translate if a near enough English equivalent exists ('cloak' for *burka*, 'village' for *aoul*, etc.), regretting the loss of local colour which Tolstoy's Russian reader would savour in these – to him familiar – exotic words. Some terms cannot be adequately

* Anyone wishing to read a detailed history of the Russian campaigns in the Caucasus can do no better than turn to the readable and stirring account given in J. F. Baddeley's *The Russian Conquest of the Caucasus* (1908).

translated and a list of these, together with a few words whose meanings could not be satisfactorily conveyed in the text, is given here:

Bairam	Islamic festival, celebrated twice in each year
Cherkeska	collarless top-coat with cartridge-pockets sewn across the breast (as worn by Cossacks, who adopted it from the mountaineers)
Chikhir	Caucasian red wine
Djigit	daredevil horseman, trick-rider; (by extension) fine fellow
Ghazavat	holy war
Kunak	friend (one obligated by bonds of hospitality and protection)
Naib	deputy governor, lieutenant
Nuker	bodyguard, attendant
Papakha	Caucasian sheepskin cap, often very tall
Sardar	governor, viceroy
Shariat	Muslim written law
Tarikat	the 'Path' by which Muslims through prayer and abstinence may attain spiritual knowledge and perfection
Yakshi	good

I was walking home through the fields. It was midsummer. The hay had been carried from the meadows and they were just preparing to cut the rye.

There is a delightful variety of flowers at this time of year: downy, sweet-scented clover, red, white and pink; impudent daisies; milky white ox-eyes with bright yellow centres and their unpleasant, musty, heady odour; yellow charlock with its honeyed smell; tall-standing, tulip-like Canterbury bells, mauve and white; vetches; neat scabious, yellow, red, pink, and mauve; plantains with their pinky down and faint pleasant smell; cornflowers, bright blue in the sunshine when young but paler and redder at evening and as they grow old; and the delicate, almond-scented bindweed flower which blooms and fades in a moment.

I picked a large bunch of different flowers and was walking homewards when I noticed in the ditch a wonderful crimson thistle in full bloom. It was the kind which in our parts is called the Tartar-thistle and reapers are careful to cut around it or if one is accidentally cut they throw it out of the straw so as not to prick their hands on it. I thought I would pick this thistle to put in the middle of my bunch of flowers. I climbed into the ditch and after brushing away a furry bumble-bee, which had worked its way into the centre of the flower and fallen into a sweet and languorous sleep, I set about picking the flower. However, this was no easy matter: it was not just that the stalk pricked me at every turn, even through the handkerchief which I had wrapped round my hand; it was so terribly tough that I was five minutes struggling with it, breaking through the fibres one by one. When at last I succeeded in plucking the flower the stalk was in shreds and the flower itself no longer seemed as fresh and beautiful as before. And, apart from that, it was too crude and clumsy to go with the delicate flowers I had in my bunch. I was sorry that I had needlessly destroyed a flower which had been fine where it was, and threw it away. But what strength and vigour, I thought, recalling the effort it had cost me to pluck it. How stoutly it defended itself, and how dearly it sold its life.

The way home was through a fallow field of black earth which had just been ploughed. I walked along the dusty, gently rising black-earth road. The ploughed field was squire's land and very large, so that on either side of the road and on up the slope you could see nothing but black evenly furrowed fallow land, as yet unharrowed. The ploughing was well done and there was not a plant or blade of grass to be seen across the whole field: it was all black. What a cruel, destructive creature man is. How many different living creatures and plants he has destroyed in order to support his own life, I thought, instinctively looking for some sign of life in the midst of this dead black field. Ahead of me to the right of the road there was a small bush of some kind. When I got nearer I saw it was a Tartar-thistle, like the one whose flower I had idly picked and thrown away.

The Tartar-thistle bush consisted of three shoots. One had been broken off and the remnant of stalk stuck out like a severed arm. There was a flower on each of the other two. The flowers had once been red, but were now black. One stalk was broken and its upper half with the soiled flower at the end hung down; the other, though caked with black mud, still stood erect. It was evident that the whole bush had been run over by a cart wheel and had then picked itself up again: for that reason it was standing crookedly, but still it was standing. It was like having part of its body torn away, its innards turned inside out, an arm pulled off, and an eye plucked out. But still it was standing and would not surrender to man who had destroyed all its brethren around.

What strength! I thought. Man has conquered everything, destroyed millions of plants, but still this one will not give in.

And an old tale of the Caucasus came to my mind, part of which I saw myself, part heard from eye-witnesses, and part created in my imagination. The tale as I recalled and pictured it was as follows.

1

IT was the end of 1851.

On a cold November evening Hadji Murat rode into Makh-ket, a Chechen village hostile to the Russians, which lay wreathed in the fragrant smoke of dung fires.

The straining chant of the muezzin had just ended and in the pure, smoke-laced mountain air, over the lowing of cattle and bleating of sheep which picked their way through the honey-comb of jostling huts in the village, you could distinctly hear from the fountain below the guttural tones of men in argu-ment and the voices of women and children.

This Hadji Murat was the *naib* of Shamil, a man famed for his exploits, who whenever he rode out was always accom-panied by his standard and some dozens of his murids making show of their horsemanship. Now, wrapped in a hood and felt cloak from beneath which a rifle stuck out, Hadji Murat rode with a single murid, doing his best to pass unobserved and care-fully studying the faces of passing locals with his quick black eyes.

Coming to the centre of the village Hadji Murat did not take the street leading on to the square but turned left into a narrow lane. When he reached the second house, which was built into the side of the hill, he stopped and looked around. There was nobody on the veranda at the front of the house but on the flat roof behind the freshly plastered clay chimney lay a man with a sheepskin coat over him. Hadji Murat gave him a gentle prod with the handle of his whip and clicked his tongue. From under the coat rose an old man in a nightcap and a tattered jacket which was shiny with age. His lashless eyes were red and watery and he blinked to get them open. Hadji Murat gave the customary greeting '*Salam aleikum*' and revealed his face.

'*Aleikum salam*' said the old man with a toothless smile as he recognized Hadji Murat. He got up on his thin legs and began directing his feet into the wooden-heeled shoes that stood by the chimney. Having put his shoes on, he unhurriedly donned the wrinkled coat of plain sheepskin and came backwards down the ladder which was leant against the roof. As he put on his coat and climbed down the old man shook his head on his lean, wrinkled, sunburnt neck and champed toothlessly all the time. Reaching the ground, he hospitably took Hadji Murat's bridle and his right stirrup. But Hadji Murat's murid, a sharp powerful fellow, swiftly dismounted, pushed the old man aside and took his place.

Hadji Murat got off his horse and walked with a slight limp on to the veranda. A boy of fifteen or so came quickly out of the door towards him, and stared in surprise at the visitors with his shining eyes, which were black as ripe currants.

'Run to the mosque and fetch your father,' ordered the old man and, going ahead, he opened for Hadji Murat the light, creaking door into the house. As Hadji Murat went in, there came through an inner door a thin, lean, middle-aged woman wearing blue trousers and a jacket over a yellow smock. She was carrying some cushions.

'Your coming is a happy omen,' she said, and bending over she spread the cushions along the front wall for the guests to sit on.

'May your sons live long,' answered Hadji Murat, taking off his cloak, rifle and sword and handing them to the old man.

The old man carefully hung the rifle and sword on nails next to the weapons of the master of the house and between two

large basins which gleamed on the smooth plaster of the clean-
ly whitewashed wall.

Hadji Murat straightened the pistol at the back of his belt,
went over to the cushions the woman had laid out and, drawing his *cherkeska* round him, sat down. The old man squatted
opposite him on his bare heels, closed his eyes and lifted his
hands with upturned palms. Hadji Murat did the same. Then
after a prayer they both drew their hands across their faces,
bringing them together at the tip of their beards.

'*Ne khabar?*' Hadji Murat asked the old man – that is, 'What
news?'

'*Khabar yok*' – 'Nothing new,' the old man answered, his
red lifeless eyes looking not in Hadji Murat's face but at his
chest. 'I live at the bee-garden. I have just come today to visit
my son. He will know.'

Hadji Murat could see that the old man was unwilling to say
what he knew and what Hadji Murat needed to know. He
nodded and asked no more.

'There is no good news,' the old man began. 'All that is new
is that the hares are all taking counsel to see how they can drive
off the eagles. And the eagles go on killing them one by one.
Last week the Russian dogs burnt the people's hay on the
Michik, curse them,' wheezed the old man venomously.

Hadji Murat's murid came in, strode softly across the mud
floor on his powerful legs, and, as Hadji Murat had done, took
off his cloak, rifle and sword and hung them on the nails along
with Hadji Murat's weapons, retaining only his dagger and
pistol.

The old man pointed at him and asked 'Who is he?'

'He is my murid. His name is Eldar,' said Hadji Murat.

'It is well,' said the old man and indicated a place for Eldar
on the felt rug next to Hadji Murat.

Eldar sat down cross-legged and with his handsome sheep's
eyes stared silently at the face of the now talkative old man
who was telling how the week before their men had captured

two soldiers, one of whom they had killed and the other sent to Shamil in Vedeno. Hadji Murat listened inattentively, keeping an eye on the door and listening for sounds outside. Steps were heard on the veranda at the front of the house. The door creaked and the master of the house came in.

Sado, the master of the house, was a man of about forty with a small beard, long nose, and eyes which were as black though not as shining as those of his son, the fifteen-year-old boy who had gone to fetch him and who now came in with his father and sat by the door. Taking off his wooden shoes at the door, Sado pushed his old well-worn *papakha* to the back of his head, which was long unshaved and sprouted a growth of black hair, and at once squatted facing Hadji Murat.

Just as the old man before him, he closed his eyes, lifted his upturned hands, and after saying a prayer wiped his hands over his face. Only after this did he speak. He said that Shamil had ordered Hadji Murat to be taken dead or alive, that Shamil's messengers had set out only the day before, that the people were frightened to disobey Shamil's commands, and that it was necessary therefore to take care.

'In my house as long as there is life in me no harm shall come to my *kunak*,' said Sado. 'But when you are in the open – what then? We must give it thought.'

Hadji Murat listened attentively and nodded his approval. When Sado had finished, he said:

'Very well. I must now send someone with a letter to the Russians. My murid will go, but he will need a guide.'

'I will send my brother Bata,' said Sado. He turned to his son. 'Tell Bata to come.'

The nimble-footed boy sprang up like a jack-in-the-box, and with a flurry of arms raced from the house. In ten minutes he was back with a wiry, short-legged Chechen, tanned black by the sun, who wore a yellow *cherkeska* with splitting seams and tattered cuffs and black leggings which hung round his ankles. Hadji Murat greeted the new arrival and came straight to the point, asking briefly:

'Can you get my murid through to the Russians?'

'Yes, I can,' replied Bata, speaking quickly and cheerfully. 'I can manage everything. No other Chechen could get through the way I can. He might go, and promise everything, but do nothing. But I can.'

'Good,' said Hadji Murat. 'For your service you shall have three,' he said, holding out three fingers.

Bata nodded to show that he understood, but said that he did not value the money and was ready to serve Hadji Murat for the honour of doing so. Everyone in the mountains knew Hadji Murat and the way he had beaten the Russian pigs.

'All right,' said Hadji Murat. 'A long rope is good – a speech is better short.'

'I will say no more,' said Bata.

'Where the Argun bends there is a clearing on the side opposite the cliff. There are two haystacks there. Do you know the place?'

'Yes, I know it.'

'I have three horsemen waiting for me there,' said Hadji Murat.

'*Aya*,' said Bata, nodding.

'Ask for Khan-Mahoma. Khan-Mahoma knows what to do and what to say. He has to be taken to the Russian commander, to the prince Vorontsov. Can you do that?'

'Yes, I will take him.'

'Take him and bring him back. You can do that?'

'Yes, I can do that.'

'You will take him and return to the forest. I will be there.'

'All this I shall do,' said Bata. He got up, put his hands to his chest and left.

'We must send someone to Gekhi too,' said Hadji Murat to his host after Bata had gone. 'In Gekhi we need . . .' he took hold of one of the cartridge cases on the breast of his *cherkeska*, but stopped speaking and dropped his hand on seeing two women come in.

One of the women was Sado's wife, the same thin, middle-aged woman who had put out the cushions. The other was a young girl dressed in red trousers and a green jacket with loops of silver coins hanging across her breast. A silver rouble hung from the rather short, broad plait of coarse black hair that fell between her shoulders down her thin back; she had the same black, currant-like eyes as her father and brother and they shone merrily out of her young face which was trying to look serious. She did not look at the visitors, though it was obvious that she felt their presence.

Sado's wife carried a low round table on which were tea, patties, pancakes in butter, cheese, *churek* – bread made in a flat loaf – and honey. The girl carried a basin, ewer and towel.

Neither Sado nor Hadji Murat spoke while the women, moving quietly in their red unsoled slippers, set out before the guests the refreshments they had brought. As long as the women were in the room Eldar sat still as a statue, his sheep's eyes fixed on his crossed legs. Only when they had gone and their soft footsteps had died away on the other side of the door did Eldar give a sigh of relief and Hadji Murat take one of the cartridge cases from the front of his *cherkeska*, unplug the bullet and draw out a rolled-up note which lay underneath.

'Give this to my son,' he said, showing the note to Sado.

'Where does the answer go?' Sado asked.

'To you, and you will pass it on to me.'

'It shall be done,' said Sado and transferred the note to a cartridge case on his own *cherkeska*. Then he picked up the ewer and moved the basin towards Hadji Murat. Hadji Murat turned back the sleeves of his jacket over his muscular arms, which were white above the wrist, and placed his hands under the stream of cold clear water which Sado poured from the ewer. Then after wiping his hands dry on the clean, rough towel he turned to the food. Eldar did the same, and while his guests ate Sado sat facing them, several times thanking them for their visit. His son, who sat by the door and never for a moment took his black shining eyes off Hadji Murat, smiled as if confirming with his smile his father's words.

Although it was over twenty-four hours since he had last eaten, Hadji Murat ate only a little bread and cheese, and some honey which he scooped out and spread on his bread with a small knife taken from beneath his dagger.

'Our honey is good. It is a year of years for honey: it is plentiful and good,' said the old man, obviously pleased that Hadji Murat was eating his honey.

'Thank you,' said Hadji Murat, moving away from the food.

Eldar was still hungry, but like his murshid he left the table and handed Hadji Murat the basin and ewer.

Sado knew that he was putting his life at stake by receiving Hadji Murat, because after his quarrel with Shamil an announcement had gone out to all who lived in Chechnia forbidding them on pain of death to receive Hadji Murat. Sado knew that at any moment the villagers might learn of Hadji Murat's presence in his house and demand his surrender. But he was actually pleased rather than concerned by that. Sado considered it his duty to protect his guest, his *kunak*, even if it should cost him his life, and he rejoiced and prided himself on doing what was proper.

'As long as you are in my house and my head is on my shoulders, no harm shall come to you,' he told Hadji Murat once more.

Hadji Murat looked intently into his shining eyes and saw that it was true. He said with some solemnity:

'May life and happiness be yours.'

Sado silently pressed his hand to his chest in gratitude for Hadji Murat's kindly words.

When he had closed the shutters and kindled some logs in the fireplace Sado left the guest-room feeling particularly cheerful and keyed up and went to the part of the house occupied by his family. The womenfolk, not yet asleep, were talking of the dangerous visitors who were spending the night in their guest-room.

2

THE same night, ten miles from the village where Hadji Murat was staying, three soldiers and an N.C.O. left the frontier fort of Vozdvizhenskoe by the Shakhgiri gate. They were dressed as soldiers commonly were at that time in the Caucasus: in sheepskin coats and *papakhas*, with rolled greatcoats across their shoulders and large top-boots coming above the knee. At first the soldiers went along the road with shouldered arms, but after some 500 yards they left the road and, with their boots rustling the dry leaves, went some twenty paces to the right. They stopped by a broken plane tree whose black trunk was visible even in the darkness. It was this tree that the Russians generally used as a listening post.

The bright stars which had seemed to be floating over the tree-tops while the soldiers were going through the forest now stood still, shining brightly through the bare branches of the trees.

'It's dry, that's one good thing,' said Panov, the corporal, unslinging his long rifle with fixed bayonet and leaning it with a rattle against the tree trunk. The three soldiers did the same.

'Sure enough, I've lost it,' grumbled Panov in annoyance. 'Either I left it behind or else it fell out on the way.'

'What is it you are looking for?' asked one of the soldiers, in a jolly, cheerful voice.

'My pipe, damme. I don't know where it's got to.'

'Have you got the stem all right?' asked the cheerful soldier.

'Yes, here's the stem.'

'Why not just shove it in the ground?'

'That's no good.'

'We'll fix it in a jiffy.'

Smoking in a listening post was forbidden, but this was hardly a listening post; it was more a kind of forward sentry post which was placed there to ensure that the Chechens did not move up a cannon unnoticed, as had happened in the past, and shoot at the fort. This being so, Panov saw no need to go without his smoke and fell in with the suggestion made by the cheerful soldier. The latter took a knife out of his pocket and began digging at the ground. When he had made a small hollow, he patted it smooth, fixed the pipe-stem, filled the hollow with tobacco, pressed it firm – and the pipe was ready. A sulphur match flared, momentarily lighting the prominent cheek-bones of the cheerful soldier lying flat on his stomach. The pipe-stem wheezed, and Panov caught the pleasant aroma of kindled tobacco.

'Fixed it?' he asked, rising to his feet.

'Course I have.'

'Good lad, Avdeev! You're a regular genius. How about it, then?'

Avdeev rolled on to his side to make room for Panov, releasing the smoke from his mouth.

When they had had their smoke, the soldiers began talking.

'I hear the company commander's had his hand in the till again. Gambling debts, I suppose . . .?' said one soldier in a lazy drawl.

'He'll pay it back,' said Panov.

'Of course he will. He's a good officer,' agreed Avdeev.

'Oh, he's good, all right,' the soldier who had started the conversation went on gloomily. 'But if you ask me, the whole company ought to have it out with him and tell him that if he's taken some money he must say how much and when he's going to pay it back.'

'It must be as the company decides,' said Panov, breaking away from his pipe.

'That's right,' agreed Avdeev. 'It's the company which has the say.'

'But look, we've got to buy in oats and get boots for the spring. For that we need money, and if he's taken it . . .' persisted the disgruntled soldier.

'I say it's as the company wants,' repeated Panov. 'It's not the first time it's happened: he'll pay it back all right.'

At that time in the Caucasus each company ran its own economy through a chosen committee. The company received an official allowance of 6 roubles 50 kopeks per man and saw to its own provisioning: planted cabbages, cropped hay, had its own carts and took pride in showing off the company's well-fed horses. The company funds were kept in a cash-box, the keys of which were held by the company commander, and it was a common occurrence for the company commander to borrow from these funds. That had happened now and it was this that the soldiers were talking about. Nikitin, the gloomy one, wanted the company commander called to account, while Panov and Avdeev thought this unnecessary.

Nikitin had a smoke after Panov, then spread out his greatcoat and sat down, leaning against the tree. The soldiers fell silent. The only sound was that of the wind stirring in the treetops high overhead. Suddenly through this steady gentle sound came the whining, shrieking, weeping and laughing cries of jackals.

'There they go, off again, curse 'em,' said Avdeev.

'They're laughing at you and your ugly mug,' came the thin Ukrainian voice of the fourth soldier.

Again all was quiet except for the wind which stirred the branches of the trees, now hiding, now revealing the stars beyond.

'What about you, Antonych?' the cheerful Avdeev suddenly asked Panov. 'Do you ever get fed up?'

'How do you mean – fed up?' replied Panov without enthusiasm.

'Well, sometimes I get that fed up I don't know what I might do to myself.'

'Go on with you,' said Panov.

'Like when I blew all that money drinking – it was only because I was fed up. It just got on top of me, so I had the notion to go and get drunk.'

'It's often worse after you've been drinking.'

'It was too. But what can you do?'

'What is it you're fed up about then?'

'Me? I'm home-sick.'

'Were you well off then?'

'No, we weren't exactly rich, but we lived well. It was a good life.'

And Avdeev began telling the story he had told Panov many times before.

'You see, I joined up voluntary in place of my brother,' said Avdeev. 'He had four kids, and I was only just married, and Mother wanted me to go. And I thought, it's all the same to me, maybe they'll remember a good turn. So I went to see the master. He was a good man, our master, and he said to me "Good lad! You do that!" So I went and joined up in place of my brother.'

'Well, that's fine,' said Panov.

'But now I'm fed up, Antonych. Don't you see? And what gets me down most of all is why I joined up instead of my brother. Now he's living like a lord and I lead a dog's life. And the more I think about it, the worse it gets. That's a sin, I suppose.'

Avdeev said nothing for a while, then asked:

'What about another smoke?'

'Why not – you set it up.'

But the soldiers were not to get their smoke. As soon as Avdeev got up and was about to fix the pipe again, through the rustling of the wind came the sound of footsteps on the roadway. Panov took his rifle and prodded Nikitin with his foot. Nikitin rose and picked up his greatcoat. The third soldier, Bondarenko, also got up.

'My, what a dream I just had, mates . . .'

Avdeev hissed at Bondarenko, and the soldiers became dead still, listening. The soft footsteps of men not wearing boots drew closer. The crackling of leaves and dry twigs in the darkness became clearer and clearer. Then came the sound of voices talking in that strange guttural tongue spoken by the Chechens. Now the soldiers not only heard, but could see two shadows passing through the trees. One was shorter, the other taller. As they came abreast of the soldiers, Panov with his rifle at the ready stepped into the roadway with his two comrades.

'Halt! Who goes there?' he cried.

'Chechen, friendly,' said the shorter of the two. This was Bata. 'No gun. No sword,' he said, pointing to himself. 'We see prince.'

The taller one stood by his companion, saying nothing. He also had no weapons on him.

'It's a scout, so he'll have to go to the C.O.,' Panov explained to his comrades.

'Prince Vorontsov, must see. Very big business,' said Bata.

'All right, all right, we'll get you there,' said Panov. 'Well now, what about it – you,' he said to Avdeev, 'you take them with Bondarenko, hand them over to the orderly officer and come back here. Watch your step and make them go in front. They're smart, these cropheads, if you don't watch them.'

'What's this for then?' said Avdeev, feinting a thrust with his rifle and bayonet. 'One prod with this and he's done for.'

'But what good is he if you bayonet him?' said Bondarenko. 'Come on, quick march.'

When the footsteps of the two soldiers and the scouts had died away, Panov and Nikitin returned to their former position.

'What the devil brings them out at night?' said Nikitin.

'Must be something important,' said Panov. 'It's got chilly, though,' he added and unrolling his greatcoat, he put it on and sat against the tree.

A couple of hours later Avdeev and Bondarenko came back.

'Well, did you hand them over all right?' asked Panov.

'Yes. They were still awake up at the C.O.'s, so they took them straight along. Really good lads they are too, these crop-heads. They really are! I got talking to them splendid.'

'You would, of course,' said Nikitin, disgruntled.

'They really are just like Russians. One is married. Got a missus? I ask. Yes, he says. Any nippers? Yes, he says. Many? Just a couple, he says. We had a fine talk. Good lads!'

'Oh, yes, good lads,' said Nikitin. 'You just come up against him on your own and he'll cut your tripes out.'

'It should soon be getting light,' said Panov.

'Yes, the stars are going faint,' said Avdeev, sitting down.

And they lapsed again into silence.

3

THE windows of the barracks and the soldiers' billets had long been in darkness, but in one of the best houses of the fort all the windows were still ablaze. This was the house of the commander of the Kura regiment, Prince Semen Mikhailovich Vorontsov, son of the commander-in-chief and an imperial *aide-de-camp*. Vorontsov lived there with his wife, Marya Vasilevna, a celebrated St Petersburg beauty, and in this small Caucasian fort he lived in greater style than anyone before him. To Vorontsov and particularly to his wife the life they led there was not merely modest, but full of all manner of deprivations; the local inhabitants on the other hand were astonished at the extraordinary luxury in which they lived.

It was midnight now, and in the large drawing-room with its carpeted floor and curtains drawn across the doors the hosts sat with their guests playing cards at a card-table lit by four candles. One of those playing was Vorontsov himself, a fair-haired colonel with a long face, wearing the ciphers and aiguillettes of an *aide-de-camp*; his partner was a graduate of St Petersburg University, a morose-looking young man with tousled hair, recently engaged by Princess Vorontsov as tutor to her small son by her first husband. Playing against them were two officers: one was Poltoratsky, a company commander with a broad ruddy face, who had formerly been in the guards, the other the regimental adjutant, who sat very straight with a frigid look on his handsome face. Marya Vasilevna herself, a full-bodied beauty with large eyes and black eyebrows, sat by Poltoratsky, touching his legs with her crinoline and looking over his cards. In the way she spoke and looked and smiled, in every movement of her body and in the scent of her perfume there was something that made Poltoratsky oblivious of everything but the sense of her proximity and he made blunder after blunder to the increasing annoyance of his partner.

'Oh no, that really is too bad! You have hung on to the ace again!' said the adjutant, his face flushing all over, as Poltoratsky played the ace to his partner's trick.

As if just waking up, Poltoratsky gazed uncomprehendingly at the displeased adjutant with his wide-set, black, good-natured eyes.

'You must forgive him,' said Marya Vasilevna with a smile. To Poltoratsky she said: 'You see, I told you.'

'But what you told me was quite wrong,' replied Poltoratsky, smiling.

'*Was* it?' she said and smiled too. This answering smile so much agitated and delighted Poltoratsky that he flushed crimson, snatched up the cards and began shuffling them.

'It isn't your turn to shuffle,' said the adjutant severely, and with his white, ringed hand himself began dealing the cards as if his sole concern was to be rid of them as quickly as possible.

The prince's valet came into the drawing-room and told the prince that the orderly officer wished to see him.

'Excuse me, gentlemen,' said Vorontsov, speaking Russian with an English accent. 'Marie, will you take my place?'

'Does no one mind?' asked the princess, with a rustle of silk rising quickly and lightly to her full imposing height and smiling the radiant smile of a happy woman.

'I am always agreeable to everything,' said the adjutant, very pleased that he would now be playing against the princess who had no idea of the game. Poltoratsky simply spread his hands and smiled.

The rubber was ending when the prince returned to the drawing-room. He was unusually cheerful and elated.

'Do you know what I suggest?' he said.

'No, what?'

'That we have some champagne.'

'I never say no to that,' said Poltoratsky.

'That would be very nice,' said the adjutant.

'Vasilii, bring some champagne,' said the prince.

'What were you wanted for?' asked Marya Vasilevna.

'It was the orderly officer and someone he had with him.'

'Who was it? What did they want?' asked Marya Vasilevna hastily.

Vorontsov shrugged. 'I am not able to say,' he said.

'You are not able to say,' repeated his wife. 'We shall see about that!'

Champagne was brought in. The guests all had a glass, and, having finished their game and settled their debts, began to take leave.

'Is it your company detailed for forest clearing tomorrow?' the prince asked Poltoratsky.

'Yes, it is. Why?'

'Then we shall meet tomorrow,' said the prince with a half-smile.

'Delighted,' said Poltoratsky, not really following what Vorontsov was saying and concerned only that he was about to press Marya Vasilevna's large white hand.

Marya Vasilevna, as always, not only pressed Poltoratsky's hand firmly, but shook it hard as well. She again reminded him of the mistake he made in leading diamonds and gave him a smile that seemed to Poltoratsky charming, tender and significant.

Poltoratsky walked home in that uplifted mood which can only be understood by men such as he, brought up in high society, when after months of isolated camp life they again meet a woman from their old milieu – and a woman at that like Princess Vorontsov.

On reaching the house which he shared with a fellow officer, he gave the outer door a shove, but found it locked. He knocked. The door did not open. Annoyed at this, he began kicking and beating at the locked door with his sword. Footsteps sounded inside and Vavilo, Poltoratsky's serf servant, undid the latch.

'What did you go and lock up for, you idiot?'

'Aleksei Vladimirovich, really you can't . . .'

'Drunk again! I'll show you I really can . . .'

He was about to hit Vavilo, but changed his mind.

'To hell with you. Light me a candle.'

'Yesshir, straight away.'

Vavilo was in fact the worse for drink, and this was because he had been to the quartermaster's name-day party. When he got home he started thinking how different his life was from that of Ivan Makeich, the quartermaster. Ivan Makeich had money coming in, was married and in a year's time was hoping to get his discharge. But Vavilo had been taken into domestic service by his master as a boy and here he was now past forty with no wife and living his life in army camps with his feckless master. Poltoratsky was a good master, he did not hit him much, but what kind of a life was it? He's promised I can have my freedom when he gets back from the Caucasus. But where is there for me to go when I am free? It's a dog's life, thought Vavilo. And he had felt so tired that he had secured the latch to keep out intruders and gone to sleep.

Poltoratsky went into the bedroom which he shared with his fellow officer, Tikhonov.

'How did you get on? Lose?' asked Tikhonov, waking up.

'Not at all. I won seventeen roubles and we had a bottle of Cliquot.'

'And you gazed at Marya Vasilevna?'

'And I gazed at Marya Vasilevna,' repeated Poltoratsky.

'It will soon be time to get up,' said Tikhonov. 'We have to be off at six.'

'Vavilo,' shouted Poltoratsky. 'Call me at five, and make sure I'm awake.'

'How am I supposed to wake you up when you hit me?'

'You wake me up, I tell you. Understand?'

'Very well.'

Vavilo went out taking their boots and clothes.

Poltoratsky got into bed, smiling as he lit a cigarette and put out the candle. In the darkness he saw before him the smiling face of Marya Vasilevna.

At the Vorontsovs' they did not settle down straightaway either. After the guests had gone, Marya Vasilevna went up to her husband, stopped in front of him and [speaking in French] said severely:

'Well, are you going to tell me what it is all about?'

'But, my dear ...'

'Don't "my dear" me! It was an envoy, wasn't it?'

'I still can't tell you.'

'You can't? Then I'll tell you what it was myself!'

'You?'

'Was it Hadji Murat? Well, was it?' said the princess, who for several days had heard of the negotiations with Hadji Murat and presumed that her husband had been visited by Hadji Murat himself.

Vorontsov could not deny it, but disappointed his wife when he said that it had not been Hadji Murat himself but only a scout coming to say that Hadji Murat would come over to him the next day at the place detailed for forest clearing.

The young Vorontsovs, both husband and wife, were very glad of this event, which broke the monotony of life in the fort. They talked a while about how pleased Vorontsov's father would be to receive the news, then, after two, they went to bed.

4

AFTER the three sleepless nights he had spent fleeing from the murids sent by Shamil to capture him, Hadji Murat fell asleep the moment Sado left after bidding him goodnight. He slept fully dressed, resting on one arm, his elbow sunk deep in the red down cushions his host had provided for him. Eldar slept a short distance away, by the wall. He lay on his back, with his strong young limbs stretched out so that his full chest, surmounted by the black cartridge-cases of his white *cherkeska*, was higher than his blue, freshly shaved head which was thrown back and had slipped off its cushion. His upper lip with its faint covering of down pouted like a child's and seemed to be sipping something as it rose and fell. He slept as Hadji Murat did – fully dressed with his pistol and dagger in his belt. The dying fire burnt in the fireplace, and a night-light glowed faintly in the recess of the stove.

In the middle of the night the guest-room door creaked and at once Hadji Murat was on his feet, pistol in hand. Into the room came Sado stepping softly over the mud floor.

'What is it?' asked Hadji Murat, alert as if he never slept at all.

'We have to think,' said Sado, squatting down in front of Hadji Murat. 'A woman on a roof saw you come. She told her husband and now it's all over the village. A neighbour has just been to see my wife, and she says the old men are meeting at the mosque and want to stop you.'

'I must go,' said Hadji Murat.

'The horses are ready,' said Sado and went swiftly out.

'Eldar,' whispered Hadji Murat, and Eldar, on hearing his name but chiefly on hearing his murshid's voice, sprang powerfully to his feet, straightening his *papakha*. Hadji Murat put on his weapons and cloak. Eldar did the same. Then both went out on to the veranda. The black-eyed boy brought their horses. At the clatter of hooves along the beaten roadway a head poked from the door of a neighbouring house and some person ran with wooden shoes tapping up the hill to the mosque.

There was no moon, but the stars shone brightly in the black sky and in the darkness you could make out the roof tops of the houses and, standing above the other buildings, of the mosque and minaret at the top of the village, where a buzz of voices could be heard.

Hadji Murat, swiftly grasping his rifle, put his foot into the narrow stirrup, silently, inconspicuously swung his body over and without a sound took his seat on the high padded saddle.

'May God reward you!' he said to Sado, feeling for the other stirrup with an accustomed movement of his right foot. He lightly touched the boy holding his horse with his whip to tell him to stand away. The boy stepped back, and the horse, as if knowing what it had to do, set off at a brisk walk, out of the lane and on to the main street. Eldar rode behind. Sado in a fur top-coat, his arms swiftly swinging, followed them almost at a run, switching from side to side of the narrow street. At the end of the village a shadow moved across the road, then another.

'Halt! Who is it? Stop!' cried a voice, and several men blocked the roadway.

Instead of stopping, Hadji Murat snatched his pistol from

his belt and spurred his horse straight at the men blocking the way. They scattered, and without looking back Hadji Murat set off down the road at a fast amble with Eldar following at a quick trot. A couple of shots rang out behind them, the bullets whistled past without touching Hadji Murat or Eldar. Hadji Murat rode on at the same pace. After about 300 yards he pulled up his gently panting horse and listened. Ahead and below was the sound of rushing water. Behind he could hear the cocks in the village answering each other. Over these noises he heard the beat of horses' hoofs and the sound of voices getting closer. Hadji Murat touched his horse and set off at the same steady ambling pace.

The riders behind were galloping and soon caught up with him. There were about twenty mounted men: the villagers who had decided to detain Hadji Murat or at least clear themselves with Shamil by showing they had tried. When they were near enough to be seen in the darkness Hadji Murat stopped, dropped his reins and, undoing the cover of his rifle with a practised move of his left hand, drew the gun out with his right. Eldar did the same.

'What do you want?' Hadji Murat shouted. 'You want to capture me, do you? Come on, take me then!' And he raised his rifle. The villagers stopped.

Rifle in hand, Hadji Murat began descending the gully. The horsemen followed, keeping their distance. When Hadji Murat reached the far side of the gully the men following him called on him to listen to what they had to say. Hadji Murat replied with a shot from his rifle and put his horse into a gallop. When he stopped there was no longer any sound of pursuit; the village cocks could not be heard either, but the sound of running water in the forest and the occasional lament of the eagle owl had grown more distinct. The black wall of the forest was now quite close. This was the forest where Hadji Murat's murids were awaiting him. As he came up to the trees, Hadji Murat halted, took a deep breath and whistled.

He stopped and listened. After a minute a similar whistle came from the forest. Hadji Murat turned off the track and rode into the trees. When he had gone about a hundred yards he saw through the trees a fire with shadowy figures sitting round it, and a saddled horse in hobbles half lit by the light of the fire.

One of the men by the fire rose quickly and, coming up to Hadji Murat, took hold of the rein and one stirrup. This was Khanefi, an Avar, Hadji Murat's sworn brother who was in charge of his affairs.

'Put out the fire,' said Hadji Murat, dismounting. The men began scattering the fire, stamping out the burning wood.

'Has Bata been here?' asked Hadji Murat, walking over to a cloak spread on the ground.

'Yes, he was here. He went off long ago with Khan-Mahoma.'

'Which road did they take?'

'That one,' replied Khanefi, pointing in the direction opposite to the way Hadji Murat had come.

'That's all right,' said Hadji Murat. He took off his rifle and began loading it. 'We must keep a look-out. I was pursued,' he said to one of the men putting out the fire.

This man was Gamzalo, a Chechen. He came over to the cloak, picked up a rifle that lay in its cover there and without a word walked to the edge of the clearing to the point where Hadji Murat had entered it. Eldar had dismounted; he took his horse and Hadji Murat's and tethered them to the trees with their heads pulled up high; then, like Gamzalo, with his rifle on his back he posted himself at the other end of the clearing. The fire was now out and the forest looked less black than before and, though faint, there were stars shining in the sky.

Looking at the stars and seeing the Pleiades already half way up the sky, Hadji Murat reckoned it was well past midnight and long since time for his nightly prayers. He asked Khanefi to bring the ewer which he always carried in his saddle-bags and, putting on his cloak, went down to the water.

When he had taken off his shoes and performed the ritual washing, Hadji Murat stood on the cloak in his bare feet, then facing eastwards knelt, sitting back on his legs, and said the usual prayers with eyes closed and ears blocked by his fingers.

When he had finished his prayers he returned to his place, where the saddle-bags were, sat down on the cloak, and with his elbows on his knees and head bent forward he fell to thinking.

Hadji Murat had always trusted in his luck. When planning some venture he was always perfectly sure in advance that he would succeed – and he always did. With few exceptions it had been this way throughout his turbulent life of fighting. And he hoped it would be this way now. With the troops which Vorontsov would give him he could see himself attacking Shamil, making him his prisoner and taking his revenge. He could see the Russian tsar rewarding him, and he would rule once more, not only in Avaria but all over Chechnia which would submit to him. Thinking these thoughts, without noticing it he fell asleep.

He dreamt of descending on Shamil with his men to the sound of singing and cries of 'Hadji Murat comes upon you!'; he dreamt of seizing Shamil and his wives and he heard the wives weeping and sobbing. He woke up. The chant of 'La ilaha',* the shouts of 'Hadji Murat comes upon you', the weeping of Shamil's wives – these were the whining, crying and laughing of the jackals which had woken him up. Hadji Murat lifted his head, looked at the sky now lightening in the east between the trees, and asked the murid sitting near by what news there was of Khan-Mahoma. Hearing that he was still not back, Hadji Murat lowered his head and again dozed off.

He was woken by the cheerful voice of Khan-Mahoma who had returned with Bata from his mission. Khan-Mahoma at once sat down by Hadji Murat and began telling him how they

*The opening phrase of the Muslim creed *La ilaha illa allah* – 'there is no God but God . . .'

had come upon the soldiers and been taken direct to the prince, how he had talked in person to the prince, who had been delighted at the news and promised to meet them the next day across the Michik at the Shali clearing, where the Russians would be tree-felling. Khan-Mahoma was continually interrupted by Bata who kept adding details of his own.

Hadji Murat questioned them closely about the exact words used by Vorontsov in answer to his proposal to go over to the Russians. Khan-Mahoma and Bata replied in unison that the prince had promised to receive Hadji Murat as a guest and to be responsible for his well-being. Hadji Murat also asked about the way there, and after Khan-Mahoma had assured him that he knew the way well and could take him straight to the place, Hadji Murat took out his money and paid Bata his promised three roubles. He told his men to get from the saddle-bags his gold-inlaid weapons and his *papakha* with the turban, and instructed his murids to clean themselves up so as to look well when they came to the Russians. While they cleaned their weapons, saddles, harness and horses, the stars faded, it became quite light, and an early-morning breeze stirred in the air.

5

EARLY that morning while it was still dark two companies under the command of Poltoratsky, equipped with axes, marched out seven miles beyond the Shakhgiri gate, and at first light, after posting a line of sharpshooters, they began their tree-felling operation. By eight o'clock the mist, mingling with the fragrant smoke of green branches that hissed and crackled on the camp fires, began to rise and the felling parties, who had been unable to see more than five yards and had so far only heard each other, could now see the fires and the tree-littered road that passed through the forest. The sun appeared intermittently as a bright blob in the mist. In a clearing a little way from the road sat a group of men using drums as seats. These were Poltoratsky and his subaltern Tikhonov, two officers of No. 3 Company and Baron Frézier, a former horse-guards officer and comrade of Poltoratsky at the Corps of Pages, who had been reduced to the ranks on account of a duel. Food wrappings, cigarette-ends and empty bottles lay round the drums. The officers had had some vodka and something to eat and were now drinking porter. A drummer was opening the eighth bottle. Poltoratsky for all his lack of sleep was in that particular mood of animation and jovial unconcern which always came on him when he was with his men and his comrades in a spot where there might be danger.

The officers were having a lively discussion about the latest news, the death of General Sleptsov. Nobody there saw his death as the supreme moment of his life – the moment of its ending and return to the source from which it came – they only saw in it the gallantry of a dashing officer who had charged, sword in hand, at the mountaineers and furiously cut them down.

Everybody (especially the officers who had seen action) knew and had opportunity to know that warfare at that time in the Caucasus – or at any time anywhere – never actually involved the hand-to-hand fighting with swords which is always supposed to occur and invariably appears in descriptions (when there *is* fighting with swords or bayonets it only means cutting down and bayoneting men in flight); nevertheless the officers accepted this fiction and it gave them the cool pride and gaiety which they felt as they sat on the drums, some in dashing poses, others quite unassumingly, smoking, drinking and jesting, with never a thought for death which might at any moment strike them as it had Sleptsov. And in fact while they were talking, as if to justify their expectation, there came from the left of the road the sharp, attractive, exhilarating crack of a rifle shot and a bullet whistled gaily through the misty air and thudded into a tree. There were a few ponderous bangs as the soldiers' muskets returned the enemy fire.

'Ho, ho!' cried Poltoratsky gaily. 'That's in the picket line. Here's a stroke of luck for you, Kostya, old boy,' he said to Frézier. 'Go back to your company. We'll lay on a lovely battle and get you a commendation.'

The demoted baron leapt to his feet and went smartly off into the area of smoke where his company was. Poltoratsky was brought his little dark-bay Kabarda horse, mounted, then, mustering his company, led it off towards the picket line where the firing was. The picket line was on the edge of the forest where the ground fell away into a bare gully. The wind was blowing towards the forest and not only the near slope of the gully but also its farther side were clearly visible.

As Poltoratsky came up to the pickets the sun peeped through the mist and several horsemen could be seen on the far side of the gully a couple of hundred yards away on the edge of another belt of thin forest. These were the Chechens who had pursued Hadji Murat and who wanted to see him arrive for his meeting with the Russians. One of them had fired a shot at the pickets, and some of the soldiers had replied. The Chechens drew back and the firing ceased. But when Poltoratsky came up with his company he ordered them to open fire, and no sooner was the order given than from all along the picket line came a merry exhilarating rattle of musket fire with prettily spreading puffs of smoke. The soldiers were delighted with this diversion and hastily reloaded, discharging one shot after another. The Chechens were evidently put on their mettle and galloped forward in turn to let off a few shots at the soldiers. One of the shots wounded a soldier – it was Avdeev, the soldier who had been in the listening post. When his comrades got to him he lay face down swaying rhythmically with both hands clutching a wound in his stomach.

'I was just going to load and I heard a thud,' said the soldier who had been paired with Avdeev. 'I looked round and saw he'd dropped his gun.'

Avdeev was in Poltoratsky's company and Poltoratsky, seeing the group of soldiers, rode up to him.

'Are you hit, lad?' he asked. 'Whereabouts?'

Avdeev made no reply.

'I was just going to load, sir,' began the soldier paired with Avdeev, 'when I heard a thud. I looked round and saw he'd dropped his gun.'

Poltoratsky clicked his tongue.

'Too bad. Does it hurt much, Avdeev?'

'No, it doesn't hurt, but I can't walk. If I could have a drink, sir.'

Vodka, or rather the liquor drunk by soldiers in the Caucasus, was produced and Panov, frowning severely, brought a tot of it to Avdeev. Avdeev started to drink, but at once pushed it away.

'I can't get it down. You have it,' he said.

Panov drank what was left. Avdeev made another effort to get up, but again sank back. A greatcoat was spread out and Avdeev was laid on it.

'Sir, the colonel is coming,' said the sergeant-major to Poltoratsky.

'All right. You carry on,' said Poltoratsky and with a switch of his whip set off at a brisk trot to meet Vorontsov.

Vorontsov was riding his chestnut English thoroughbred stallion and was accompanied by the regimental adjutant, a Cossack and a Chechen interpreter.

'What's been happening here?' he asked Poltoratsky.

'A party of Chechens came out and attacked the pickets,' Poltoratsky replied.

'I know, and it was all arranged by you.'

'It really wasn't me, prince,' said Poltoratsky, smiling. 'They came of their own accord.'

'I hear a soldier was wounded?'

'Yes. A great pity. He's a good man.'

'Is it bad?'

'Seems like it. He got it in the stomach.'

'And do you know where I am going?' asked Vorontsov.

'No, I don't.'

'And can't you even guess?'

'No.'

'Hadji Murat has come over and is just going to meet us.'

'Never!'

'He sent us a scout yesterday,' said Vorontsov, with difficulty suppressing a delighted smile. 'He is supposed to be waiting for me now at the Shali clearing, so you post your riflemen up as far as the clearing and then come to me.'

'Very good, sir,' said Poltoratsky, raising his hand to his *papakha*, and rode back to his company. He moved the picket line on the right-hand side himself and ordered the sergeant-major to do the same on the left. In the meantime four soldiers carried the wounded man back to the fort.

Poltoratsky was already on his way back to Vorontsov when he noticed a group of horsemen closing on him from behind. He stopped and waited for them.

At their head on a white-maned horse rode an impressive-looking man wearing a white *cherkeska*, a *papakha* wound with a turban, and weapons mounted with gold. This man was Hadji Murat. He rode up to Poltoratsky and said something to him in Tatar. Poltoratsky raised his eyebrows, spread his hands to indicate that he could not understand, and smiled. Hadji Murat smiled back at him, and Poltoratsky was struck by the childish good-nature of his smile. It was not at all what Poltoratsky had expected the fearsome mountaineer to be like. He had expected someone grim, cold and distant, yet here was this totally unaffected person smiling so good-naturedly that he did not seem to be a stranger at all but an old familiar friend. The only remarkable thing about him was the wide-spaced eyes which looked you calmly and acutely in the eye.

There were four men in Hadji Murat's suite. One of these was Khan-Mahoma, who had gone to see Vorontsov the night before. He was ruddy and round-faced, with bright, black, lidless eyes, and a beaming look of happiness. One of the

others was stocky with a lot of hair and eyebrows that met together. This was Khanefi, a Tavlistani, who looked after all
Hadji Murat's property. He was leading a spare horse which
carried tightly packed saddle-bags. The other two men of
Hadji Murat's suite were particularly striking: one was a
young, handsome fellow, slim-waisted like a woman, but
broad in the shoulders, with the beginnings of a light-brown
beard and eyes like a sheep – this was Eldar; the other was
blind in one eye, had neither eyebrows nor eyelashes, wore a
trimmed ginger beard and had a scar running across his nose
and face – this was the Chechen Gamzalo.

Vorontsov had come into view along the road and Poltoratsky pointed him out to Hadji Murat. Hadji Murat set off
in his direction and when he came up to him put his right hand
to his chest and said something in Tatar, at the same time halt-
ing his horse. The Chechen interpreter translated:

'He says he surrenders himself to the will of the Russian
tsar. He wants to serve him, he says, and wanted to long ago,
but Shamil would not let him.'

After listening to the interpreter, Vorontsov extended to
Hadji Murat his suède-gloved hand. Hadji Murat looked at the
hand and hesitated for a moment, then shook it firmly and
spoke again, looking at the interpreter and Vorontsov in
turn.

'He says he wanted to come only to you, because you are
the son of the *sardar*. He much respects you.'

Vorontsov nodded his thanks. Hadji Murat said something
else, pointing to his suite.

'He says these men are his murids, and will serve the Russians
as he will.'

Vorontsov turned and nodded to them as well.

The merry Khan-Mahoma, with his lidless black eyes, also
nodded and said something to Vorontsov which was evidently
funny, for the shaggy-haired Avar smiled, baring his bright
white teeth. The red-haired Gamzalo merely flashed his single

red eye at Vorontsov for a second, then fixed his gaze once more on his horse's ears.

When Vorontsov and Hadji Murat, accompanied by his followers, rode back to the fort, the soldiers relieved from picket duty were standing in a group and made comments as they passed:

'How many souls that devil's done for, and now you just see how they'll butter him up,' said one.

'What do you expect? He was Shamble's chief lootenant, he was. Now, I daresay . . .'

'That young one's a proper *djigit*, that's a fact.'

'Just look at him with the ginger hair. He's got a vicious look in his eye.'

'A right dog he'll be.'

They all particularly noticed the red-haired one.

At the site of the tree-felling the soldiers nearest the road ran over to watch. An officer shouted at them, but Vorontsov stopped him.

'Let them have a look at their old acquaintance. Do you know who this is?' he asked one of the soldiers nearest to him, speaking slowly in his English accent.

'No, sir.'

'It's Hadji Murat. Have you heard of him?'

'That I have, sir. We've given him many a licking.'

'Yes, and he's given as good as he's got.'

'Indeed he has, sir,' replied the soldier, pleased with the chance to converse with his commanding officer.

Hadji Murat realized that they were talking about him and a merry smile gleamed in his eyes. Vorontsov returned to the fort in the very best of spirits.

6

VORONTSOV was very pleased that it was he and no one else who was responsible for the defection and reception of the man who, after Shamil, was Russia's principal and mightiest enemy. There was only one snag, and that was that the military commander in Vozdvizhenskoe was General Meller-Zakomelsky, and strictly speaking the whole affair should have been conducted through him. Vorontsov had handled it entirely on his own without making any report to him, and so there could be some unpleasantness. The thought of this somewhat marred Vorontsov's pleasure.

On reaching his house Vorontsov left Hadji Murat's murids in the hands of the regimental adjutant and took Hadji Murat himself inside.

Princess Marya Vasilevna, elegantly dressed and smiling, met Hadji Murat in the drawing-room together with her son, a good-looking, curly-headed boy of six. Hadji Murat put his hands to his breast and through the interpreter who had come in with him said somewhat ceremoniously that as the prince received him in his home he considered himself his *kunak* and the whole family of a *kunak* was as sacred as the *kunak* himself. Marya Vasilevna liked both the look and bearing of Hadji Murat, and she was even more disposed in his favour by the way he flushed and turned red when she gave him her large white hand. She invited him to sit down and after enquiring if he drank coffee ordered some to be served. But when the coffee was brought Hadji Murat declined it. He understood a little Russian, but could not speak it, and when he did not understand he smiled, and his smile appealed to Marya Vasilevna just as it had to Poltoratsky. Meanwhile, Marya Vasilevna's curly bright-eyed son (whom she called Bulka) stood by his mother with his eyes fixed on Hadji Murat, of whom he had heard as a great warrior.

Leaving Hadji Murat with his wife, Vorontsov went to the regimental office to make arrangements for notifying the higher authorities of Hadji Murat's defection. After writing a report to General Kozlovsky, commander of the Left Flank, in Grozny, and a letter to his father, Vorontsov hurried home, afraid that his wife would be annoyed at his having imposed on her this strange, terrible man who needed careful handling so as neither to offend nor to encourage him too much. But he need not have worried. Hadji Murat was seated in an arm-chair with Bulka (Vorontsov's stepson) on his knee, tilting his head as he listened attentively to the interpreter's translation of what the laughing Marya Vasilevna was saying. Marya Vasil-evna was telling Hadji Murat that if he were to give to every *kunak* whatever he happened to praise then he would soon be going round in the state of Adam . . .

When Vorontsov came in, Hadji Murat put Bulka off his knee – which surprised and upset the boy – and he rose, his playful expression at once giving way to a stern and serious one. He sat down only when Vorontsov did. Going back to their conversation he replied to Marya Vasilevna that such was their law that one must give to a *kunak* any object that he took a liking to.

'Your son – my *kunak*,' he said in Russian, stroking Bulka's curly hair, the boy having once more climbed on his knee.

'He really is charming, this brigand of yours,' Marya Vasilevna said to her husband in French. 'Bulka was admiring his dagger so he made him a present of it.'

Bulka showed the dagger to his stepfather.

'It's very valuable,' said Marya Vasilevna [again in French].

'We must find an opportunity to make him a present, too,' Vorontsov replied.

Hadji Murat sat with lowered eyes, stroking the boy's curls and saying:

'*Djigit, djigit.*'

'It's a beautiful dagger, beautiful,' said Vorontsov, half unsheathing the sharpened steel dagger which was grooved down the centre. 'Thank you.'

'Ask him if there is anything I can do for him,' he said to the interpreter.

The interpreter translated, and Hadji Murat at once replied that he wished for nothing, but requested that he might now be given some place where he could pray. Vorontsov called his valet and told him to see to Hadji Murat's request.

As soon as Hadji Murat found himself alone in the room allotted to him his countenance changed: the look of pleasure, the shifting expressions of tenderness and solemnity vanished and a worried look appeared.

His reception by Vorontsov was much better than he had expected. But the better the reception the less Hadji Murat trusted Vorontsov and his officers. He had all kinds of fears, and one was that he would be seized and sent in chains to Siberia or simply be killed, and he was therefore on his guard.

Eldar came in and he asked him where his murids were quartered, where the horses were, and whether they had had their weapons taken from them.

Eldar answered that the horses were in the prince's stable, that Hadji Murat's men had been put in one of the out-buildings, their weapons had been left them and they were being given food and tea by the interpreter.

Hadji Murat shook his head in bewilderment, and taking off his outer clothes, knelt to pray. When he finished praying he ordered his silver dagger to be brought, put on his clothes and belt, and sat with his feet up on the ottoman to await events.

A little after four o'clock he was summoned to dinner with the prince.

At dinner, Hadji Murat ate nothing except some pilaff, which he took from that part of the dish from which Marya Vasilevna had served herself.

'He is afraid we might poison him,' Marya Vasilevna said to her husband. 'He took his from the same place as I did.'

And she at once turned to Hadji Murat and asked through the interpreter when he would next pray. Hadji Murat raised five fingers and pointed to the sun.

'Soon, then.'

Vorontsov took out his Bréguet watch and pressed the spring. The watch struck a quarter past four. Hadji Murat was evidently intrigued by the striking of the watch and asked if Vorontsov would make it strike again and allow him to see it.

'Here is an opportunity. Give him the watch,' Marya Vasilevna said to her husband [in French].

Vorontsov promptly offered it to Hadji Murat. He put his hand to his heart and took it. He pressed the spring a few times, listened and shook his head approvingly.

After dinner the prince was told that Meller-Zakomelsky's *aide-de-camp* was there.

The *aide-de-camp* informed the prince that the general had heard of Hadji Murat's defection and was very displeased at having received no report of the matter and that he required Hadji Murat to be brought to him forthwith. Vorontsov said that the general's order would be carried out. He then told Hadji Murat through the interpreter what the general wanted and asked him to go with him to Meller.

When she discovered the purpose of the *aide-de-camp*'s visit, Marya Vasilevna realized at once that there was liable to be some unpleasantness between her husband and the general. Despite her husband's efforts to dissuade her she made ready to accompany him and Hadji Murat to the general.

'It would be much better if you stayed at home. It is my affair, not yours.'

'You cannot stop me going to see the general's wife.'

'You could see her some other time.'

'But I want to see her now.'

There was nothing for it but to agree and the three of them set off together.

When they went in Meller, grimly polite, conducted Marya

Vasilevna to his wife and ordered his *aide-de-camp* to take Hadji Murat into the drawing-room and keep him there until further orders.

'After you,' he said to Vorontsov, opening the door to his study and letting the prince go in first.

Once inside he stood in front of the prince and, without inviting him to sit down, said:

'I am military commander here and therefore all negotiations with the enemy must be conducted through me. Why did you not report this business of Hadji Murat to me?'

'A scout came and told me that Hadji Murat wanted to give himself up to me,' said Vorontsov, turning pale with emotion in expectation of rough treatment by the furious general, but also himself infected by his anger.

'I want to know why you did not report it.'

'I was going to do so, Baron, but . . .'

'You don't address me as "Baron", but as "your excellency".'

And the baron suddenly gave vent to his long suppressed annoyance and delivered himself of all the feeling that had been building up inside him.

'I haven't served the Emperor for twenty-seven years just so that people who joined the service yesterday can use their family connections to take charge of things that are none of their business, and that under my very nose.'

'Your excellency, I beg you not to speak unjustly . . .' Vorontsov interrupted him.

'I am saying what is true, and I will not have . . .' the general began more irritably than before.

At that moment there was a rustle of skirts and Marya Vasilevna came into the room followed by a rather short lady of unassuming appearance, the wife of Meller-Zakomelsky.

'Now, now, Baron. Simon never meant to cause you any trouble,' said Marya Vasilevna.

'That is not what I am saying, Princess . . .'

'Well, I think it would be best to call the matter closed. You know – "an uneasy war is better than peace". Oh dear, what am I saying . . .' She laughed.

And the angry general succumbed to the enchanting smile of the beautiful Marya Vasilevna. A smile flickered beneath his whiskers.

'I confess I was wrong,' said Vorontsov, 'but . . .'

'Well, I was too hasty myself,' said Meller and gave the prince his hand.

Peace was restored and it was decided to leave Hadji Murat with Meller for the time being and then dispatch him to the commander of the Left Flank.

Hadji Murat sat in the next room and although he did not understand what they were saying he understood all that was necessary: that they were quarrelling about him and that his defection from Shamil was a matter of immense importance for the Russians and that therefore, provided they did not exile or kill him, he could demand a lot from them. In addition, he understood that although Meller-Zakomelsky was the commander, he counted for less than Vorontsov, his subordinate, and that it was Vorontsov, not Meller-Zakomelsky, who mattered. As a result, when Meller-Zakomelsky summoned Hadji Murat and began interrogating him, Hadji Murat's manner was proud and dignified. He said that he had come out of the mountains in order to serve the White Tsar and that he would give a full account of things only to the tsar's *sardar*, that is to the commander-in-chief, Prince Vorontsov, in Tiflis.

7

THE wounded Avdeev was taken to the hospital, a small building with a boarded roof on the way out of the fort, and put into an empty bed in the general ward. There were four other patients in the ward: a typhus case tossing feverishly on his bed, a man with malaria, pallid, with dark rings under his eyes, waiting for the next paroxysm and yawning continuously, and two men wounded in a raid three weeks earlier – one in the hand (he was walking about), the other in the shoulder (he sat on his bed). Except for the man with typhus they all gathered round the new arrival and questioned the men who brought him.

'It might be grapeshot the way they fire sometimes and nobody gets hurt, but this time there weren't more than half a dozen shots,' said one of the bearers.

'One had his name on it.'

'Ah!' Avdeev gave a sudden loud groan, fighting the pain as they began putting him on the bed. When they had laid him there he frowned and groaned no more, only kept up a continuous twitching with his feet. He held his hands to his wound and gazed fixedly into space.

The doctor arrived and ordered the wounded man to be turned over so that he could see if the bullet had passed out through his back.

'What's this?' the doctor asked, pointing to the criss-cross of white scars on Avdeev's back and buttocks.

'That's old stuff, sir,' said Avdeev, moaning.

These were the marks of the punishment he had received for misapplying the money he had got drunk on.

Avdeev was turned over again and for some time the doctor probed in his stomach. He found the bullet but could not extract it. After dressing the wound and fixing it with sticking plaster, the doctor left. All the time his wound was being probed and dressed Avdeev lay with his teeth clenched and eyes closed, but when the doctor had gone he opened his eyes and looked around in surprise. His eyes were looking towards the other patients and the orderly, but he appeared to see not them, but some other thing that surprised him greatly.

Avdeev's comrades Panov and Seregin came. He still lay there, staring ahead in surprise. It was a long time before he recognized his comrades, although he was looking directly at them.

'Any message you want sent home, Pete?' asked Panov.

Avdeev was looking Panov in the face, but he made no reply.

'I asked if you wanted any message sent home,' repeated Panov, touching Avdeev's cold, broad-boned hand.

Avdeev seemed to come to.

'Ah, Antonych is here.'

'Yes, I'm here. Is there no message you want sent home? Seregin could write it.'

'Seregin,' said Avdeev, with difficulty shifting his gaze to Seregin. 'You'll write it? . . . Then say this – "Your son Peter has passed away." I envied my brother. I was telling you last night. Well, now I'm glad. Let him be. Good luck to him, I'm glad. Write that.'

After this he said nothing for a long time, his eyes fixed on Panov.

'Did you find your pipe, then?' he asked suddenly.

Panov shook his head and did not answer.

'Your pipe, your pipe – did you find it?' Avdeev repeated.

'It was in my knapsack.'

'There now! Now let me have a candle. I'm going to die,' said Avdeev.

Just then Poltoratsky came to inquire after his man.

'Feeling bad, old chap?' he asked.

Avdeev closed his eyes and shook his head. His face with its high cheek-bones was pale and stern. He did not answer, only repeated again to Panov:

'Get me the candle. I'm dying.'

They placed a candle in his hand but his fingers would not bend, so they put it between his fingers and held it for him. Poltoratsky left. Five minutes after he had gone the orderly put his ear to Avdeev's chest and said that he was dead.

In the report dispatched to Tiflis Avdeev's death was described in the following manner: 'On 23 November two companies of the Kura Regiment proceeded from the fort for tree-felling. In the early afternoon a considerable force of mountaineers made a sudden attack on the felling-party. The pickets began to withdraw and at this point No. 2 Company charged the enemy with fixed bayonets and routed them. In the course of this action two privates were slightly wounded and one killed. The mountaineers' losses were about a hundred killed and wounded.'

8

ON the day that Avdeev died in the hospital at Vozdvizhenskoe his old father, the wife of his brother (the one he had joined the army for), and his elder brother's daughter, a girl of marriageable age, were threshing oats on the frost-bound threshing-floor. There had been a thick fall of snow the evening before and a hard frost overnight. The old man had woken at cock-crow and, seeing the bright moonlight through the frosted pane, had got down from his bed over the stove, put on his boots, his fur-lined coat and cap and gone to the threshing-barn. For some two hours he worked there before going back to the house and rousing his son and the women-folk. When the women arrived the threshing-floor was already cleared. A wooden shovel was stuck in the white powdery snow and by it an upturned besom; sheaves of oats were laid out in two rows, sheaf-heads together, forming a long line across the clean floor. They sorted out the flails and began threshing, rhythmically timing their strokes: the old man struck hard with his heavy flail, crushing the straw, the girl beat steadily from overhead, and the son's wife did the turning.

The moon went down and it began to grow light. They had almost finished the line when the elder son Akim, in a sheep-skin jacket and cap, came out to them.

'What are you shirking for?' his father shouted at him, pausing from his threshing and leaning on his flail.

'I've got to muck out the horses.'

'I've got to muck out the horses,' his father mimicked. 'Your old mother can do that. Get a flail. You've got too fat. Drunken sot!'

'Not your liquor though, was it?' muttered his son.

'What's that you say?' asked the old man menacingly, frowning and missing a stroke with his flail.

Akim said nothing, took a flail and the work went on with four flails going thwack-thwack-thwack-thud, as the old man's heavy flail followed the other three.

'Your neck's that fat anybody would think you was gentry. There's not enough on me to keep my trousers up,' said the old man, missing a stroke and just moving the swingle in the air to keep the rhythm.

They got to the end of the line and the women began raking off the straw.

'Peter was a fool to go off into the army for you. If you were a soldier they'd knock some sense into you, and Peter was worth five of your sort at home.'

'Oh, don't keep on, Dad,' said his daughter-in-law, tossing aside the crushed bindings.

'It's all very well. I'm supposed to feed six mouths and there's not a stroke of work from any of you. Peter, he used to do two men's work, not like . . .'

Along the path trodden in the snow from the house came the old woman, crunching over the snow in new bast shoes which she wore over tightly wrapped woollen leggings. The two men raked the unwinnowed grain into a heap while the women swept up.

'The elder sent round to say everybody's wanted at the master's for carrying bricks,' said the old woman. 'I've got some breakfast ready. You'll be going, I suppose.'

'All right. You harness the roan and go,' the old man said

to Akim. 'And see I'm not called to book on your account like I was the other day. Just you keep Peter in mind.'

'When he was home you were always on at him,' Akim this time snapped back at his father. 'And now he's gone you've got your knife into me.'

'And it's no more than you deserve,' said his mother no less angrily. 'You're not a patch on our Peter.'

'All right, all right,' said Akim.

'It isn't all right. You go and drink the money for the flour and then say it's all right.'

'What's the good of harping on what's past?' said the daughter-in-law, and they all set down their flails and went to the house.

The bad blood between father and son had begun long ago, soon after Peter had been sent off as a recruit. Even then the old man had a feeling that he had given a cuckoo for a hawk. Certainly it was right in law as the old man saw it that a man without children should go before a man with a family. Akim had four children and Peter none, but when it came to work Peter was like his father: handy, smart, strong, tough and, above all, industrious. He was always working. Like his father, he would never go by anyone working without lending a hand – he would scythe a couple of swaths, load a wagon of hay, cut down a tree or chop a pile of wood. The old man was sorry to lose him but there was no other way. Going for a soldier was like dying. Once a soldier he was gone for good: there was no point in fretting yourself with memories. Only occasionally when, as today, he wanted to get in a dig at his elder son did the old man recall Peter. His wife often thought about her younger boy and for a long time – more than a year – she had been asking her husband to send him a little money. But the old man never made any answer.

The Avdeevs' holding was a prosperous one and the old man had money put away, but he would never take the step of touching his savings. Hearing him speak of Peter now, his wife decided to ask him again and suggest he might send him something when he sold the oats, if only a rouble. This she did. After the others had gone off to work at the master's and she was alone with her husband she persuaded him to send Peter a rouble out of the money for the oats. So when from the pile of winnowed oats twelve quarters had been taken and tipped on to sacking in three sledges and the sacking carefully fastened with wooden pins she gave the old man a letter she had dictated to the sexton and he promised to put a rouble with it and send it off when he was in the town.

The old man, dressed in a new sheepskin coat, caftan and clean white woollen leggings, took the letter, put it in his pouch and, after saying a prayer, got into the leading sledge and set off for the town. His grandson rode on the last sledge. In the town the old man got the doorkeeper to read him the letter and he listened attentively and with approval.

In her letter Peter's mother first sent him her blessing, then greetings from everybody, news of his godfather's death and finally told him that Aksinya (his wife) 'no longer wants to live with us and has gone off to live her own life. They say she is doing well and living respectable.' The letter mentioned the rouble gift they were sending and ended with the following words straight from the heart of the grieving old woman who had told the sexton with tears in her eyes to write them down just as she said them:

'And Peter, my sweet, my own dear boy, I have cried my eyes out grieving for you. Why did you ever go and leave me, my own darling boy?' At this point the old woman had let out a wail and burst into tears.

'That will do,' she said.

And it was left like that in the letter, but Peter was fated never to receive the news that his wife had left home, or the rouble, or his mother's last words. The letter and money came back with the announcement that Peter had been killed in action 'defending Tsar, Fatherland and the Orthodox Faith'. That was how the military clerk put it.

On receiving this news the old woman wailed for as long

as she had time, then set about her work. The following Sunday she went to church and handed out pieces of communion bread 'to good souls that they might pray for God's servant Peter'.

Aksinya, his wife, also lamented when she heard of the death of her 'dear husband with whom she had known but a year of married life'. She was sorry for Peter and sorry for the way her whole life had been ruined. In her lament she recalled 'Peter Mikhailovich, his curly fair hair, his love, and the hard life she would have with their orphaned Vanka', and she reproached her Peter bitterly for having pity on his brother, but not on her he had left unhappily 'to shift among strangers'.

In her heart of hearts Aksinya was glad of Peter's death. She was expecting again from the bailiff in whose house she lived, and now nobody could abuse her, and the bailiff would be able to marry her just as he promised when trying to win her round.

9

PRINCE MIKHAIL VORONTSOV, brought up in England as son of the Russian ambassador, was a man of rare European education for a high Russian official of that time; he was ambitious, gentle and kindly towards his subordinates and a subtle courtier in dealing with his superiors. He had no conception of life without authority and submission. He held all the highest ranks and orders and was credited with being a skilful general, victor even over Napoleon at Craonne. In 1851 he was over seventy, but very well preserved; he was brisk in his movements and – the most important thing – he retained all the agility of his subtle and engaging mind, which he applied to maintaining his authority and establishing and extending his popularity. He possessed great wealth (his own and that of his wife, who was a Countess Branitsky), received an enormous salary as viceroy, and spent most of his money on fitting out his palace and gardens on the southern shore of the Crimea.

On the evening of 7 December 1851 a courier's *troika* drove up to his palace in Tiflis. The weary officer, black with dust, who brought the news from General Kozlovsky of Hadji Murat's defection to the Russians, walked past the sentries, stretching the cramp from his legs, and entered the broad portico of the viceroy's palace. It was six o'clock and Vorontsov was about to go into dinner when the courier's arrival was announced to him. He received him at once and so arrived a few minutes late for dinner. As Vorontsov entered the drawing-room the dinner-guests – there were about thirty of them, some sitting round Princess Vorontsov, others standing in groups near the windows – all stood up and turned towards him. Vorontsov wore his usual black military frock-coat with no epaulettes, only shoulder straps and a white cross at his throat. There was an affable smile on his clean-shaven, foxy face and he screwed up his eyes as he surveyed those present.

He came into the room with soft hurried steps, apologized to the ladies for being late, exchanged greetings with the men, and then went up to the Georgian princess Manana Orbeliani, a good-looking woman of forty-five, oriental in build, tall and portly, to whom he gave his arm to conduct her to dinner. Princess Vorontsov gave her arm to a visiting general with gingery hair and bristling whiskers. The Georgian prince escorted Countess Choiseul, Princess Vorontsov's friend; Dr Andreevsky, the *aides-de-camp* and others, with or without ladies, followed these three couples in. Footmen wearing caftans with stockings and shoes moved the chairs for the guests as they sat down and a butler ceremoniously ladled steaming soup from a silver tureen.

Vorontsov sat in the middle of the long table. Opposite him were his wife and the visiting general, on his right sat the lady he had brought in, the beautiful Orbeliani, and on his left was a young Georgian princess, a shapely, dark, ruddy-cheeked girl, brilliantly adorned, who smiled continuously.

'Excellent, my dear,' replied Vorontsov [in French] to his wife's inquiry what news the courier had brought. 'Simon has had a stroke of good fortune.'

And he began recounting so that all at the table could hear the startling news (totally unexpected to all but himself who knew that negotiations had been going on for some time) – that the celebrated Hadji Murat, Shamil's most courageous supporter, had surrendered to the Russians and would be brought in a day or two to Tiflis.

There was a hush and everyone listened, even the younger ones – the *aides-de-camp* and officers who sat at the ends of the table and had just before been quietly laughing about something.

When Vorontsov had finished speaking, his wife asked her neighbour, the red-haired general with bristling whiskers:

'Did you ever meet this Hadji Murat, General?'

'Oh, several times, Princess.'

And the general told the story of how after Gergebil had been captured by the mountaineers in 'forty-three Hadji Murat had come upon General Passek's column and almost before their eyes killed Colonel Zolotukhin.

Vorontsov listened to the general, smiling agreeably, evidently pleased to hear him holding forth. But his face suddenly took on a vacant, sombre look.

The general was in full flow and had begun recounting another episode in which he had encountered Hadji Murat.

'Your excellency will remember it,' said the general. 'It was in the "Hard Tack" expedition* – he was the one who ambushed us during the relief.'

*During the campaign conducted by Vorontsov in 1845 Russian troops occupied Shamil's stronghold of Dargo, but were virtually cut off in hostile territory. One episode in the campaign was the dispatch of

'Where was that?' enquired Vorontsov, screwing up his eyes.

The fact was that the gallant general had mentioned the word 'relief' in reference to the action in the ill-fated Dargo campaign when a whole column under Vorontsov's command would actually have been wiped out if fresh troops had not come to their relief. Everyone knew that the Dargo campaign, led by Vorontsov, in which the Russians had suffered heavy casualties and lost several guns, had been a shameful affair, and because of this if ever it was mentioned in the presence of Vorontsov it was only in the terms used by Vorontsov in his dispatch to the tsar, which presented it as a brilliant feat of Russian arms. To use the word 'relief' was a direct reminder that it was not a brilliant achievement, but a blunder that had cost many lives. Everyone realized this: some pretended to be unaware of the implications of what the general said, some waited in apprehension of what would come next, while others smiled and exchanged glances.

Only the red-haired general with the bristling whiskers failed to notice anything amiss and, carried away by his tale, calmly replied to Vorontsov's question:

'In the relief, your excellency.'

And once launched on a favourite subject the general gave a detailed account of how 'this fellow Hadji Murat had cut the column so neatly in two, that if the relief had not come' – he seemed to repeat the word 'relief' with special affection – 'none of us would have got out alive, for . . .'

The general never finished, because Manana Orbeliani, seeing the situation, interrupted him to ask whether his quarters in Tiflis were comfortable. The general in surprise looked round at everyone and at his *aide-de-camp* who was shooting him hard meaning glances from the end of the table. It suddenly dawned on him. Without replying to the princess, he frowned,

---

troops from Dargo to escort a column bringing much-needed supplies – this was the 'Hard Tack' expedition, in which both the supply train and the escorting troops suffered heavy losses.

stopped speaking and hurriedly began eating the elegant food on his plate, swallowing it whole, unaware of what it was or even how it tasted.

There was general embarrassment, but the awkward situation was saved by the Georgian prince, a very stupid man, but as a sycophant and courtier remarkably subtle and astute, who was sitting on the other side of Princess Vorontsov. As if nothing had happened he loudly began telling the story of Hadji Murat's abduction of the widow of Akhmet-Khan of Mekhtuli.

'He went into the village by night, took what he came for and galloped off with his whole band.'

'But why this woman in particular?' asked the Princess.

'Her husband was his enemy. Hadji Murat hunted after him, but the khan died before he ever caught up with him so he took revenge on his widow.'

The princess translated this into French for her old friend the Countess Choiseul, who was sitting by the Georgian prince.

'*Quelle horreur!*' said the countess, closing her eyes and shaking her head.

'Not at all,' said Vorontsov, smiling. 'I heard that he treated his prisoner with chivalrous respect and then let her go.'

'Yes, for a ransom.'

'Naturally. But nonetheless he behaved like a perfect gentleman.'

The prince's words set the tone for further anecdotes about Hadji Murat. Those in attendance realized that the more they emphasized the importance of Hadji Murat, the more agreeable it would be to Vorontsov.

'The man's daring is astonishing. He's quite remarkable.'

'He really is. In 'forty-nine he raided Shura and plundered the shops in broad daylight.'

An Armenian at the end of the table who had been in Shura at the time gave the details of this feat of Hadji Murat.

Most of the dinner passed in tales about Hadji Murat. They

all vied with each other to praise his courage, cleverness, and magnanimity. Someone recounted an incident when he had ordered the killing of twenty-six captives, but even then there was the usual reply:

'It can't be helped. *À la guerre comme à la guerre.*'

'He is a very considerable man.'

'If he had been born in Europe he might have been another Napoleon,' said the Georgian prince with the gift for flattery.

He knew that any mention of Napoleon would please Vorontsov: it was for his victory over Napoleon that Vorontsov wore the white cross round his neck.

'Well, perhaps not Napoleon, but at least a dashing cavalry general, certainly,' said Vorontsov.

'If not Napoleon, Murat.'

'He's got the same name – Hadji Murat.'

'Now that Hadji Murat has defected that will be the end of Shamil,' said someone.

'They can tell they haven't got a chance now,' said someone else ('now' meaning 'with Vorontsov in command').

'It's all thanks to you,' said Manana Orbeliani.

Prince Vorontsov tried to restrain the showers of flattery which were beginning to overwhelm him. But he found it agreeable and was in an excellent mood when he escorted his partner into the drawing-room.

After dinner as coffee was being served in the drawing-room Vorontsov was especially pleasant to everyone and going up to the general with the bristling ginger whiskers made every effort to show that he had not noticed his gaffe.

After circulating among all his guests, the prince sat down to play cards. He only played the old-fashioned game of *l'hombre*. Playing with him were the Georgian prince, the Armenian general (who had learnt the game from Vorontsov's valet), and Dr Andreevsky, who was well known for the power he wielded.

Vorontsov placed at his elbow a gold snuff-box with a

portrait of Alexander I, broke open the glossy cards and was about to lay them out, when his valet, an Italian called Giovanni, came in with a letter on a silver tray.

'Another courier has arrived, your excellency.'

Vorontsov put down the cards, with a word of apology unsealed the letter and began reading.

The letter was from his son. He gave in it an account of Hadji Murat's defection and the brush he had had with Meller-Zakomelsky.

The princess came over and asked what was in her son's letter.

'He has had a contretemps with the local commander. Simon was in the wrong. "But all is well that ends well",' he said, handing the letter to his wife. He turned then to his respectfully waiting partners and requested them to take their cards.

When the first hand had been dealt Vorontsov opened his snuff-box and did what he always did when in an especially good mood: he took a pinch of French snuff into his aged wrinkled white hand, lifted it up and placed it in his nose.

10

THE next day, when Hadji Murat came to be received by Vorontsov, the prince's waiting-room was full of people. There was the general with bristling whiskers of the previous evening, wearing full uniform and decorations, who had come to take his leave; there was a regimental commander who was under threat of court-martial for misappropriations from the regiment's victualling account; there was a wealthy Armenian, a protégé of Dr Andreevsky, who held the concession for selling vodka and was now seeking a renewal of the contract; there was a woman in black, the widow of an officer who had been killed, who had come to ask if she might receive a

pension or have her children supported by the state; there was
a Georgian prince in magnificent Georgian costume who was
trying to solicit for himself a church estate that had fallen
vacant; there was a district commissioner with a large scroll
containing the plans of a new way to subjugate the Caucasus;
and there was a khan, whose sole purpose in coming was to
be able to say at home that he had visited the prince.

All waited their turn and one by one were conducted into
the prince's study by a handsome, fair-haired boy, who was
Vorontsov's *aide-de-camp*.

When Hadji Murat, limping slightly, strode briskly into the
waiting-room, all eyes turned to him and he heard his name
whispered in different corners of the room.

He was wearing a long white *cherkeska* over a brown jacket,
the collar of which was decorated with fine silver lace. He had
on black cloth leggings and soft leather boots of the same
colour which fitted tightly over his feet like gloves; on his
shaven head he wore a *papakha* wound with a turban – the
same turban which had led to his arrest by General Klugenau
after Akhmet-Khan had informed on him and which had been
the cause of his going over to Shamil. Hadji Murat walked
quickly across the parquet floor of the waiting-room, his
slender frame swaying from the slight limp which was caused
by his having one leg shorter than the other. His widely set
eyes looked calmly straight ahead and appeared to see no one.

The handsome *aide-de-camp* greeted him and asked him to
take a seat while he announced him to the prince. But Hadji
Murat declined and remained standing with feet apart and one
hand at his dagger, scornfully surveying those present.

Prince Tarkhanov, the interpreter, went up to Hadji Murat
and began talking. Hadji Murat replied curtly, reluctantly. A
Kumyk prince who was lodging a complaint about the district
commissioner came out of Vorontsov's study, followed by the
aide-de-camp who summoned Hadji Murat, took him to the
study door and showed him in.

Vorontsov received Hadji Murat standing at the edge of his desk. The old white face of the commander-in-chief was not smiling as it had been the day before, rather it was stern and solemn.

On entering the large room with its enormous desk, large windows and green shutters, Hadji Murat put his rather small sunburnt hands to his chest where the sides of his white *cherkeska* met and with lowered eyes, speaking deliberately, distinctly and respectfully in Kumyk, which he knew well, he said:

'I surrender to the mighty protection of the great tsar and of yourself. I promise to serve the White Tsar faithfully, to the last drop of my blood, and I hope to be of service in the war against Shamil, who is my enemy and yours.'

Vorontsov listened to the interpreter, then looked at Hadji Murat. Hadji Murat, too, looked Vorontsov in the face.

As they met, the eyes of these two men said much that words could not express and not at all what the interpreter had said. Without a word passing between them each stated the plain truth about the other: Vorontsov's eyes declared that he did not believe a single word of what Hadji Murat had said, that he knew he was the enemy of everything Russian and always would be, and that he was submitting now only because he was forced to. Hadji Murat understood this, but nonetheless assured him of his loyalty. At the same time his own eyes were saying that this old man ought to be thinking about death rather than war, but, old as he was, he was sly and he would have to be on his guard. Vorontsov understood, too, but nonetheless explained to Hadji Murat what he considered necessary for a successful outcome of the war.

'Tell him,' said Vorontsov to the interpreter (he used the familiar mode of address in Russian as he did to all young officers), 'tell him that our sovereign is as gracious as he is mighty and will probably grant my request to pardon him and take him into his service. Have you said that?' he asked, looking at Hadji Murat. 'Until I know the gracious decision of my master, tell him that I undertake to receive him and to make his stay with us agreeable.'

Hadji Murat again pressed his hands to the middle of his chest and animatedly began speaking.

The interpreter conveyed what he said, which was that before, in 1839, when he had governed Avaria, he had faithfully served the Russians and would never have broken faith with them had it not been for his enemy Akhmet-Khan, who had wished to destroy him and had falsely denounced him to General Klugenau.

'Yes, yes, I know,' said Vorontsov (who, if he had ever known, had long since forgotten it). 'I know,' he said, sitting down and waving Hadji Murat to an ottoman by the wall. But Hadji Murat remained standing, signifying with a shrug of his powerful shoulders that he would not presume to sit in the presence of so important a person.

'Akhmet-Khan and Shamil are both my enemies,' Hadji Murat continued, turning to the interpreter. 'Tell the prince that Akhmet-Khan is dead, I could not revenge myself on him, but Shamil is alive and I shall not die till I have settled scores with him,' he said, frowning and clenching his jaws.

'Yes, of course,' said Vorontsov composedly. 'How does he intend to settle with Shamil?' he asked the interpreter. 'And do tell him he can sit down.'

Hadji Murat again refused a seat and in reply to the question that was conveyed to him he said that he had come over to the Russians for the very purpose of helping them destroy Shamil.

'Good, good,' said Vorontsov. 'What is it exactly he wants to do? Do please sit down . . .'

Hadji Murat sat down and said that if they would only send him to the Lezghian Line and give him a force of men he would guarantee to raise the whole of Daghestan and Shamil would have to give in.

'Yes, good idea. That could be done,' said Vorontsov. 'I will think it over.'

The interpreter told Hadji Murat what Vorontsov said. Hadji Murat became pensive.

'Tell the *sardar*,' he said, 'that my family are in the hands of my enemy and as long as they are in the mountains my hands are tied and I cannot help. If I move openly against Shamil he will kill my wife, my mother and my children. The prince has only to rescue my family, give some prisoners in exchange for them, and I will destroy Shamil or die in the attempt.'

'Good, good,' said Vorontsov. 'We will think it over. For the present he should go to the chief-of-staff and make a detailed statement of his present position, his intentions and his wishes.'

Thus ended the first meeting between Hadji Murat and Vorontsov.

That evening there was a performance of an Italian opera in the new theatre which was decorated in oriental style. Vorontsov was in his box when the conspicuous limping figure of Hadji Murat wearing a turban appeared in the stalls. He came in with Loris-Melikov, one of Vorontsov's *aides-de-camp* who had been attached to him, and took his seat in the front row. Hadji Murat sat through the first act with oriental, Muslim dignity, expressing no surprise, seeming rather indifferent; he then rose and calmly surveying the audience, went out, the centre of everyone's attention.

The following day was Monday, the Vorontsovs' customary 'at home' evening. In the large brightly lit ballroom there was music, played by an orchestra. Young women, and women not so young, in dresses which revealed their necks, their arms and practically their bosoms too, spun in the embrace of men in brightly-coloured uniforms. At the mountainous buffet footmen in red frock-coats, stockings and shoes, served champagne and handed confections to the ladies. The *sardar*'s wife who, despite her advancing years, was also half-naked, walked among her guests, smiling affably, and through the interpreter said a few kindly words to Hadji Murat, who was regarding the guests with the same indifference he had shown in the theatre the day before. The hostess was followed by other women with their bodies exposed who came up to Hadji Murat and stood shamelessly before him, smiling and asking the same question: how did he like what he saw? Vorontsov himself, wearing epaulettes and aiguillettes, the white cross at his throat and the ribbon of an order, came up to him and asked the same question, evidently assured as were all who asked that Hadji Murat could not fail to like what he saw. And Hadji Murat replied to Vorontsov as he replied to everyone else: that they had none of this – without saying if it was good or bad that this was so.

At the ball too Hadji Murat made an effort to speak to Vorontsov about ransoming his family, but Vorontsov pretended not to hear and walked away. Loris-Melikov later explained to Hadji Murat that it was not the place for talking business.

When it struck eleven, Hadji Murat checked the time on the watch he had been given by Marya Vasilevna and asked Loris-Melikov if he might go. Loris-Melikov said that he could, but that it would be better if he stayed. Despite this, Hadji Murat did not stay and drove back to the quarters that had been assigned to him in the phaeton provided for his use.

11

ON the fifth day of Hadji Murat's stay in Tiflis Loris-Melikov, the viceroy's *aide-de-camp*, came to see him on orders from the commander-in-chief.

'My head and my hands are glad to serve the *sardar*,' said Hadji Murat with his usual diplomatic expression, inclining his head and putting his hands to his chest. 'Tell me your command,' he said, looking Loris-Melikov kindly in the eyes.

Loris-Melikov sat down in the armchair by the table, Hadji Murat sank on to the low ottoman opposite him and, resting his hands on his knees, bent his head forward and listened attentively to what Loris-Melikov said. Loris-Melikov, who spoke Tatar fluently, told him that the prince, although he knew Hadji Murat's past, wished to have a full account of it from him personally.

'You tell me,' said Loris-Melikov, 'and I will write it down, then I will translate it and the prince will send it to the tsar.'

Hadji Murat was silent for a moment (he never interrupted anyone speaking and always waited after they had finished to see if they would say more); he then raised his head, tossing back his *papakha*, and smiled with that special, child-like smile with which he had earlier captivated Marya Vasilevna.

'Yes, I can do that,' he said, evidently flattered by the idea that his story would be read by the tsar.

'Start from the beginning and tell me everything. There is no need to hurry,' said Loris-Melikov, taking a notebook from his pocket.

'I can do this, but there is much, very much to tell. Many things happened,' said Hadji Murat.

'If it is too much for one day you can finish it on another,' said Loris-Melikov.

'Shall I start at the beginning?'

'Yes, at the very beginning: where you were born, where you lived.'

Hadji Murat lowered his head and sat like that for a long time. Then he picked up a stick lying by the ottoman, drew from beneath his ivory-handled, gold-mounted dagger a steel knife, sharp as a razor, and began carving the stick, at the same time telling his story.

'Write this down. I was born in Tselmes, a small village, the size of an ass's head, as we say in the mountains,' he began. 'Not far from us – two shots' distance – was Khunzakh, where the khans lived. Our family was on very close terms with them. My mother had been nurse to the eldest khan, Abununtsal-Khan, and that is how I became connected with them. There were three khans: Abununtsal-Khan, who was foster-brother to my brother Osman, Umma-Khan, who was my own sworn brother, and Bulach-Khan, the youngest, the one Shamil threw over the cliff. But that was later. When I was about fifteen the murids began coming round the villages. They beat on stones with wooden swords and cried out "Muslims, *Ghazavat*!" All the Chechens went over to the murids and the Avars began to as well. I lived in the palace then. I was like a brother of the khans: I did whatever I wanted and was rich. I had horses, weapons, and money, too. I enjoyed life and gave no thought to anything. And so I lived until Kazi-Mullah was killed and Hamzad took his place. Hamzad sent envoys to the khans to say that if they did not accept the *Ghazavat* he would destroy Khunzakh. It needed careful thought. The khans feared the Russians and were afraid to accept the *Ghazavat*, so the khanoum sent me and her second son Umma-Khan to Tiflis to ask the chief commander of the Russians to help us against Hamzad. The chief commander was Rosen, Baron Rosen. He did not see me or Umma-Khan. He had us told that he would help, but he did nothing. Only his officers began visiting us and playing cards with Umma-Khan. They gave him wine to drink and took him to evil places and he lost all that he had playing cards with them. In body he was strong as an ox and brave as a lion, but in spirit he was weak like water. He would have lost the last of his horses and weapons, if I had not taken him away. After Tiflis I thought differently and tried to persuade the khanoum and young khans to take up the *Ghazavat*.

'What made you think differently?' asked Loris-Melikov. 'Did you not like the Russians?'

For a moment Hadji Murat said nothing.

'No, I did not like them,' he said firmly. He closed his eyes. 'And another thing happened that made me want to accept the *Ghazavat*.'

'What was that?'

'Near Tselmes the khan and I came upon three murids. Two

got away, but the other one I killed with my pistol. When I went to take his weapons he was still alive. He looked up at me. "You have killed me," he said. "For me it is well. But you are a Muslim, you are young and strong. Accept the *Ghazavat*. It is God's command." '

'And did you accept it?'

'No, I did not. But I began to think,' said Hadji Murat, taking up his story again. 'When Hamzad came up to Khunzakh, we sent old men to him to say that we would accept the *Ghazavat*, but that he should send us a learned man to explain how we were to uphold it. Hamzad had the old men shaved of their whiskers, their nostrils pierced and sent them back with small cakes hung to their noses. The old men said that Hamzad was willing to send a sheikh to instruct us in the *Ghazavat*, but only on condition that the khanoum sent him her youngest son as a hostage. The khanoum trusted Hamzad and sent him Bulach-Khan. He received him well and sent a message to us summoning the older brothers too. He said that he wished to serve the khans as his father had served their father. The khanoum was weak and foolish and headstrong as all women are who live by their own will. She was afraid to send both her sons and sent only Umma-Khan. I went with him. A mile or so from his camp his murids met us, singing, shooting and showing off their riding tricks. And when we arrived Hamzad came out of his tent, went up to Umma-Khan's stirrup and received him like a khan. He said "I have done no harm to your house and wish none. I ask only that you do not kill me or prevent me from bringing people to the *Ghazavat*. And I will serve you with all my warriors as my father served your father. Let me dwell in your house. I will assist you with my advice and you can do as you wish." Umma-Khan was slow-witted in speech. He did not know what to say and was silent. Then I said that if it were as Hamzad said he should go to Khunzakh, and the khanoum and khan would receive him with honour. But I was cut short, and it was now I had my first clash with Shamil. He was there by the Imam and said to me, "No one asked you. Let the khan answer." I said no more, and Hamzad took Umma-Khan into his tent. Then Hamzad summoned me and told me to go with his envoys to Khunzakh. So I went. The envoys tried to persuade the khanoum to send her eldest son to Hamzad as well. I saw their treachery and told the khanoum not to send him. But a woman has as much wit as an egg has hair. The khanoum trusted them and told her son to go with them. Abununtsal did not want to. Then she said: "I see you are afraid." Like a bee she knew where the sting hurt most. Abununtsal flushed. He said nothing more to her and ordered his horse to be saddled. I went with him. Hamzad welcomed us even better than he had Umma-Khan. He came two shots' distance down the hill to meet us. Horsemen with pennants rode after him chanting "*La ilaha illa allah*", shooting and making show with their horses. When we reached the camp Hamzad took the khan into his tent. I stayed with the horses. I was down the hill when suddenly there was shooting in Hamzad's tent. I ran up to it. Umma-Khan was flat on his face in a pool of blood and Abununtsal was fighting the murids. Half his face had been cut away and was hanging down. He had hold of it with one hand and held his dagger in the other, cutting down anyone who came near. I saw him cut down Hamzad's brother and he was just going for another of them but the murids started shooting and he fell.'

Hadji Murat stopped. His tanned face flushed a reddish brown and his eyes turned bloodshot.

'Fear came upon me and I ran away.'

'You did?' said Loris-Melikov. 'I thought you were never afraid of anything.'

'Afterwards I was not. Ever since I have remembered the shame of that day and when I remember it I am afraid no more.'

12

'THAT is enough for now. I must pray,' said Hadji Murat. He took Vorontsov's watch from the inner breast-pocket of his *cherkeska*, carefully touched the spring and, cocking his head and suppressing a childish smile, he listened. The watch chimed twelve times and one quarter.

'My *kunak* Vorontsov *peshkesh* – gave me,' he said smiling. 'A good man.'

'Yes, he is a good man,' said Loris-Melikov. 'And it is a good watch too. You say your prayers then, and I will wait.'

'*Yakshi*, it is well,' said Hadji Murat, and went to his bedroom.

When he was alone Loris-Melikov wrote down in his notebook the substance of what Hadji Murat had told him, then lit a cigarette and walked round the room. As he came to the door opposite the bedroom Loris-Melikov heard the animated voices of men talking rapidly in Tatar. He guessed it would be Hadji Murat's murids, so opened the door and went in.

The room had that particular sour leathery smell characteristic of the mountaineers. Sitting by the window on his cloak spread on the floor was the one-eyed, ginger-haired Gamzalo in a tattered greasy jacket, tying a bridle. He was speaking heatedly in his hoarse voice, but when Loris-Melikov came in he immediately fell silent and, taking no notice of him, continued with his task. Standing opposite him was the cheerful Khan-Mahoma, who kept repeating something with his white teeth grinning and a sparkle in his black lashless eyes. The handsome Eldar, with sleeves rolled up over his powerful arms, was scouring the girth straps of a saddle hanging on a nail. Khanefi, who did most of the work and looked after the domestic side of things, was not in the room. He was in the kitchen cooking dinner.

Greeting Khan-Mahoma, Loris-Melikov asked him what they were arguing about.

'He still goes on praising Shamil,' said Khan-Mahoma, giving Loris his hand. 'He says Shamil is a great man: a scholar, holy man, and *djigit*.'

'How can he forsake him and still praise him?'

'He did and he does,' grinned Khan-Mahoma, his eyes sparkling.

'Do you then reckon him a holy man?' asked Loris-Melikov.

'If he was not a holy man the people would not listen to him,' Gamzalo retorted.

'Mansur was a holy man, but not Shamil,' said Khan-Mahoma. 'He was a real holy man. When he was Imam the people were different. He went into the villages and the people came out to him, they kissed the hem of his *cherkeska*, repented of their sins and vowed to do no evil. The old men said that in those times everyone lived like a holy man; people did not smoke and drink or miss their prayers, they pardoned offences, yes, even bloodshed. In those days a man who found money or anything else would tie it to a pole and stand it by the road. And God made the people prosper in all things then, not like today,' said Khan-Mahoma.

'In the mountains people don't drink and smoke today either,' said Gamzalo.

'Your Shamil is a *lamoroi*,' said Khan-Mahoma, with a wink to Loris-Melikov.

Lamoroi was a scornful term for the mountaineers.

'A *lamoroi* lives in the mountains, and that is where the eagles live,' replied Gamzalo.

'Good man! You got me nicely there,' said Khan-Mahoma with a grin, enjoying the apt retort of his opponent.

Seeing the silver cigarette-case in Loris-Melikov's hand, he asked him for a cigarette. Loris-Melikov remarked that surely they were not allowed to smoke. Khan-Mahoma winked and with a nod towards Hadji Murat's bedroom said that it was all right as long as nobody saw. And he straightaway began to smoke, without inhaling, awkwardly shaping his red lips as he blew out the smoke.

'It is bad,' said Gamzalo sternly and left the room. Khan-Mahoma gave a wink in his direction and while he smoked questioned Loris-Melikov about the best place to buy a silk jacket and a white *papakha*.

'Have you got such a lot of money, then?'

'I have money enough,' replied Khan-Mahoma winking.

'Ask him where he got it,' said Eldar, turning his handsome smiling face towards Loris.

'I won it,' said Khan-Mahoma and launched into the tale of how the day before he had been strolling in Tiflis and had come on a group of Russian batmen and Armenians playing heads-or-tails. There was a lot of money in the kitty: three pieces of gold and a lot of silver. Khan-Mahoma got the hang of the game at once and jingling the coppers in his pocket joined the circle, saying he would play for the lot.

'The lot? But you never had that much, did you?' asked Loris-Melikov.

'All I had was twelve kopeks,' said Khan-Mahoma, grinning.

'And what if you had lost?'

'I had this.'

Khan-Mahoma pointed to his pistol.

'Would you have given them that?'

'What for? I would have run for it and killed anybody who tried to stop me. And that would be that.'

'So you won?'

'*Aya.* I took the lot and went.'

Loris-Melikov understood Khan-Mahoma and Eldar perfectly. Khan-Mahoma was a wag, a rake, with no idea how to use the brimming life within him, always cheerful, frivolous, playing with life – his own and that of others; for him coming over to the Russians was all part of the game one day, but he might equally well go back to Shamil the next. Eldar too was perfectly easy to understand. This was a man completely devoted to his murshid, cool, strong and tough. It was only Gamzalo that Loris-Melikov was unable to make out. He could see that he was devoted to Shamil and that he also felt an insuperable loathing, scorn, disgust and hatred for all Russians. Because of this Loris-Melikov could not understand why he had come over to the Russians. The same thought occurred to him as was held by some of those in higher authority – that Hadji Murat's defection and the tale of his enmity towards Shamil were a blind, and that his only reason for surrendering was to spy out the weak points in the Russian defences before making off to the mountains once more and directing Shamil's forces to the places where the Russians were less strong. Gamzalo's whole being seemed to support this supposition. The others and Hadji Murat himself know how to hide their intentions, thought Loris-Melikov. But Gamzalo with his unconcealed hatred gives the game away.

Loris-Melikov tried talking to him. He asked if he found it dull here. But Gamzalo went on with what he was doing and casting a sideways glance at Loris-Melikov with his single eye barked hoarsely and abruptly:

'No, it's not dull.'

All other questions he answered in the same manner.

While Loris-Melikov was in the room, Hadji Murat's fourth murid came in – the Avar Khanefi, with face and neck thick with hair and a shaggy barrel chest which might have been covered with fur. He was the workman, unthinking, stalwart, always engrossed in his work, and, like Eldar, unquestioningly obedient to his master.

When he came into the *nukers'* room to fetch some rice Loris-Melikov stopped him and asked where he came from and how long he had served Hadji Murat.

'Five years,' answered Khanefi. 'We come from the same

village. My father killed his uncle and they were going to kill me,' he said, calmly looking Loris-Melikov in the face from under his eyebrows, which grew together in a single line. 'Then I asked them to take me as a brother.'

'What does that mean: take you as a brother?'

'For two months I neither shaved my head nor cut my nails, then I went to them. They sent me in to Patimat, his mother. She gave me her breast to suck and I became his brother.'

Hadji Murat's voice sounded in the next room. Eldar knew at once that he was calling, wiped his hands and hastened with long strides into the drawing-room.

'He wants you,' he said, coming back.

And Loris-Melikov, giving the cheerful Khan-Mahoma another cigarette, went in to Hadji Murat.

13

WHEN Loris-Melikov came into the drawing-room Hadji Murat greeted him with a cheerful look.

'Shall we go on then?' he said, seating himself on the ottoman.

'By all means,' said Loris-Melikov. 'I have just called in on your *nukers* and had a talk with them. One of them is a cheerful fellow,' Loris-Melikov added.

'Yes, Khan-Mahoma is a light-minded man,' said Hadji Murat.

'I liked the young man, the good-looking one.'

'Oh, Eldar. He is young and hard, like iron.'

For a moment they were silent.

'Shall I go on then?'

'Yes, please do.'

'I told you how they killed the khans. Well, they killed them, and Hamzad rode into Khunzakh and set himself up in the palace of the khans,' Hadji Murat began. 'The khanoum, their mother, was still left. Hamzad sent for her. She began to rebuke him. He gave a sign to his murid Aselder and he felled her from behind and killed her.'

'But why should he have her killed?' asked Loris-Melikov.

'What else could he do? If the front legs are over the back legs must follow. The whole family had to be wiped out, and that is what they did. Shamil killed the youngest khan: he threw him down a cliff. The whole of Avaria submitted to Hamzad: my brother and I alone would not submit. We had to have his blood for that of the khans. We pretended to submit, but our only thought was how we could have his blood. We took counsel with our grandfather and decided to wait for a time when Hamzad left the palace and we would lie in wait and kill him. But someone heard us and told Hamzad. He sent for our grandfather and said to him: "See now, if it is true that your grandsons plot evil against me, you and they shall hang on the same gallows. I am doing God's work and no one shall hinder me. Go and remember what I have said." Grandfather came home and told us. We decided then not to wait but to do our deed in the mosque on the first day of the feast. Our comrades refused, so there was just my brother and me. We took a pair of pistols each, put on our cloaks and went to the mosque. Hamzad came in with thirty of his murids, all with drawn swords. At Hamzad's side was Aselder, his favourite murid, the one who had cut off the khanoum's head. When he saw us, he shouted at us to take off our cloaks. He came up to me, my dagger was in my hand – I killed him and went for Hamzad. But already my brother Osman had shot him. Hamzad was still alive and went for my brother with his dagger, but I got him in the head and finished him off. There were thirty murids, and two of us. They killed Osman, but I fought them off, jumped out of the window and got away. When it was known that Hamzad had been killed the whole people rose up and the murids fled, and any who did not were all killed.'

Hadji Murat stopped and breathed in deeply.

'All this was very good,' he continued, 'but then everything went wrong. Shamil took the place of Hamzad. He sent envoys to say I must join him against the Russians, and if I refused he said he would destroy Khunzakh and kill me. I told him I would not go to him nor let him come at me.'

'Why would you not join him?' asked Loris-Melikov.

Hadji Murat frowned and did not answer at once.

'I could not. The blood of my brother Osman and of Abununtsal-Khan was on his head. I did not go to him. Rosen, the general, sent to me: he made me an officer and commander of Avaria. All this was good, but before that Rosen had put Avaria under Mahomet-Mirza, the khan of Kazikumykh, and afterwards under Akhmet-Khan. And Akhmet-Khan hated me. He had tried to marry his son to the khanoum's daughter Saltanet. They refused him and he thought I was to blame. So he took hate against me and sent his *nukers* to kill me, but I got away. Then he accused me falsely to General Klugenau. He said I forbade the Avars to supply wood to the soldiers, and he also said that I had donned the turban – this turban,' said Hadji Murat, pointing to the turban on his *papakha*, 'and that this meant I had gone over to Shamil. The general did not believe him and said I should be left alone. But when the general went away to Tiflis Akhmet-Khan took matters into his own hands. With a company of soldiers he seized me and had me put in chains and tied me to a gun. Six days they kept me like that, and on the seventh day they untied me and took me to Shura. They took me under guard – forty soldiers with loaded muskets. My hands were tied and the order was to kill me if I tried to escape. I knew that. As we were getting close, near Moksokh, the path was narrow and on the right-hand side there was a drop of three or four hundred feet. I moved away from the soldier to the right on to the edge of the cliff. The soldier tried to stop me, but I jumped over and dragged him after me. He was killed outright, but as you see I survived. Ribs, head, arms, leg – all broken. I tried to crawl, but could not. I came over giddy and fell asleep. I woke up soaked in blood. A shepherd saw me, he called some people and they took me to a village. My ribs and head got better, and so did my leg, except it was shorter.'

Hadji Murat stretched out his crooked leg.

'It gets me about and that is good enough,' he said. 'The people heard about me and came to visit me. I got better and moved to Tselmes. The Avars wanted me to come and rule them again,' said Hadji Murat with calm and confident pride. 'And I agreed to do so.'

Hadji Murat quickly rose, and getting a folder from his saddle-bags, took out two letters yellow with age which he handed to Loris-Melikov. Loris-Melikov read them. The first letter was as follows:

'Ensign Hadji Murat: You served under me and I was well satisfied and thought you to be a good man. I was recently informed by Major-General Akhmet-Khan that you were a traitor, that you had donned the turban, that you were in league with Shamil and that you had instructed the people to disobey the Russian authorities. I ordered you to be arrested and brought to me, but you ran away. Whether this makes things better or worse I do not know, since I do not know whether or not you are guilty. Heed now what I say. If your conscience is clear towards the great tsar, if you are guilty of nothing, then appear before me. You have nothing to fear from anyone – I am your protector. The khan will not harm you: he is himself under my command, so you have nothing to fear.'

Klugenau went on to say that he always kept his word and was just, and he again urged Hadji Murat to return.

When Loris-Melikov finished the first letter, Hadji Murat took the other one, but before handing it to Loris-Melikov he told him how he had answered the first letter.

'I wrote and told him that I wore the turban not for Shamil but to save my soul. I wrote that I had no desire to go over to

Shamil and could not do so because through him my father, brothers and kinsmen had been killed, but neither could I go back to the Russians since they had dishonoured me. At Khunzakh while I was tied up some cur —— on me. And I could not go over to the Russians until this man had been killed. But most of all I was afraid of that double-dealer Akhmet-Khan. Then the general sent me this letter,' said Hadji Murat, handing Loris-Melikov the second faded sheet.

'You replied to my letter and I thank you,' read Loris-Melikov. 'You write that you are not afraid to come back, but are prevented by the dishonour inflicted on you by a *giaour*. I can assure you that the Russian law is just, and you yourself will witness the punishment of the man who dared to offend you – I am already having this investigated. Listen, Hadji Murat. I have just cause to be dissatisfied with you, because you do not trust me and my honour. However, this I excuse you, knowing as I do the generally mistrustful nature of you mountaineers. If your conscience is clear, if you really have donned the turban only to save your soul, then you are in the right and can boldly face the Russian government and myself. You may rest assured that the man who dishonoured you will be punished, that *your property will be returned*, and that you will see and know what the Russian law means. And besides, Russians take a different view of things and consider it no disgrace to you that some scoundrel dishonoured you. I have myself allowed the people of Gimri to wear the turban and I take a right view of their deeds. So, I repeat, you have nothing to fear. Come back with the man I am now sending to you. He is loyal to me, and is *not the servant of your enemies*, but the friend of a man who enjoys the special consideration of the government.'

Klugenau then once more urged Hadji Murat to return.

'I did not trust this letter,' said Hadji Murat when Loris-Melikov had finished reading. 'And I did not go to Klugenau. For me the main thing was to be revenged on Akhmet-Khan and that I could not do through the Russians. At that time Akhmet-Khan surrounded Tselmes, wishing to capture me or to kill me. I did not have enough men and could not fight him off. It was just then that an envoy brought me a letter from Shamil. He promised to help me beat off Akhmet-Khan and kill him, and he offered to make me ruler of all Avaria. I gave it much thought and went over to Shamil. And ever since I have been fighting the Russians.'

Hadji Murat then gave an account of all the actions he had fought. They were very numerous and Loris-Melikov knew part of them already. All his campaigns and raids were astonishing for the extraordinary swiftness of his movements and the boldness of his attacks, which were always successful.

'There was never any friendship between me and Shamil,' said Hadji Murat, as he ended his story, 'but he feared me and had need of me. It so happened then that someone asked me who would be Imam after Shamil, and I said it would be the man whose sword was sharp. This was passed on to Shamil and he decided to get rid of me. He sent me to Tabasaran and I went and carried off a thousand sheep and three hundred horses. But he said the thing I had done was wrong and he replaced me as *naib* and commanded me to send him all the money I had. I sent him one thousand gold pieces. He sent his murids and took away all my property. Then he summoned me, but I knew that he wanted to kill me and did not go. He sent his men to capture me, but I fought my way out and came over to Vorontsov. Only I did not bring my family. My mother, my wife and my son are with Shamil. Tell the *sardar*: while my family is there I can do nothing.'

'I will tell him,' said Loris-Melikov.

'See to it, do everything you can. All I have is yours if only you will help me with the prince. I am bound hand and foot and the end of the rope is in Shamil's hand.'

With these words Hadji Murat ended his story to Loris-Melikov.

14

ON 20 December Vorontsov wrote the following letter to Chernyshev, the Minister of War. He wrote in French.

'My dear Prince, I did not write to you with the last post, since I wished first to decide what course to follow with Hadji Murat and I was also unwell for two or three days. In my last letter I informed you of Hadji Murat's arrival here: he arrived in Tiflis on the 8th; I met him the following day and for eight or nine days I had talks with him and considered what eventually he might do for us and particularly what we should do about him now. He is much concerned about the fate of his family and says with what seems to be perfect candour that as long as his family are in Shamil's hands he is paralysed and cannot do us any service to show his gratitude for the pardon and good reception we have given him. The uncertainty concerning those dear to him has thrown him into a state of feverish anxiety and those persons whom I detailed to reside with him assure me that he does not sleep at night, eats practically nothing, is continually praying, and asks only for permission to go riding with a few Cossacks – for him the only possible diversion and exercise, which the habit of years has made a necessity. Every day he has come to ask me if I have any news of his family and he begs me to collect all the prisoners we have on the various lines of the frontier and offer them to Shamil in exchange, together with a small sum of money which he would provide himself. There are people who would give him money for this purpose. His constant theme has been: first rescue my family, and then give me the chance to serve you (he thinks on the Lezghian Line would be best); if in a month I fail to do you a major service, you may punish me as you think fit.

'I have told him that all this seems to me very reasonable and that in fact there are many people on our side who would be reluctant to trust him if his family did remain in the mountains rather than under our care, where they would be a guarantee of his good faith. I said that I would do all I could to collect the prisoners held in our frontier posts and that although our regulations prevented me from adding any ransom money to what he might raise himself I might find some other means to assist him. I then frankly expressed my view that in no event would Shamil release his family and that Shamil might tell him so outright, promising him a free pardon and reinstatement if he returned, but threatening to kill his mother, wife and six children if he did not. I asked if he could honestly say what he would do if he received such a declaration from Shamil. Hadji Murat raised his eyes and hands to heaven and said that everything was in the hands of God, but that he would never put himself in the power of his enemy, because he was perfectly certain that he would not be pardoned by Shamil and that his days then would be numbered. As for the destruction of his family he doubted whether Shamil would undertake this lightly: firstly, so as not to render Hadji Murat an even more desperate and dangerous enemy, and secondly, because there were many people in Daghestan, some with considerable influence, who would dissuade him. He ended by saying several times over that whatever may be God's will for the future, he for the present was only concerned with the ransom of his family; that he begged me for God's sake to help him and allow him to return to the neighbourhood of Chechnia, where with the permission and assistance of our military command he could have contact with his family and receive regular information about their condition and about possible means to secure their release; that many persons and even some *naibs* in that part of enemy territory are more or less loyal to him; that among the people as a whole – neutrals as well as those under Russian authority – he can, with our help, easily establish contacts, which would be extremely useful for achieving the purpose by which he is driven day and night and whose fulfilment will bring him peace of mind and enable him to act for our benefit and to reward the trust we have shown him. He wants to be returned to Grozny with an escort of twenty or thirty brave Cossacks, who could protect him against his enemies and for us provide a guarantee of the sincerity of his intentions.

'You will realize, my dear Prince, that I have been much perplexed by all this, for whatever steps I take, a grave responsibility falls upon me. It would be exceedingly rash to trust him entirely. But if we wished to deprive him of all means for escape we should have to lock him up, and in my view this would be neither just nor politic. News of such a measure would quickly spread throughout Daghestan and it would be very damaging to our interests there since it would discourage all those – and there are many – who are prepared to go more or less openly against Shamil and who take a special interest in the situation of the most courageous and resourceful of the Imam's lieutenants, who has found himself obliged to place himself in our hands. Once we treat Hadji Murat as a prisoner the beneficial effect of his desertion of Shamil will be totally lost to us.

'I think therefore that I could not have acted otherwise than I did, though conscious that I might be held guilty of a major error of judgement if Hadji Murat should decide to go off again. In service life and in such involved affairs as this it is difficult, if not impossible, to follow a clear-cut course without risking error and accepting responsibility, but once the course looks clear one should follow it regardless of the consequences.

'I request you, my dear prince, to present this matter for his Imperial Majesty's consideration, and I shall be happy if our sovereign master is gracious enough to approve my action. I have communicated all that I have written above to General Zavodovsky and General Kozlovsky to aid him in his direct relations with Hadji Murat, whom I have informed that he should do nothing and go nowhere without Kozlovsky's approval. I told him that it would be better still from our point of view if he took to riding out with our escort, since Shamil might otherwise spread it abroad that we are keeping him under lock and key. But in suggesting this I made him promise that he would never go to Vozdvizhenskoe since my son, to whom he first surrendered and whom he considers his *kunak* (i.e. friend), is not in command there and there might be some misunderstanding. In any case, Vozdvizhenskoe is too near to a large population hostile to us, while Grozny is convenient in every respect for the contacts he wishes to have with his agents.

'Besides the twenty picked Cossacks who at his own request will never leave his side, I have also sent with him Captain Loris-Melikov, a worthy, distinguished and highly intelligent officer who speaks Tatar; he knows Hadji Murat well and appears to enjoy his full confidence. During the ten days he spent here Hadji Murat resided in the same house as Lieutenant-Colonel Prince Tarkhanov, who is commander of the Shusha district and here at present on official business. He is a truly worthy man in whom I have every confidence. He has also won Hadji Murat's trust and, since he speaks excellent Tatar, he has been our sole intermediary during the talks we have had on the most delicate and secret matters.

'I asked Tarkhanov's advice about Hadji Murat and he entirely agreed with me that it is a matter either of acting as I have done, or of putting him in prison and keeping him in the strictest possible confinement (since once you treat him badly he would be hard to hold), or else of removing him right out of the country. But both the last two measures would not merely destroy the whole benefit to us of Hadji Murat's quarrel with Shamil, it would also inevitably put an end to any development of the mountaineers' discontent with Shamil and to the possibility of their rising against him. Prince Tarkhanov told me that he was himself convinced Hadji Murat was telling the truth and that Hadji Murat firmly believes Shamil will never forgive him and, despite any promise of pardon, would have him executed. The only thing which caused Tarkhanov concern in his dealings with Hadji Murat was Hadji Murat's devotion to his religion, and he is frank about the possibility that Shamil might work on him from this angle. But, as I already said above, Shamil will never make Hadji Murat believe that, if he returned, he would not kill him at once or within a short time.

'And that, my dear prince, concludes what I wished to tell you concerning this episode in our local affairs.'

15

VORONTSOV'S report was dispatched from Tiflis on 24 December. On the eve of the New Year, 1852, the courier – with a dozen worn-out horses and bloodied coachmen's noses left behind him – delivered it to Prince Chernyshev, then Minister of War.

And on 1 January Chernyshev took Vorontsov's report with various other papers to the Emperor Nicholas.

Chernyshev did not like Vorontsov for a number of reasons – the universal esteem in which he was held, his enormous wealth, the fact that Vorontsov was a real aristocrat while he, Chernyshev, was a mere *parvenu*, and principally because of the special favour showed him by the Emperor. Because of this Chernyshev took every opportunity to do what he could to damage Vorontsov. In his last report on Caucasian affairs he had caused Nicholas to be displeased with Vorontsov over the fate of a small column which through the laxness of the higher command had been practically wiped out by the mountaineers. On this occasion he intended to present Vorontsov's proposals concerning Hadji Murat in an unfavourable light. He wished to suggest to the Emperor that Vorontsov, who was always protecting and even indulging the natives, especially to the detriment of the Russians, had acted unwisely; that in all probability Hadji Murat had surrendered merely in order to spy out our defences and that it would therefore be best to send him into central Russia and make use of him only after his family had been rescued from the mountains, when one could be quite certain of his loyalty.

But Chernyshev's plan failed for the simple reason that on the morning of 1 January Nicholas was in a particularly bad mood and out of sheer contrariness would not have accepted any proposal from anyone. Still less was he inclined to accept the proposal of Chernyshev, whom he only tolerated because for the time being he regarded him as indispensable, but knowing how he had attempted to bring ruin on Zakhar Chernyshev during the Decembrists' trial and take over his property, he considered him a thorough-going scoundrel. So because of Nicholas's bad mood Hadji Murat remained in the Caucasus and his fate was not affected as it might have been had Chernyshev made his report at some other time.

It was half-past nine when in the haze of a twenty-degree frost Chernyshev's fat, bearded coachman in a blue velvet pointed cap drove up to the side entrance of the Winter Palace on the box of a small sledge identical to that in which the Emperor himself rode. He gave an amicable nod to his friend, Prince Dolgoruky's coachman, who, having dropped his master, had already been waiting a long time at the palace entrance with his reins tucked under his fat quilted rump while he rubbed his chilled hands.

Chernyshev was wearing a greatcoat with a soft grey beaver collar and a cocked hat with a plume of cock's feathers worn in the regulation manner. Throwing back the bearskin rug, he carefully lifted out his numbed feet (he wore no galoshes and took pride in never doing so) and, livening, walked with jingling spurs along the carpet and through the door respectfully opened before him by the porter. In the hall an old footman hastened forward to relieve him of his greatcoat, after which Chernyshev went to a mirror and carefully removed his hat from his curled wig. After regarding himself in the mirror he gave a twist to his curls at the front and sides with a familiar touch of his aged hands, straightened his cross, aiguillettes and the large epaulettes with the imperial cipher and, moving feebly on his aged, unresponsive legs, he began to climb the shallow, carpeted staircase.

Passing doors at which footmen in ceremonial dress obsequiously bowed to him, Chernyshev entered the Emperor's ante-room. He was respectfully greeted by the duty *aide-de-camp*, who had been recently appointed and was resplendent with his new uniform, epaulettes, aiguillettes and his ruddy, as yet unjaded, face with its trim black moustache and the hair at his temples combed forwards just like the Emperor's. Prince Vasilii Dolgoruky, the deputy Minister of War, with a bored look on his dull face (bedecked with moustache, side-whiskers and hair combed forwards at the temples just like the Emperor's), rose and greeted Chernyshev as he entered.

'*L'empereur?*' Chernyshev asked the *aide-de-camp*, with an inquiring glance at the door of the Emperor's study.

'His Majesty has just returned,' the *aide-de-camp* answered, evidently pleased with the sound of his own voice, then, gliding so softly that a glass of water on his head would not have spilled, he went to the door which swung silently open and, demonstrating with his whole being the veneration he felt for the place he was entering, he disappeared through the door.

Dolgoruky meanwhile had opened his dispatch-case and was checking through the papers inside.

Chernyshev, knitting his brow, walked up and down, easing his legs and remembering all the things he had to report to the Emperor. He was by the study door when it opened once more and the *aide-de-camp* appeared, even more resplendent and respectful than before, and signalled to the Minister and his Deputy that they should go in to the Emperor.

The Winter Palace had long since been restored after the fire, but Nicholas continued to reside on the upper floor. The study in which he received ministers and the most senior officials who came to report to him was a very tall room with four big windows. A large portrait of Alexander I hung on the main wall. Two bureaux stood between the windows. Along the walls were several chairs and in the middle of the room an enormous desk, with an armed chair for Nicholas and ordinary chairs for his visitors.

Nicholas sat at his desk in a black frock-coat with shoulder straps and no epaulettes, his huge figure with its tightly-laced paunch thrown back in his chair. Without moving, he gazed lifelessly at his visitors. His long white face with the huge sloping forehead that bulged between the smoothly brushed hair at his temples (which was so artistically joined to the *toupée* covering the bald patch on his head) was particularly cold and fixed that day. His eyes, which were always dull, looked duller than usual; his lips compressed beneath the up-turned points of his moustache, his plump cheeks freshly shaved around the regular sausage-shaped side-whiskers and supported by his tall collar, and his chin pressed down on the collar gave his face a look of displeasure, even of anger. The cause of this mood was tiredness. And the cause of his tiredness was that the night before he had attended a masked ball. Wearing his Horse Guards helmet topped with a bird, he had moved among the throng that pressed towards him but timidly withdrew before his huge, assured figure, and he had met again the masked lady – the one who at the previous ball had roused his senile passion by her white skin, beautiful figure, and tender voice, and who had then vanished after promising to meet him at the next masked ball. At yesterday's ball she had approached him and he did not let her go. He took her to the private chamber kept ready for this purpose, where they could be alone. Without speaking, Nicholas reached the door of the chamber and looked round for the attendant, but he was not there. Nicholas frowned and pushed the door open himself, allowing his partner to go in first.

'There is someone there,' said the masked lady, stopping. The chamber was indeed occupied. Sitting close to each other on a velvet couch were an Uhlan officer and a pretty young woman with blonde curls in a domino with her mask removed. Seeing the angry figure of Nicholas drawn up to its full height, she hastily replaced her mask, and the Uhlan officer, transfixed with horror, not rising from the couch, stared blankly at Nicholas.

However accustomed Nicholas was to the terror he inspired in others, he always found it agreeable and sometimes took pleasure in confounding his terror-struck victims by addressing them in a paradoxically gentle way. He did so on this occasion.

'You are a bit younger than me, my boy,' he said to the officer, who was numb with terror. 'You can make room for me.'

The officer sprang to his feet, going pale and red in turn, and bending low, silently followed his partner out of the chamber, leaving Nicholas alone with his lady.

The latter turned out to be a pretty and innocent girl of twenty, the daughter of a Swedish governess. She told Nicholas that ever since she was a child she had been in love with him from his portraits, that she worshipped him and had decided at all costs to make him take notice of her. And now she had succeeded and, as she put it, she wanted nothing else. The girl was conveyed to the place where Nicholas customarily kept his assignations with women and he spent over an hour with her.

That night when he had returned to his room and got into the hard, narrow bed, on which he prided himself, and covered himself with his cloak, which he considered (and declared) to be as famous as Napoleon's hat, he was unable to get to sleep. He recalled the frightened and exalted look on the white face of the girl, then he thought of the powerful, rounded shoulders of his regular mistress Nelidova and compared the two of them. That it was wrong for a married man to engage in debauchery was something that never occurred to him and he would have been very surprised if anyone had condemned him for it. But though he was convinced that what he had done was right and proper, it still left a nasty taste in his mouth, and in order to suppress this feeling he turned his mind to a subject which never failed to soothe him – his own greatness.

Although he had gone to sleep late, he rose, as always, before eight. He performed his usual toilet, rubbed his large, well-fed body with ice and said his prayers, repeating the familiar prayers he had said as a child – 'Mother of God', 'I believe', 'Our Father' – attaching no significance to the words. He then went out by the side entrance on to the embankment wearing a greatcoat and peaked cap.

Half-way along the embankment he met a law school student dressed in uniform and hat who was enormously tall like himself. Seeing the uniform of the law school, which he detested for its freethinking ways, Nicholas frowned, but his displeasure grew less as he noted the tallness of the student, the keenness with which he stood to attention and the exaggerated pointing of his elbow as he saluted.

'What is your name?' he asked.

'Polosatov, your Majesty.'

'You are a fine fellow.'

The student still stood with his hand at the salute. Nicholas stopped.

'Do you want to join the army?'

'No, your Majesty.'

'Idiot!'

Nicholas turned away and walked on. He began talking to himself aloud, saying whatever came into his head. 'Koperwein, Koperwein,' he repeated several times – it was the name of the girl of the previous night. 'Squalid business.' He was not thinking what he was saying, but by listening to himself as he spoke he stifled his feeling of unease. 'What would Russia be without me?' he said to himself, sensing a return of his feeling of dissatisfaction. 'And not only Russia, but what would Europe be without me?' And he thought of his brother-in-law, the King of Prussia, and how feeble and stupid he was, and shook his head.

As he came back towards the steps he saw the Grand-duchess Elena Pavlovna's carriage with a footman in red drive up to the Saltykov entrance. For him Elena Pavlovna was the embodiment of those futile people who spent their time talking not only about science and poetry, but also about government, and had the idea that people were capable of governing themselves better than he, Nicholas, could. He knew that however much he trod these people down they would keep raising their heads. And he remembered his brother Mikhail who had recently died. A feeling of vexation and sadness came over him. He frowned darkly and again began whispering whatever came into his head. He stopped doing so only when he entered the palace. He went to his apartments, smoothed his side-whiskers, the hair at his temples and the *toupée* on his crown in front of the mirror, and then, giving a twirl to his moustache, he went straight to the study where he received reports.

He received Chernyshev first. Chernyshev at once saw from Nicholas's face and especially his eyes that he was in a particularly bad mood that day and, knowing of Nicholas's activities the night before, he realized the cause. After a chilly greeting Nicholas invited Chernyshev to sit down and fixed him with his lifeless eyes.

The first matter in Chernyshev's report concerned the peculations of certain commissariat officials which had come to light; then there was the matter of transferring troops on the Prussian frontier; then the question of New Year awards for certain persons omitted from the first list; then came Voront-sov's report about the surrender of Hadji Murat; and finally the unpleasant case of a student at the Medical Academy who had attempted to kill one of the professors.

Nicholas pressed his lips together in silence and, smoothing his papers with his large white hands, one of which had a single gold ring on the third finger, he listened to the report about the peculations, his eyes fixed on Chernyshev's forehead and the lock of hair above it.

Nicholas was convinced that everyone was engaged in pecu-lation. He knew that in the present case he would have to punish the officials and decided to send them all to serve as common soldiers, but he also knew that this would do nothing to stop the officials who replaced them doing the same thing. Officials had it in their nature to steal, he had a duty to punish them, and however irksome it was he conscientiously carried this duty out.

'It seems there is only one honest man in Russia,' he said.

Chernyshev understood at once that this single honest man was Nicholas himself and gave an approving smile.

'Such must be the case, your Majesty,' he said.

'Leave it and I will write in the decision.' said Nicholas, taking the paper and putting it on the left side of his desk.

Chernyshev then began on the matter of the awards and of the transfer of troops. Nicholas looked through the list, deleted a few of the names on it, and then gave brief, decisive instruc-tions for the movement of two divisions to the Prussian fron-tier.

Nicholas could never forgive the King of Prussia the consti-tution he had granted after 1848 and therefore, while professing in letters and speeches the most amicable feelings for his brother-in-law, he considered it prudent to maintain troops on the Prussian border. The troops might be required in the event of a popular uprising in Prussia (on every hand Nicholas saw the prospect of uprisings); he could then advance them to the defence of his brother-in-law's throne, just as he had moved his troops in to defend Austria against the Hungarians. The troops on the border were also necessary to add weight and import to any advice he gave to the Prussian king.

'Yes, what would Russia be now without me?' he thought once more.

'Well, what else is there?' he asked.

'A courier from the Caucasus,' said Chernyshev and he reported what Vorontsov had written about the surrender of Hadji Murat.

'So,' said Nicholas. 'That is a good start.'

'Your Majesty's plans are clearly beginning to bear fruit,' said Chernyshev.

Nicholas was particularly gratified by this praise of his strategic skill, because although he took pride in his skill as a strategist, deep down he was aware that in fact he had none. He wished now to hear himself praised in more detail.

'What is your view, then?' he asked.

'My view is that if we had followed your Majesty's plan sooner – gradual, if slow, advance, clearing the forest and destroying food supplies – then the Caucasus would have been subdued long ago. I put down Hadji Murat's surrender entirely to this. He has realized that they cannot hold out any longer.'

'That is true,' said Nicholas.

The plan for achieving a slow advance into enemy territory by forest clearance and the destruction of food supplies had been put forward by Ermolov and Velyaminov. It was the exact opposite of Nicholas's own plan, which proposed the immediate seizure and destruction of the brigands' nest where Shamil had his residence and which had led to the Dargo expedition of 1845 that had cost so many lives: despite this, however, Nicholas also claimed credit for the policy of slow advance by forest clearing and destruction of supplies. One would have supposed that in order to believe that the plan of slow advance was his plan, he would find it necessary to conceal the fact that he had actually insisted on carrying out the operation of 1845 which was its complete opposite. But he did not conceal it and, despite the obvious contradiction, prided himself both on his plan for the 1845 expedition and on the plan for slow advance. The blatant, unceasing flattery of those around him had so far detached him from reality that he was no longer aware of his own inconsistency and ceased to relate his words and actions to reality, logic or plain common sense, fully convinced that all his decisions, however senseless, unjust and inconsistent they were in fact, became sensible, just and consistent simply by virtue of having been made by him.

It was the same with his decision in the case of the medical student to which Chernyshev turned after his report on the Caucasus.

The facts of the case were that the student had retaken an examination which he had failed twice before and when once more the examiner failed him the student, a neurotic type, considering the result unfair, seized a penknife and in a fit of frenzy attacked the professor, inflicting a few trivial wounds.

'What is his name?' asked Nicholas.

'Brzezowski.'

'A Pole?'

'He is of Polish origin and a Catholic,' replied Chernyshev.

Nicholas frowned.

He had done much harm to the Poles and to explain this it was necessary to believe that all Poles were scoundrels. Nicholas considered that to be so and hated the Poles in proportion to the harm he had done them.

'Just wait a moment,' he said and, shutting his eyes, bent his head.

Chernyshev had heard this many times before. He knew that when Nicholas wished to decide some major problem he had only to concentrate for a few moments and inspiration would come to him and the perfect decision would be spontaneously made, as if dictated by some inner voice. Nicholas was now considering how he might best assuage his malice for the Poles which had been roused afresh by this case of the student and, prompted by his inner voice, he made the following decision. Taking the report, he wrote in his bold hand: 'Warrants the death penalty. But in Russia, thank God, there is no capital punishment. And it is not for me to introduce it. Let him run the gauntlet – twelve times through 1,000 men. Nicholas.' He signed his name with an enormous unnatural flourish.

Nicholas knew that 12,000 lashes meant not only certain, painful death, it was also a piece of excessive cruelty, since 5,000 lashes would suffice to kill even the strongest man. But he liked to be implacably cruel – as he liked to reflect that there was no capital punishment in Russia.

When he had finished writing, he pushed his decision on the student across to Chernyshev.

'There. Read it,' he said.

Chernyshev read it and bent his head in token of his respectful amazement at the sagacity of the decision.

'And have all the students brought on to the square to see him punished,' added Nicholas.

'It will be good for them,' he thought. 'I will destroy this revolutionary spirit, root and branch.'

'I will attend to it,' said Chernyshev, and after a brief silence and adjustment of his hair he returned to the report on the Caucasus.

'What answer should be made then to Prince Vorontsov?'

'Keep firmly to the system I have laid down – destroy the Chechens' homes and harry them with raids,' said Nicholas.

'What are your orders concerning Hadji Murat?' asked Chernyshev.

'Well, doesn't Vorontsov say he wants to use him in the Caucasus?'

'Isn't that rather risky?' said Chernyshev, avoiding Nicholas's gaze. 'I'm afraid Vorontsov is too trusting.'

'What would you think then?' retorted Nicholas sharply, seeing through Chernyshev's intention to present Vorontsov's proposal in a disadvantageous light.

'I would think it safer to send him into Russia.'

'You would think that, would you?' taunted Nicholas. 'Well, I don't. I agree with Vorontsov. Write to him to that effect.'

'Very well,' said Chernyshev and, rising, began to take his leave.

Dolgoruky, who throughout the audience had spoken only a few words in reply to questions put by Nicholas on the troop movements, also withdrew.

After Chernyshev Nicholas received Bibikov, the Governor-General of the Western Provinces, who had come to take leave of the Emperor. Nicholas approved the measures taken by Bibikov against the peasants who had refused to embrace Orthodoxy and ordered him to try all the recalcitrants by court-martial – which meant condemning them to run the gauntlet. He also ordered that the editor of a newspaper be conscripted into the army for printing information about the transfer to crown ownership of several thousand state peasants.

'I am doing this because I consider it necessary,' he said. 'And I will not have it discussed.'

Bibikov was fully aware of the harshness of the orders for dealing with the Uniate peasants and the injustice of transferring state peasants (the only free peasants at that time) to crown ownership – to be, that is, serfs of the imperial family. But it was impossible to object. To fail to agree with any of Nicholas's instructions would mean the total loss of the brilliant position he now held which had taken forty years to achieve. And for that reason he humbly bowed his black, greying head in token of his obedience and readiness to fulfil his Majesty's cruel, senseless and dishonest wishes.

When he had dismissed Bibikov, Nicholas, with a sense of duty well done, stretched, looked at the clock and went to

dress for his *sortie*. He put on uniform complete with epaulettes, orders and sash and went out into the reception rooms
where over a hundred people – men in uniform and women
in elegant, low-cut dresses – all in their appointed places,
tremblingly awaited his appearance.

With his lifeless gaze, chest puffed out, and tight-laced
paunch swelling out below and above its corseting, Nicholas
came out to the waiting courtiers and, sensing that all eyes
were turned with trembling obsequiousness on him, put on
an even more dignified air. As he encountered familiar faces
and recalled who was who, he stopped and spoke a few words
in Russian or French and, piercing them with his cold, lifeless
gaze, listened to what they said.

Having accepted their good wishes for the New Year,
Nicholas went into the chapel.

Just as the laity had done, so too God through his servitors
greeted and praised Nicholas, and, however tedious these
greetings and praises had become to him, Nicholas received
them as his due. All this had to be because on him depended
the well-being and happiness of the whole world, and although
it wearied him he could not refuse the world his help. When
at the end of the Eucharist the splendid deacon, with his well-
combed hair and beard, intoned the words 'Grant, God, many
years . . .' which were taken up by the beautiful voices of the
choristers, Nicholas looked round and, catching sight of Nelidova standing by the window with her magnificent shoulders,
gave her best over the girl of the previous night.

After the Eucharist he called on the Empress and passed
some minutes with his family, joking with his children and
his wife. He then went through the Hermitage to see Volkon-
sky, the Minister of the Court, and among other things instructed him to pay from his special fund an annual pension to
the mother of the girl of the previous night. From there he set
off on his usual morning drive.

Dinner that day was served in the Pompeian Hall. Apart

from Nicholas and Mikhail, the younger sons of the Emperor, the guests were Baron Liven, Count Rzhevussky, Dolgoruky, the Prussian ambassador, and an *aide-de-camp* of the King of Prussia.

While waiting for the Emperor and Empress to appear, the Prussian ambassador and Baron Liven engaged in an interesting discussion about the recent disquieting news from Poland. [They spoke in French.]

'Poland and the Caucasus are the two running sores of Russia,' said Liven. 'We have to keep almost 100,000 men in each of these countries.'

The ambassador feigned surprise.

'You say Poland,' he said.

'Yes, indeed, it was a master-stroke on Metternich's part to encumber us with ...'

At this point the Empress came in with her shaking head and fixed smile, followed by Nicholas.

At table Nicholas told them of Hadji Murat's surrender and said that in consequence of his orders to constrict the mountaineers by clearing the forest and building forts the war in the Caucasus would soon be over.

The ambassador, having exchanged a fleeting glance with the Prussian *aide-de-camp*, with whom he had the same morning discussed Nicholas's unfortunate weakness of considering himself a great strategist, warmly applauded the plan as further evidence of Nicholas's great strategic skill.

After dinner Nicholas went to the ballet, where hundreds of unclad women paraded in tights. One in particular took his fancy and summoning the ballet-master, Nicholas thanked him and instructed that he should be presented with a diamond ring.

The following day when Chernyshev came with his report, Nicholas once more confirmed his instructions to Vorontsov that with the surrender of Hadji Murat he should step up the raids on Chechnia and hem it in with a line of military posts.

Chernyshev wrote to Vorontsov to this effect and another

courier – wearing out horses and bloodying coachmen's noses – galloped off to Tiflis.

16

IN prompt execution of Nicholas's instructions a raid on Chechnia was carried out in January 1852.

The column detailed to make the raid consisted of four infantry battalions, two squadrons of Cossacks and eight guns. The column advanced along the road, flanked on either side by a continuous line of sharpshooters in high boots, sheepskin jackets and *papakhas*, who marched with shouldered muskets and cartridge-belts over their shoulders, climbing up and down the gullies that crossed their way. As always, the column advanced through hostile territory with the minimum of noise. Only occasionally the guns clanked as they jolted over a shallow ditch, or a limber-horse – understanding nothing of orders to keep silent – snorted, or an irate officer shouted in a hoarse subdued voice, berating his men for extending the flank lines or being too close or too far from the column. Only once was the silence broken, when a goat with a grey back and white rump and belly leapt out of a thorn patch between the column and the flank line, followed by a he-goat with similar markings and small horns thrown back on its shoulders. With bounding strides, tucking their forelegs up to their chests, these handsome frightened animals ran so close towards the column that some of the soldiers chased them, laughing and shouting, hoping to stick them with their bayonets, but the goats turned back, darted through the flank line and flew off like birds into the hills, pursued by a few regimental dogs.

It was still winter, but the sun was beginning to reach higher in the sky and by midday, when the column after its early-morning start had covered seven or eight miles, it was hot and it hurt to look at the steel of the bayonets and the sudden glinting lights that flashed like miniature suns on the brass of the guns.

Behind the column lay the clear, swift river they had just crossed, ahead cultivated fields and meadows with shallow gullies running across them, further ahead lay black, mysterious hills covered with forest and beyond them projecting crags, then high on the horizon the ever enchanting, ever changing snow-clad mountains sparkling like diamonds.

At the head of No. 5 Company in a black frock-coat and *papakha* with his sword slung from his shoulder marched the tall handsome figure of Butler, an officer recently transferred from the guards. He was feeling cheerful – a feeling compounded of *joie de vivre*, mortal danger, eagerness for action, and the consciousness of being part of one enormous whole controlled by a single will. This was Butler's second action and it was pleasant to think that at any moment they would be under fire and that he would not duck when a cannon-ball passed overhead or pay heed to the whistling bullets, but rather, as before, he would lift his head higher and with smiling eyes look round at his fellow-officers and men and talk very casually about something completely different.

The column turned off the good road on to a little-used one which passed through fields of maize stubble. They were now nearing the forest, when – it was impossible to see where from – a cannon-ball whistled ominously overhead and landed in a maize-field by the side of the road half-way down the baggage-train, showering it with earth.

'It's starting,' said Butler with a merry smile to the officer by his side.

And sure enough, after the cannon-shot a dense throng of mounted Chechens carrying pennants appeared out of the trees. In the middle of them was a large green standard and the old company sergeant-major, who had a very good eye, informed the short-sighted Butler that it must be Shamil himself. The Chechens rode down the hill and appeared on the rise above the next gully on the right; they began descending into it. The little general wearing a warm black frock-coat and a *papakha* with a large white tassel rode up to Butler's company on his ambler and ordered him to move rightwards against the descending horsemen. Butler quickly led his company in the direction indicated, but before they reached the bottom of the gully he heard behind him two cannon-shots, one after the other. He looked round and saw two clouds of blue-grey smoke rise over the cannon and drift along the gully. The Chechens, who had evidently not been expecting artillery, turned back. Butler's company opened fire on the retreating mountaineers, and the whole gully was clouded with gun-smoke. Only higher up, out of the gully, could one see the mountaineers retreating hastily and firing to keep off the pursuing Cossacks. The column continued to advance after the mountaineers and on the slope of the next gully they came upon the village.

Butler and his company entered the village at the double after the Cossacks. The inhabitants were all gone. The soldiers were ordered to burn the corn and hay and the houses too. An acrid layer of smoke spread through the village; in the smoke soldiers rushed about carrying off what they could find from the houses, but chiefly chasing and shooting the chickens which the villagers had been unable to take with them. The officers sat down away from the smoke, and had lunch and something to drink. The sergeant-major brought them honeycombs on a board. There was no sound of the Chechens. Soon after midday the order was given to withdraw. The companies formed into column at the back of the village and Butler had to bring up the rear. As soon as they moved off, the Chechens reappeared and followed, firing parting shots into the column.

When the column reached open ground the mountaineers fell back. None of Butler's men was wounded and on the way back he was in a most cheerful and jolly mood.

After fording the river they had crossed in the morning the column marched on, stretching across the maize-fields and meadows; the chorus-leaders of each company came to the front and the sound of songs burst forth. There was no wind, the air was fresh and pure and so clear that the snowy mountains seventy miles off seemed no distance away, and when the singers stopped you heard the even tramp of feet and the clank of the guns as the background against which the songs began and ended. The song sung in Butler's No. 5 Company had been made up by one of the cadets in honour of the regiment and was sung to the tune of a dance with the refrain: 'Sharpshooters, sharpshooters! We're the best, we're the best!'

Butler was on horseback riding alongside his immediate superior, Major Petrov, with whom he shared quarters. He was feeling delighted that he had decided to leave the guards and go off to the Caucasus. His main reason for leaving the guards had been that after losing heavily at cards in St Petersburg he was completely broke. He feared that if he stayed in the guards he would be unable to stop himself gambling and he had nothing left to lose. Now that was all over and done with. He had a different life now, a good, dashing life. He had forgotten all about being ruined and the debts he could not pay. The Caucasus, the war, the men, the officers, this brave, good-natured, hard-drinking Major Petrov – it all seemed to him so splendid that at times he could hardly believe he was not in St Petersburg, in some smoke-laden rooms staking his bets as he played against the bank, hating the banker and feeling that pressing pain in his head, rather than here in this marvellous country among these fine fellows of the army of the Caucasus.

'Sharpshooters, sharpshooters! We're the best, we're the best!' sang the chorus-leaders. His horse strode merrily along to the music. Trezorka, the shaggy, grey company dog, with its tail up and a busy look, ran ahead of Butler's company as if in command. Butler was feeling bright, cheerful and at ease. War, as he saw it, was simply a matter of subjecting himself to danger, risking death, and in return gaining awards and the respect of his comrades here and of his friends in Russia. The other face of war – the men, officers and mountaineers killed and wounded – oddly never occurred to him. To maintain his poetic view of war he even subconsciously avoided looking at the dead and wounded. It was the same today – on the Russian side three men were killed and twelve wounded. He went past a dead body lying on its back and only out of the corner of his eye did he observe the odd position of the wax-like hand and the deep-red blotch on the head: he did not look closer. The mountaineers as far as he was concerned were just daredevil horsemen you had to defend yourself against.

'Well, there you are, old chap,' said the major, between songs. 'Not like your way of things in Petersburg – with your "right dress!", "left dress!". We've done a job of work, and now home. Dear old Masha will have a pie for us and some decent cabbage-soup. That's the life, isn't it? Come on, let's have "At morn's first light",' he said, giving the order for his favourite song.

The major lived with the daughter of the camp surgeon. She used to be known as Mashka, but then became Marya Dmitrievna. She had no children and was a good-looking, blonde woman of thirty with a mass of freckles. Whatever her past, she was now the major's faithful companion and looked after him like a child, which was just what the major needed, since he frequently drank himself into a stupor.

When they reached the fort everything was as the major had anticipated. Marya Dmitrievna produced a solid, tasty meal for him, Butler and two officers from the column they had invited to join them, and the major ate and drank till he was past talking and went off to his bedroom to sleep. Butler, who was also tired, but well content and somewhat tipsy after too much *chikhir*, went off to his room, and was hardly undressed before he fell into an unbroken, dreamless sleep, with one hand under his handsome, curly head.

17

THE village laid waste by the raiding party was the one in which Hadji Murat had spent the night before going over to the Russians.

Sado, with whom he had stayed, took his family away to the mountains when the Russians approached the village. When he came back he found his house destroyed: the roof was caved in, the door and the post supporting the veranda were burnt, and the inside befouled. His son, the good-looking boy with shining eyes who had regarded Hadji Murat with such rapture, was brought in to the mosque dead on the back of a horse draped with a cloak. He had been bayoneted in the back. The fine-looking woman who had waited on Hadji Murat during his visit stood over her son with her hair loose and the smock she was wearing rent at the chest to reveal her old, sagging breasts. She stood clawing her face till the blood ran and wailing without stop. Sado took a pick and shovel and went with his kinsmen to dig a grave for his son. The old grandfather sat by the wall of the ruined house, whittling a stick and gazing blankly into space. He had just come back from his bee-garden. The two small hayricks he had there were burnt; the apricot and cherry trees which he had planted and tended were broken and scorched; and, worst of all, every one of his hives had been burnt together with the bees. The wailing of women sounded in every house and in the square where two more bodies were brought. The young children wailed with their mothers. The hungry animals howled, too, and there was nothing to give them. The older children played no games and watched their elders with frightened eyes.

The fountain had been befouled, evidently on purpose, so no water could be drawn from it. The mosque, too, had been defiled and the mullah and his pupils were cleaning it out.

The village elders gathered in the square and squatted on

their heels to discuss the situation. Nobody spoke a word of hatred for the Russians. The emotion felt by every Chechen, old and young alike, was stronger than hatred. It was not hatred, it was a refusal to recognize these Russian dogs as men at all, and a feeling of such disgust, revulsion and bewilderment at the senseless cruelty of these creatures that the urge to destroy them – like the urge to destroy rats, venomous spiders or wolves – was an instinct as natural as that of self-preservation.

The villagers were faced with a choice: either to remain as before and by terrible exertions restore all that had been created with such labour and so easily and senselessly destroyed, while every minute expecting a repetition of the same thing, or they could act contrary to the law of their religion and, despite the revulsion and scorn they felt for the Russians, submit to them.

The old men prayed and resolved unanimously to send envoys to ask Shamil for help, and straightaway they set about rebuilding what had been destroyed.

18

THE second day after the raid, not too early, Butler went out into the street by way of the back door, intending to have a stroll and a breath of fresh air before his morning tea, which he normally took with Petrov. The sun was already clear of the mountains and it was painful to look at the white daub houses where it shone on the right-hand side of the street. It was, though, as cheering and soothing as ever to look leftwards at the black tree-clad mountains rising higher and higher in the distance and, visible beyond the ravine, the lustreless chain of snow-capped mountains pretending as always to be clouds.

Butler looked at the mountains, filled his lungs, and felt happy to be alive and to be just who he was, living in this beautiful world. He was quite happy, too, about his conduct in the previous day's action, both during the advance and in particular during the march back when things were quite hot; and he was happy to recall the way Masha, otherwise Marya Dmitrievna (the woman Petrov lived with) had entertained them after they had got back from the raid, and the especially unaffected, kindly way she had treated everyone, being particularly nice to him, it had seemed. With her thick plait of hair, her broad shoulders, full bosom, and kindly beaming face covered with freckles, Marya Dmitrievna could not help attracting Butler who was a young, vigorous, unmarried man, and he even had an idea that she was keen on him. But he thought it would be a shabby way to treat his simple, good-natured comrade and always behaved towards Marya Dmitrievna with the utmost simplicity and respect and it gladdened him that he did so. He was thinking of this just now.

His thoughts were disturbed by the drumming of many horses' hoofs on the dusty road ahead of him. It sounded like several horsemen galloping. He raised his head and saw at the end of the street a party of riders approaching at a walk. There were a couple of dozen Cossacks with two men riding at their head: one wore a white *cherkeska* and a tall *papakha* wound with a turban, the other was a dark, hook-nosed officer in the Russian service, dressed in a blue *cherkeska* with a lavish amount of silver on his clothing and weapons. The horseman in the turban rode a handsome palomino with a small head and beautiful eyes; the officer was mounted on a tall, rather showy Karabakh. Butler, who was very keen on horses, appreciated at a glance the resilient power of the first rider's horse and stopped to find out who they were. The officer spoke to him.

'That house of commandant?' he asked, pointing with his whip at Ivan Matveevich's (Petrov's) house, and betraying by his accent and defective grammar his non-Russian origin.

'Yes, that's it,' said Butler. 'And who might that be?' he

asked, going closer to the officer and with a glance indicating the man in the turban.

'That Hadji Murat. He come here and stay with commandant,' said the officer.

Butler knew about Hadji Murat and that he had surrendered to the Russians, but he had never expected to see him here, in this small fort.

Hadji Murat was looking at him in a friendly fashion.

'How do you do. *Koshkoldy*,' said Butler, using the Tatar greeting he had learnt.

'*Saubul*,' replied Hadji Murat, nodding. He rode across to Butler and offered his hand from which his whip hung on two fingers.

'Commandant?' he asked.

'No, the commandant is inside. I'll go and fetch him,' Butler said to the officer, going up the steps and pushing at the door.

But the 'front door', as Marya Dmitrievna called it, was locked. Butler knocked, but getting no reply went round by the back way. He called for his batman, but got no answer, and being unable to find either of the two batmen went into the kitchen. Marya Dmitrievna was there, with face flushed, her hair pinned up in a kerchief and sleeves rolled up over her plump, white arms. She was cutting pie-cases from a rolled-out layer of dough as white as her arms.

'Where have the batmen got to?' asked Butler.

'Gone off drinking,' said Marya Dmitrievna. 'What is it you want?'

'I want the door opened. You've got a whole horde of mountaineers outside. Hadji Murat has come.'

'Go on, tell me another one,' said Marya Dmitrievna, smiling.

'It's not a joke. It's true. They are just outside.'

'What? Really?' said Marya Dmitrievna.

'Why should I want to make it up? Go and look – they are just outside.'

'Well, there's a thing!' said Marya Dmitrievna, rolling down her sleeves and feeling for the pins in her thick plait of hair. 'I'll go and wake up Ivan Matveevich, then!'

'No, I'll go. You, Bondarenko, go and open the door,' said Butler.

'That's all right by me,' said Marya Dmitrievna and returned to her work.

When he learnt that Hadji Murat had arrived, Petrov, who had heard already that he was in Grozny, was not in the least surprised. He sat up in bed, rolled a cigarette, lit it, and began to get dressed, loudly coughing to clear his throat and grumbling at the high-ups who had sent 'that devil' to him. When he was dressed, he ordered his batman to bring his 'medicine', and the batman, knowing what he meant, brought him some vodka.

'You should never mix your drinks,' he growled, drinking the vodka and eating a piece of black bread with it. 'I was drinking *chikhir* last night and now I've got a thick head. All right, I'm ready,' he said finally and went into the parlour, where Butler had taken Hadji Murat and the escorting officer.

The officer handed Ivan Matveevich the orders from the commander of the Left Flank in which he was instructed to take charge of Hadji Murat and, while allowing him contact with the mountaineers through scouts, to ensure that he never left the fort except with an escort of Cossacks.

Ivan Matveevich read the paper, looked hard at Hadji Murat, and studied the paper again. After several times shifting his gaze from the paper to his visitor, he finally fixed his eyes on Hadji Murat and said:

'*Yakshi, bek-yakshi.* Very well. Let him stay then. But you tell him that my orders are not to let him loose. And orders are orders. As to quarters, what do you think, Butler? We could put him in the office.'

Before Butler could reply, Marya Dmitrievna, who had come from the kitchen and was standing in the doorway, said to Ivan Matveevich:

'Why in the office? Let him stay here. We can give him the guest-room and the store-room. At least he'll be where you can keep an eye on him,' she said. She glanced at Hadji Murat, but meeting his eyes turned hurriedly away.

'Yes, I think Marya Dmitrievna is right,' said Butler.

'Go on, off with you!' said Ivan Matveevich, frowning. 'Womenfolk have no business here.'

Throughout this conversation Hadji Murat sat with his hand behind the handle of his dagger and a faintly disdainful smile on his lips. He said it mattered nothing where he lived. All he needed was what the *sardar* had granted – to have contact with the mountaineers, and he wished therefore that they be allowed access to him. Ivan Matveevich said that this would be done and asked Butler to look after their guests while something to eat was brought and the rooms made ready. He would go to the office to fill in the necessary papers and give the necessary instructions.

Hadji Murat's relations with these new acquaintances immediately became very clearly established. From their first meeting Hadji Murat felt nothing but repugnance and scorn for Ivan Matveevich and was always haughty in his treatment of him. He particularly liked Marya Dmitrievna, who cooked and served his food. He liked her simple manner, her particular, for him foreign, type of beauty, and the unconsciously conveyed attraction which she felt for him. He tried not to look at her, or to speak to her, but his eyes turned automatically towards her and followed her movements.

With Butler he struck up an immediate friendship and took pleasure in the long talks he had with him, asking Butler about his life and telling him of his own, passing on the news brought by the scouts about the situation of his family and even asking his advice as to what he should do.

The news brought by the scouts was not good. In the four days he had been at the fort they had come twice and on both occasions the news was bad.

19

SHORTLY after Hadji Murat's surrender to the Russians his family was taken to the village of Vedeno and kept there under guard waiting for Shamil to decide their fate. The women – Hadji Murat's old mother Patimat and his two wives – together with their five small children lived under guard in the house of Ibrahim Rashid, one of Shamil's captains; Yusuf, his eighteen-year-old son, was kept in a dungeon, a deep pit dug eight or nine feet into the ground, with four criminals who, like him, were awaiting Shamil's decision on their fate.

But no decision came, because Shamil was away campaigning against the Russians.

On 6 January 1852 Shamil returned home to Vedeno after a battle with the Russians in which, according to the Russians, he had been beaten and fled to Vedeno, but in which, according to the view of Shamil and all his murids, he had been victorious and put the Russians to flight. In this engagement – and it happened very rarely – he himself had fired his rifle and with drawn sword would have charged straight at the Russians if his escort of murids had not held him back. Two of them were killed at his side.

It was midday when Shamil arrived at his destination, surrounded by his party of murids showing off their horsemanship, firing rifles and pistols and chanting endlessly '*La ilaha illa allah.*'

All the people of Vedeno, which was a large village, were standing in the street and on the roofs of the houses to greet their master, and they too celebrated the event with musket and pistol fire. Shamil rode on a white Arab, which merrily sought to have its head as they neared home. The horse's harness was extremely plain with no gold or silver ornament – a red leather bridle, finely made and grooved down the middle, metal bucket stirrups and a red shabrack showing from under the saddle. The Imam wore a fur coat overlaid with brown cloth, the black fur projecting at the collar and cuffs; it was drawn tight about his tall, slim frame by a black leather strap with a dagger attached to it. On his head he wore a tall, flat-topped *papakha* with a black tassel and white turban round it, the end of which hung below his neck. On his feet were green soft leather boots and his legs were covered with tight black leggings edged with plain lace.

The Imam wore nothing at all that glittered, no gold or silver, and his tall, erect, powerful figure in its plain clothes in the midst of the murids with their gold- and silver-ornamented dress and weapons, created on the people exactly the impression of grandeur which he desired and knew how to create. His pale face, framed by his trimmed red beard, with its small, constantly screwed up eyes, wore a fixed expression as if made of stone. Passing through the village he felt thousands of eyes turned on him, but his own eyes looked at no one. The wives and children of Hadji Murat went on to the veranda with the other occupants of the house to watch the Imam's entry. Only Patimat, Hadji Murat's old mother, did not go, but remained sitting as she was on the floor of the house with her grey hair dishevelled and her long arms clasped round her thin knees, while she blinked her fiery black eyes and watched the logs burning down in the fire-place. She, like her son, had always hated Shamil, now more than ever, and had no wish to see him.

Hadji Murat's son also saw nothing of Shamil's triumphal entry. From his dark fetid pit he could only hear the shots and chanting and he experienced such anguish as is only felt by young men, full of life, when deprived of their freedom. Sitting in the stinking pit and seeing only the same wretched, filthy, emaciated creatures he was confined with, who mostly hated one another, he was overcome by a passionate envy for people who had air and light and freedom and were at this moment prancing round their leader on dashing horses and shooting and chanting in chorus '*La ilaha illa allah.*'

After processing through the village Shamil rode into a large courtyard next to an inner one where he had his harem. Two armed Lezghians met Shamil at the opened gates of the first courtyard. The yard was full of people. There were people from distant parts here on their own account, there were petitioners, and there were those whom Shamil himself had summoned for judgement. When Shamil rode in everyone in the courtyard rose and respectfully greeted the Imam with their hands placed to their chests. Some knelt and remained kneeling while Shamil crossed the courtyard from the outer to the inner gateway. Although Shamil recognized in the waiting crowd many disagreeable people and many tiresome petitioners who would be wanting his attention, he rode past them with the same stony expression on his face and went into the inner court where he dismounted alongside the veranda of his residence to the left of the gate.

The campaign had been a strain, mental rather than physical, for although he had proclaimed it a victory, Shamil knew that the campaign had been a failure, that many Chechen villages had been burnt and destroyed, and that the Chechens – a fickle and light-headed people – were wavering and some of them, nearest to the Russians, were already prepared to go over to them. It was all very difficult and measures would have to be taken, but for the moment Shamil did not want to do anything or think about anything. All he wanted was to relax and enjoy the soothing delights of family life provided by his favourite wife Aminet, a black-eyed, fleet-footed Kist girl of eighteen.

But not only was it out of the question to see Aminet at this moment – though she was only on the other side of the fence which separated the women's apartments from the men's quarters in the inner courtyard (and Shamil had no doubt that even as he dismounted Aminet and his other wives would be watching through the fence) – not only could he not go to her, he could not even lie down on a feather mattress and recover from his fatigue. Before anything else he had to perform his midday devotions. He felt not the least inclination to do so, but it was necessary that he should, not only in his capacity as religious leader of the people, but also because to him person-ally it was as essential as his daily food. So he carried out the ritual washing and praying. At the end of the prayers he sum-moned those who were waiting.

The first to come in to him was his father-in-law and teacher, Jemel-Edin, a tall fine-looking old man with grey hair, snowy white beard and a rubicund face. After a prayer to God, he began to question Shamil about the campaign and to recount what had happened in the mountains while he was away.

There were all manner of events to report – blood-feud killings, cattle-stealing, alleged breaches of the *Tarikat* – smoking tobacco, drinking wine, and Jemel-Edin also told Shamil that Hadji Murat had sent men to take his family over to the Russians, but that this was discovered and the family had been moved to Vedeno, where they were now under guard awaiting the Imam's decision. The old men were gathered in the adjoining guest-room for the purpose of con-sidering all these matters, and Jemel-Edin advised Shamil to dismiss them today since they had already waited three days for him.

Shamil took dinner in his own room, where it was brought by Zaidet, the senior of his wives, a sharp-nosed, dark, ill-favoured woman for whom he did not care. He then went into the guest-room.

There were six men in Shamil's council – old men with white, grey and ginger beards. They wore tall *papakhas* with or without turbans, new jackets and *cherkeskas* with leather belts and daggers. They rose to greet him. Shamil was a head taller than any of them. They all, including Shamil, lifted their upturned hands and with closed eyes recited a prayer, then wiped their hands across their faces, drew them down over their beards and joined them. This done, they sat down, with Shamil sitting on a higher cushion in the middle, and began their deliberations of the business in hand.

The cases of those accused of crimes were decided according to the *Shariat*: two thieves were condemned to have a hand cut off, another to have his head cut off for murder, and three were pardoned. They moved on then to the main business – to consider what measures should be taken to prevent the Chechens going over to the Russians. In order to halt these defections Jemel-Edin had drawn up the following proclamation:

'May you have peace everlasting with Almighty God. I hear that the Russians show favours to you and call for your submission. Believe them not, do not submit, but be patient. For this you will be rewarded, if not in this life, then in the life to come. Remember what happened before when your weapons were taken from you. If then, in 1840, God had not shown you the light, you would now be soldiers and carry bayonets instead of daggers, and your wives would not wear trousers and would be defiled. Judge the future by the past. It is better to die at war with the Russians than to live with the infidels. Be patient, and I shall come with the Koran and the sword to lead you against the Russians. For the present I strictly command you to have neither intention nor even any thought of submitting to the Russians.'

Shamil approved the proclamation, signed it and decreed that it should be dispatched to all parts.

When this business was finished the question of Hadji Murat was discussed. This was a very important matter for Shamil. Although he did not care to admit it, he knew that if Hadji Murat had been on his side, with his skill, daring, and courage, what had now happened in Chechnia would never have occurred. It would be good to settle his quarrel with Hadji

Murat and make use of him once again; but if that could not be done, he must still ensure that he did not aid the Russians. In either case, therefore, he must send for him and, when he came, kill him. This could be done either by sending a man to Tiflis to kill him there, or by summoning him and putting an end to him here. The only way to do that was to use Hadji Murat's family, above all his son, whom, as Shamil knew, he adored. It was therefore necessary to work through his son.

When the councillors had talked it over, Shamil closed his eyes and fell silent.

The councillors knew what this meant: Shamil was now listening to the voice of the Prophet telling him what should be done. After five minutes' solemn silence Shamil opened his eyes, screwing them more tightly than before and said:

'Fetch me the son of Hadji Murat.'

'He is here,' said Jemel-Edin.

Indeed, Yusuf, thin, pale, ragged, and stinking, still handsome though in face and figure, and with the same fiery black eyes as Patimat, his grandmother, was standing at the gate of the outer courtyard waiting to be summoned.

Yusuf did not feel about Shamil as his father did. He did not know all that had happened in the past, or if he knew, it was only at second-hand, and he could not understand why his father was so doggedly opposed to Shamil. Yusuf only wanted to go on living the easy, rakish life that he, as son of the *naib*, had led in Khunzakh, and he could see no point in being at odds with Shamil. In defiant opposition to his father he greatly admired Shamil and regarded him with the fervent veneration that was generally felt for him in the mountains. He experienced a particular feeling of awe and reverence for the Imam now as he entered the guest-room. He stopped at the door and was fixed by Shamil's screwed up eyes. He stood for a few moments, then went up to Shamil and kissed his large white hand with long fingers.

'You are the son of Hadji Murat?'

'Yes, Imam.'

'You know what he has done?'

'I know, Imam, and am sorry for it.'

'Do you know how to write?'

'I was studying to be a mullah.'

'Then write to your father and say that if he returns to me now, before *Bairam*, I will pardon him and all will be as of old. But if he will not and remains with the Russians, then ...' – Shamil frowned menacingly – 'I shall give your grandmother and mother to be used in the villages, and I shall cut off your head.'

Not a muscle twitched on Yusuf's face. He bowed his head to signify he had understood what Shamil said.

'Write that and give it to my messenger.'

Shamil was then silent and took a long look at Yusuf.

'Write that I have decided to spare you. I will not kill you but will have your eyes put out, the same as I do to all traitors. Go.'

Yusuf appeared to be calm while in the presence of Shamil, but when he was led out of the guest-room he threw himself on his escort, snatched his dagger from its sheath and tried to kill himself. But he was seized by the arms, bound and taken back to the pit.

That evening when the evening prayers were over and dusk fell, Shamil put on a white fur top-coat and passed through the fence into the part of the courtyard where his wives lived. He went straight to Aminet's room. But Aminet was not there; she was with the older wives. Trying to keep out of sight, Shamil stood behind the door of her room to wait for her. But Aminet was angry with Shamil because he had given some silk to Zaidet and not to her. She saw him come out and go to look for her in her room and she deliberately did not return to her room. She stood a long time in Zaidet's doorway, laughing quietly as she watched the white figure go in and out of her room. It was nearly time for the midnight prayers when Shamil, after waiting in vain, went back to his own quarters.

20

HADJI MURAT had been a week at the fort living in the house of Ivan Matveevich. Although Marya Dmitrievna had quarrelled with the shaggy-haired Khanefi (Hadji Murat had with him only two men: Khanefi and Eldar) and had several times ejected him from her kitchen – for which he nearly cut her throat – she evidently felt a particular respect and sympathetic concern for Hadji Murat. She no longer served him his dinner, a task she had passed on to Eldar, but she took every opportunity to see him and do anything she could to please him. She also took a very keen interest in the negotiations about his family; she knew how many wives he had, how many children and what ages they were, and each time a scout came she asked whom she could to discover how the negotiations were going.

In the course of this week Butler had become firm friends with Hadji Murat. Sometimes Hadji Murat would call on him in his room, at other times Butler would visit him. They sometimes conversed through an interpreter, otherwise they used their own resources – signs and, particularly, smiles. Hadji Murat had evidently taken a liking to Butler. This was clear from the way that Butler was treated by Eldar. Whenever Butler came into Hadji Murat's room Eldar greeted him, flashing his teeth in a cheerful grin, hastened to put cushions on his seat and helped him off with his sword if he was wearing it.

Butler also got on good terms with the shaggy-haired Khanefi, who was Hadji Murat's sworn brother. Khanefi knew many songs of the mountains and sang them well. To please Butler Hadji Murat would summon Khanefi and tell him to sing, mentioning the songs he thought good. Khanefi had a high tenor voice and sang with great clarity and expression. There was one song Hadji Murat was particularly fond of and Butler was much struck by its solemn, sad refrain. Butler asked the interpreter to tell him the words in Russian and wrote it down.

The song was about vengeance – the vengeance that Khanefi and Hadji Murat had pledged to each other.

It went as follows:

'The earth will dry on my grave, and you, my own mother, will forget me. Grave grass will grow over the graveyard and will deaden your grief, my old father. The tears will dry in my sister's eyes and sorrow will fly from her heart.

'But you, my elder brother, will not forget me till you have avenged my death. You, my second brother, will not forget me till you lie by my side.

'Bullet, you are hot and the bearer of death, but were you not my faithful slave? Black earth, you will cover me, but did I not trample you beneath my horse's hoofs? Death, you are cold, but I was your master. The earth shall take my body, and heaven my soul.'

Hadji Murat always listened to this song with his eyes closed, and, as its last lingering note faded away, he would say in Russian:

'Good song, wise song.'

With the arrival of Hadji Murat and his close acquaintance with him and his murids, Butler was even more captivated by the poetry of the peculiar, vigorous life led by the mountaineers. He got himself a jacket, *cherkeska* and leggings, and he felt he was a mountaineer too, living the same life as these people.

On the day Hadji Murat was to leave Ivan Matveevich gathered a few of the officers to see him off. The officers were sitting at two tables, one for tea, dispensed by Marya Dmitrievna, and the other laid with vodka, *chikhir* and *hors d'oeuvre*,

when Hadji Murat, armed and dressed for the road, came limping with quick, soft steps into the room.

Everyone rose and one after the other shook hands with
him. Ivan Matveevich invited him to sit on the ottoman, but
Hadji Murat thanked him and sat on a chair by the window.
He was clearly not in the least put out by the silence which fell
when he came in. He closely studied the faces of those present,
then fixed his eyes indifferently on the table with the samovar
and food on it. Petrokovsky, one of the officers more spirited
than the rest, who had not seen Hadji Murat before, asked him
through the interpreter if he had liked Tiflis.

'*Aya*,' said Hadji Murat.

'He says he does,' the interpreter answered.

'What did he like in particular?'

Hadji Murat made some reply.

'He liked the theatre best.'

'Did he enjoy the commander-in-chief's ball?'

Hadji Murat frowned.

'Every people has its own customs. Our women do not
wear such clothes,' he said, glancing at Marya Dmitrievna.

'What didn't he like?'

'We have a saying,' Hadji Murat said to the interpreter. 'A
dog asked a donkey to eat with him and gave him meat, the
donkey asked the dog and gave him hay: they both went
hungry.' He smiled. 'Every people finds its own ways good.'

The conversation stopped there. The officers began drinking
tea or eating. Hadji Murat took the glass of tea he was offered
and put it in front of him.

'Now, would you like some cream? Perhaps a bun?' asked
Marya Dmitrievna, serving him.

Hadji Murat inclined his head.

'Well, good-bye then,' said Butler, touching him on the
knee. 'When shall we meet again?'

'Good-bye, good-bye,' Hadji Murat said in Russian, smiling. '*Kunak* Bulur. I your good *kunak*. Now time – off we go,'

HADJI MURAT   241

he said, tossing his head as if to show the direction he had to go.

Eldar appeared in the doorway with something large and white over his shoulder and a sword in his hand. Hadji Murat beckoned him and Eldar with his long strides came over and gave him the white cloak and the sword. Hadji Murat took the cloak and, dropping it over his arm, gave it to Marya Dmitrievna, saying something for the interpreter to translate.

'He says: you admired the cloak – take it,' said the interpreter.

'But what for?' said Marya Dmitrievna, blushing.

'Must do. *Adat tak*, it is the custom', said Hadji Murat.

'Well, thank you,' said Marya Dmitrievna, taking the cloak. 'God grant you may rescue your son. He is a fine boy – *ulan yakshi*,' she added. 'Tell him I hope he can rescue his family.'

Hadji Murat looked at Marya Dmitrievna and nodded in approval. Then he took the sword from Eldar and gave it to Ivan Matveevich. Ivan Matveevich took it and said to the interpreter:

'Tell him he must take my brown gelding. That is all I can give in return.'

Hadji Murat waved his hand in front of his face to show that he did not want anything and would not accept it. Then he pointed first to the mountains, then to his heart, and went to the door. Everyone followed. Some of the officers, who remained inside, drew the sword and after inspecting the blade decided it was a genuine *gourda*.

Butler accompanied Hadji Murat on to the steps outside. But just then something totally unexpected happened which might have cost Hadji Murat his life but for his promptness, determination and skill.

The villagers of Tash-Kichu, a Kumyk village, held Hadji Murat in high esteem and on many occasions had come to the fort just to have a look at the celebrated *naib*. Three days before Hadji Murat's departure they sent messengers inviting him to attend their mosque on Friday. However, the Kumyk princes who resided at Tash-Kichu hated Hadji Murat and had a blood feud with him, and when they heard of the villagers' invitation they would not allow him into the mosque. The people were roused by this and there was a fight between the villagers and the princes' supporters. The Russian authorities restored peace among the mountaineers and sent a message to Hadji Murat instructing him not to attend the mosque. Hadji Murat did not go and everybody thought the matter was ended.

But at the very moment of Hadji Murat's departure, when he went out on to the steps and the horses stood waiting outside, one of the Kumyk princes, Arslan-Khan, who was known to Butler and Ivan Matveevich, rode up to the house.

Seeing Hadji Murat he drew his pistol from his belt and aimed it at him. But before Arslan-Khan could fire, Hadji Murat, despite his lameness, sprang like a cat from the steps towards him. Arslan-Khan fired and missed. Hadji Murat meanwhile had run up to him, and with one hand seized his horse's bridle and with the other pulled out his dagger, shouting something in Tatar.

Butler and Eldar rushed up to the enemies at the same time and seized them by the arms. Hearing the shot, Ivan Matveevich also appeared.

'What do you mean by this, Arslan – creating mischief in my house!' he said, on discovering what had happened. 'It's no way to behave. Have it out with each other by all means, but keep it "out" and don't go slaughtering people in my house.'

Arslan-Khan, a tiny man with a black moustache, got down from his horse, pale and shaking, and with a vicious look at Hadji Murat went off with Ivan Matveevich into the parlour. Hadji Murat went back to the horses, breathing heavily and smiling.

'Why did he want to kill you?' Butler asked him through the interpreter.

The interpreter translated Hadji Murat's reply: 'He says that it is our law. Arslan has blood to avenge on him, that is why he wanted to kill him.'

'And what if he catches up with him on his journey?' asked Butler.

Hadji Murat smiled.

'What of it? If he kills me, it will be the will of Allah. Well, good-bye,' he said once more in Russian, and grasping his horse by the withers, looked round at those seeing him off and affectionately encountered Marya Dmitrievna's eye.

'Good-bye, good lady,' he said to her. 'Thank you.'

'May God only grant you can get your family free,' repeated Marya Dmitrievna.

Hadji Murat did not understand what she said, but he understood her concern for him and nodded to her.

'Be sure you don't forget your *kunak*,' said Butler.

'Tell him I am his true friend and will never forget him,' Hadji Murat replied through the interpreter. Then, despite his crooked leg, as soon as his foot touched the stirrup he swung his body quickly and effortlessly on to the high saddle and, straightening his sword and with a customary hand fingering his pistol, he rode off from Ivan Matveevich's house with that particular proud, warlike air the mountaineers have when on horseback. Khanefi and Eldar also mounted and, after bidding friendly farewells to their hosts and the officers, set off at a trot after their murshid.

As always happens, a discussion started about the person who had left.

'He's a great fellow!'

'It was just like a wolf the way he went for Arslan-Khan. There was a completely different look on his face.'

'He will do us down,' said Petrokovsky. 'He must be a right rogue.'

'Then I wish there were more Russian rogues like him,' interposed Marya Dmitrievna with sudden annoyance. 'He was with us for a week and he couldn't have been nicer,' she said. 'Polite and wise and fair-minded he was.'

'How did you find all that out?'

'I just did.'

'Fallen for him, have you?' said Ivan Matveevich, coming in. 'It's a fact.'

'All right, so I've fallen for him. What's that to you? I just don't see why you speak ill of somebody when he is a good man. He may be a Tatar, but he is a good man.'

'Quite right, Marya Dmitrievna,' said Butler. 'Good for you to stand up for him!'

21

THE life of those living in the advanced fortresses on the Chechnia Line went on as before. In the interval there had been two alarms; foot-soldiers came running out, Cossacks and militia galloped in pursuit, but on neither occasion were they able to apprehend the mountaineers. They got away, and on one occasion at Vozdvizhenskoe drove off eight Cossack horses which were being watered and killed a Cossack. There had been no Russian raids since the one which had destroyed the village. But a major expedition into Greater Chechnia was expected following the appointment of Prince Baryatinsky as commander of the Left Flank.

On arriving in Grozny, being now in command of the whole Left Flank, Prince Baryatinsky (a friend of the Crown Prince and former commander of the Kabarda Regiment) at once assembled a force to continue the fulfilment of the Emperor's instructions which Chernyshev had communicated to Vorontsov. The column set out from Vozdvizhenskoe, where it had assembled, and took up position on the road to Kurinskoe. The troops camped there and engaged in forest clearing.

Young Vorontsov lived in a magnificent fabric tent; his

wife, Marya Vasilevna, would drive out to the camp and often stayed overnight. Baryatinsky's relations with Marya Vasilevna were a matter of common knowledge, and she was coarsely abused by the officers unconnected with the court and by the ordinary soldiers, who because of her presence in the camp were sent out on night picket duty. It was usual for the mountaineers to bring up their cannon and fire into the camp. The shots they fired mostly missed their target so as a rule no action was taken against them. But to prevent the mountaineers bringing up their guns and frightening Marya Vasilevna pickets were sent out. To go on picket every night to save a lady from being frightened was an insult and an offence, and the soldiers and the officers not received in the best society had some choice names for Marya Vasilevna.

Butler took leave from the fort and paid a visit to the column in order to see old comrades from the Corps of Pages and his regiment, now serving in the Kura Regiment or as *aides-de-camp* or adjutants on the staff. He found it all very enjoyable from the start. He stayed in Poltoratsky's tent and there found a number of people he knew who were delighted to see him. He also went to see Vorontsov, whom he knew slightly, having once served in the same regiment with him. Vorontsov made him very welcome. He introduced him to Prince Baryatinsky and invited him to the farewell dinner he was giving to General Kozlovsky, Baryatinsky's predecessor as commander of the Left Flank.

The dinner was splendid. Six tents had been brought up and pitched together in a row. Their whole length was taken up by a table laid with cutlery, glasses and bottles. It was all reminiscent of the guards officers' life in St Petersburg. They sat down to table at two o'clock. In the centre of the table sat Kozlovsky on one side, and Baryatinsky on the other. Vorontsov sat on Kozlovsky's right, his wife on his left. The whole length of the table on either side was filled by officers of the Kabarda and Kura Regiments. Butler sat by Poltoratsky and they chatted gaily and drank with the officers sitting by them. When they got to the main course and the orderlies began filling the glasses with champagne, Poltoratsky – with genuine apprehension and regret – said to Butler.

'Old "um-er" is going to make a fool of himself.'

'What do you mean?'

'Why, he's got to make a speech. And how can he?'

'Yes, old boy, it's a bit different from capturing barricades under fire. And on top of that he's got the lady next to him and all these court fellows. It really is pitiful to watch,' said the officers one to another.

But the solemn moment arrived. Baryatinsky rose and, lifting his glass, addressed a short speech to Kozlovsky. When he had finished, Kozlovsky got up and in a reasonably firm voice began to speak:

'By his Imperial Majesty's command I am leaving you, gentlemen,' he said. 'We are parting, but always consider me – um-er – present with you . . . You, gentlemen, know the truth of the – um-er – saying that you cannot soldier on your own. And so all the rewards that have come to me in my – um-er – service, everything that has been – um-er – bestowed upon me, the generous tokens of his Majesty's favour, my – um-er – position, and my – um-er – good name, all this, absolutely everything' – his voice quivered – 'I – um-er – owe to you and to you alone, my dear friends.' And his wrinkled face wrinkled still more, he gave a sob, and tears came to his eyes. 'I give you my – um-er – sincere and heartfelt thanks . . .'

Kozlovsky could not go on and stood to embrace the officers who came up to him. Everyone was very touched. The princess covered her face with her handkerchief. Prince Vorontsov pulled a face and blinked hard. Many of the officers, too, were moved to tears. And Butler, who did not know Kozlovsky well, was also unable to restrain himself. He found it all exceptionally agreeable. After this there were toasts to Baryatinsky, to Vorontsov, to the officers, to the other ranks, and finally the guests left, intoxicated by wine and the rapturous martial sentiment to which they were anyway specially inclined.

The weather was superb – sunny and calm, and the air fresh and invigorating. On every side was the sound of campfires crackling and men singing. Everyone seemed to be celebrating. Butler went to call on Poltoratsky in the most happy and serene frame of mind. Some of the officers were gathered there, a card-table had been set up and an *aide-de-camp* had gone banker with a hundred roubles. Twice Butler left the tent holding on to the purse in the pocket of his trousers, but in the end he succumbed and, despite the vow he had made to his brothers and to himself, began playing against the bank.

Before an hour was past Butler, flushed and sweating, covered with chalk, was sitting with his elbows on the table, writing down his bets beneath the crumpled cards. He had lost so much that he was now afraid of counting what was scored against him. He knew without reckoning that if he used all the pay he could get in advance and whatever his horse would fetch he could still not make up the whole of what he owed to this unknown *aide-de-camp*. He would have gone on playing, but the *aide-de-camp* put down the cards with his clean white hands and began totting up the column of chalk entries under Butler's name. Butler with embarrassment apologized that he was unable to pay all his losses immediately and said he would send the money on; as he said it he saw they were all sorry for him and everyone, even Poltoratsky, avoided his gaze. It was his last evening. All he had had to do was to avoid gambling and go to Vorontsov's where he had been invited. Everything would have been fine, he thought. But far from being fine, everything now was disastrous.

After saying good-bye to his comrades and friends, he left for home and on arriving went straight to bed and slept for eighteen hours at a stretch, as people usually do after losing heavily. Marya Dmitrievna could tell he had lost everything by his request for fifty kopeks to tip his Cossack escort, by his melancholy look and terse replies, and she set on Ivan Matveevich for giving him leave.

It was after eleven when Butler woke on the following day and when he recalled the situation he was in he would have liked to sink back into the oblivion from which he had just emerged, but this could not be done. He had to take steps to repay the 470 roubles which he owed to this total stranger. One step was to write a letter to his brother, repenting for his misdeed and begging him to send for the last time 500 roubles on account of his share in the mill which they still owned jointly. Then he wrote to a skinflint relative begging her to let him have 500 roubles, too, at whatever interest she wanted. Then he went to see Ivan Matveevich and knowing that he, or rather Marya Dmitrievna, had money, asked for a loan of 500 roubles.

'I'd be glad to: I'd let you have it like a shot, but Masha wouldn't part with it. These damned womenfolk are that tight-fisted. But you've got to get off the hook somehow. What about that sutler, hasn't he got any money?'

But there was no point even trying to borrow from the sutler, so Butler's only source of salvation was his brother or the skinflint relative.

22

HAVING failed to achieve his purpose in Chechnia, Hadji Murat returned to Tiflis. He went daily to see Vorontsov, and when Vorontsov received him he begged him to collect the mountaineers held captive and exchange them for his family. He repeated again that unless this were done he was tied and could not, as he wished, serve the Russians and destroy Shamil. Vorontsov promised in general terms to do what he could, but deferred giving a decision until General Argutinsky arrived in Tiflis and he could discuss it with him. Hadji Murat then asked Vorontsov's permission to go for a time to Nukha, a small town in Transcaucasia where he thought it would be easier to conduct negotiations about his family with Shamil and his supporters. Besides that, Nukha was a Muslim town with a mosque and it would be easier for him there to perform the prayers required by Muslim law. Vorontsov wrote to St Petersburg about this, and meanwhile allowed Hadji Murat to go to Nukha.

The story of Hadji Murat was regarded by Vorontsov, by the authorities in St Petersburg and by the majority of Russians who knew of it either as a lucky turn in the course of the war in the Caucasus or simply as an interesting episode. But for Hadji Murat, especially more recently, it was a drastic turning-point in his life. He had fled from the mountains partly to save his life and partly because of his hatred for Shamil. Despite all difficulties, he had succeeded in escaping, and initially he had been delighted with his success and actually considered his plans for attacking Shamil. But getting his family out, which he had supposed would be easy, had proved harder than he thought. Shamil had seized his family and now held them captive, promising to dispatch the women into the villages and to kill or blind his son. Now Hadji Murat was going to Nukha to try with the help of his supporters in Daghestan by guile or force to rescue his family from Shamil. The last scout to call on him at Nukha told him that the Avars who were loyal to him were going to carry off his family and bring them over to the Russians, but as they were short of men ready to undertake this they were reluctant to attempt it in Vedeno where the family was held and would only do it if they were moved from Vedeno to some other place. They would then take action while they were being moved. Hadji Murat ordered him to tell his friends that he would give 3,000 roubles for the release of his family.

At Nukha Hadji Murat was allotted a small house with five rooms not far from the mosque and the khan's palace. Living in the same house were the officers and interpreter attached to him and his *nukers*. Hadji Murat spent his time waiting for and receiving the scouts who came in from the mountains and in going for the rides he was allowed to take in the neighbourhood of Nukha.

On 8 April when he returned from riding Hadji Murat learnt that in his absence an official had arrived from Tiflis. Despite his anxiety to find out what news the official brought him, Hadji Murat did not go at once to the room where the official and the local commissioner were waiting, but went first to his own room to say his midday prayers. After he had prayed, he went into the other room which served him as a sitting-room and reception room. The official from Tiflis, a chubby state councillor called Kirillov, conveyed to him that Vorontsov wished him to be in Tiflis by the twelfth for a meeting with Argutinsky.

'*Yakshi*,' said Hadji Murat sharply.

He did not take to this official Kirillov.

'Have you brought the money?'

'Yes, I have it,' said Kirillov.

'It is for two weeks now,' said Hadji Murat, holding up ten fingers then four more. 'Give it to me.'

'You will have it directly,' said the official, getting a purse from his travelling bag. 'What does he want money for?' he said to the commissioner in Russian, presuming that Hadji Murat would not understand. But Hadji Murat did understand and looked angrily at Kirillov. As he was taking out the money Kirillov, who wanted to strike up some conversation with Hadji Murat in order to have something to report to Vorontsov on his return, asked him through the interpreter if he found life tedious in Nukha. Hadji Murat gave a scornful sideways glance at this fat little man in civilian clothes who carried no weapons, and made no answer. The interpreter repeated the question.

'Tell him I have nothing to say to him. Let him just give me the money.'

With this, Hadji Murat again sat down at the table and prepared to count the money.

When Kirillov had produced the gold ten-rouble pieces and laid out seven piles each of ten coins (Hadji Murat received 50 roubles in gold per day), he pushed them across to Hadji Murat. Hadji Murat dropped the coins into the sleeve of his *cherkeska*, rose and, as he left the room, quite unexpectedly rapped the state councillor on the top of his bald head. The state councillor leapt to his feet and commanded the interpreter to say that he had better not treat him like that because he was equivalent in rank to a colonel. The commissioner agreed. Hadji Murat merely nodded to indicate that he knew that and left the room.

'What can you do with him?' said the commissioner. 'He will stick his dagger in you, and that's that. There's no coming to terms with these devils. And he's getting his blood up, I can see.'

As soon as dusk fell two scouts, hooded to the eyes, came in from the mountains. The commissioner took them into Hadji Murat's quarters. One of the scouts was a dark, portly Tavlistani, the other a skinny old man. For Hadji Murat the news they brought was cheerless. Those of his friends who had undertaken to rescue his family were now backing out completely for fear of Shamil, who threatened the most horrifying deaths to any who helped Hadji Murat. Having heard their account, Hadji Murat put his elbows on his crossed legs, bowed his head (he was wearing his *papakha*) and for a long time was silent. He was thinking, thinking positively. He knew that he was thinking now for the last time, that he must reach a decision. Hadji Murat raised his head and, taking two gold pieces, gave one to each of the scouts.

'Go now.'

'What will be the answer?'

'The answer will be as God wills. Go.'

The scouts got up and left. Hadji Murat remained sitting on the rug, his elbows on his knees. He sat there for a long time.

'What should I do? Trust Shamil and go back to him? He is a fox and would play me false. And even if he did not, I could still not submit to this ginger-haired double-dealer. I could not because, now that I have been with the Russians, he will never trust me again,' thought Hadji Murat.

And he recalled the Tavlistan folk-tale about the falcon which was caught, lived among people and then returned to his home in the mountains. The falcon returned wearing jesses on his legs and there were bells still on them. And the falcons spurned him. 'Fly back to the place where they put silver bells on you,' they said. 'We have no bells, nor do we have jesses.' The falcon did not want to leave his homeland and stayed. But the other falcons would not have him and tore him to death.

Just as they will tear me to death, thought Hadji Murat.

'Should I stay here? Win the Caucasus for the Russian tsar, gain fame and wealth and titles?'

'Yes, I could do that,' he thought, recalling his meetings with Vorontsov and the old prince's flattering words.

'But I have to decide now, or he will destroy my family.'

All night Hadji Murat was awake, thinking.

23

HALF-WAY through the night he had made up his mind. He decided that he must flee to the mountains and with the Avars who were loyal to him force his way into Vedeno and either free his family or die in the attempt. Whether or not to bring his family back to the Russians or flee to Khunzakh with them and fight Shamil he did not decide. He knew only that he must now get away from the Russians and into the mountains. And he began at once to put this decision into effect. He took his black quilted jacket from beneath the cushion and went to his *nukers'* quarters. They lived across the hall. As soon as he stepped out into the hall, the door of which was open, he was enveloped by the dewy freshness of the moonlit night and his ears were filled by the whistling and warbling of nightingales in the garden by the house.

Hadji Murat crossed the hall and opened the door of his *nukers'* room. There was no light in the room, only the new moon in its first quarter shining through the windows. A table and two chairs stood to the side and all four *nukers* lay on rugs and cloaks spread on the floor. Khanefi was sleeping outside with the horses. Gamzalo, hearing the door creak, raised himself, looked round and, seeing it was Hadji Murat, lay down again. Eldar, however, who lay next to him sprang up and began to put on his jacket, expecting some command. Kurban and Khan-Mahoma slept on. Hadji Murat put his jacket on the table and there was the knock of something hard as he did so: the gold pieces sewn in the lining.

'Sew these in as well,' said Hadji Murat, handing Eldar the gold pieces he had received that day.

Eldar took the money and, going into the light, at once got a knife from beneath his dagger and began cutting open the lining of the jacket. Gamzalo half rose and sat with crossed legs.

'Gamzalo, tell the men to check their guns and pistols and prepare some cartridges. Tomorrow we shall travel far,' said Hadji Murat.

'There is powder and bullets. All will be ready,' said Gamzalo and he growled some incomprehensible remark.

Gamzalo knew why Hadji Murat was ordering them to get their guns loaded. Right from the start he had had only one desire, which as time went on had grown ever stronger: to kill and cut down as many of the Russian dogs as he could and escape to the mountains. He now saw that Hadji Murat wanted this, too, and he was content.

When Hadji Murat had gone, Gamzalo roused his com-

panions and all four spent the night looking over their rifles
and pistols, checking the touch-holes and flints, replacing
poor ones, priming the pans with fresh powder, filling their
cartridge pockets with measured charges of powder and bullets
wrapped in oiled rags, sharpening their swords and daggers
and greasing the blades with lard.

Near daybreak Hadji Murat again went into the hall to
fetch water to wash before praying. The singing of the nightingales as they greeted the dawn was louder and more sus-
tained than in the night. From the *nukers'* room came the even
sound of steel grating and shrilling on stone as a dagger was
sharpened. Hadji Murat ladled some water from the tub and
had reached his own door when he heard another sound
coming from the murids' room besides that of sharpening: it
was the thin voice of Khanefi singing a song Hadji Murat
knew. Hadji Murat stopped and listened.

The song told how the *djigit* Hamzad and his men drove off
a herd of white horses from the Russian side, and how later
across the Terek the Russian prince came on him and surrounded him with a great army as thick as a forest. The song
went on to tell how Hamzad slaughtered the horses and with
his men held fast behind this bloody rampart of dead horses
and fought the Russians as long as there were bullets in their
guns and daggers at their belts and blood still flowed in their
veins. But before dying Hamzad saw some birds in the sky
and cried out to them: 'You birds of the air, fly to our homes
and tell our sisters, our mothers and fair maidens that we died
for the *Ghazavat*. Tell them our bodies shall lie in no grave,
our bones will be carried off and gnawed by ravening wolves
and black crows will pick out our eyes.'

With these words, sung to a doleful refrain, the song ended,
to be followed at once by the cheerful voice of the merry
Khan-Mahoma who, as the song finished, bawled '*La ilaha illa
allah*' and let out a piercing yell. Then all was quiet and again
the only sound was the billing and singing of the nightingales

in the garden and, through the door, the even grating and occasional shrilling note of steel slipping rapidly over stone.

Hadji Murat was so lost in thought that he did not notice he was tipping the jug and spilling water over himself. He shook his head reprovingly and went into his room.

When he had finished his morning prayers, Hadji Murat checked his weapons and sat on his bed. There was nothing else to do. To ride out he had to ask permission from the commissioner. It was still dark outside and the commissioner was still asleep.

Khanefi's song reminded Hadji Murat of another song, which his mother had made up. It was about an actual event – something that had happened just after he was born, but which he had heard from his mother.

The song was this:

'Your damask blade slashed open my white breast, but I pressed to it my darling boy, and washed him in my hot blood, and the wound healed without help of herbs and roots. I did not fear death, no more will my boy-*djigit*.'

The words of the song were addressed to Hadji Murat's father. The point of it was that when Hadji Murat was born the khanoum also gave birth to a son (Umma-Khan, her second son) and sent for Hadji Murat's mother to be his wet-nurse as she had been for the khanoum's elder son Abununtsal. But Patimat had not wanted to leave her son and refused to go. Hadji Murat's father got angry and ordered her to. When she still refused he stabbed her with his dagger and would have killed her if she had not been taken away. So, after all, she did not give up her son but raised him, and made up this song about what had happened.

Hadji Murat remembered his mother singing it to him as she put him to bed alongside her, under the fur top-coat on the roof of their house, and he asked her to show him her side where the scar was. He could see his mother just as she was – not all wrinkled and grey with missing teeth as when he left her now, but young and beautiful and strong, so strong that even when he was five or six and heavy she carried him in a basket on her back to see his grandfather over the mountains.

And he remembered his grandfather with his wrinkled face and small grey beard. He was a silversmith and Hadji Murat remembered him engraving the silver with his sinewy hands and making him say his prayers. He remembered the fountain at the bottom of the hill where he went with his mother to fetch water, holding on to her trousers. He remembered the skinny dog that used to lick his face, and especially the smell and taste of smoke and sour milk when he followed his mother into the barn where she milked the cow and warmed the milk. He remembered the first time his mother shaved his head and how surprised he had been to see his little round head all blue in the shining copper basin that hung on the wall.

And remembering his childhood, he remembered too his own beloved son Yusuf, whose head he himself had shaved for the first time. Now Yusuf was a handsome young *djigit*. He remembered him as he last saw him. It was on the day he left Tselmes. His son brought his horse for him and asked if he could ride out and see him off. He was ready dressed and armed and holding his own horse by the bridle. Yusuf's young, ruddy, handsome face and everything about his tall slender figure (he was taller than his father) had seemed the very expression of youthful courage and the joy of living. His shoulders, broad for one so young, his very wide youthful hips and long slender body, his long powerful arms, and the strength, suppleness and dexterity of all his movements were a constant joy to his father and Hadji Murat always regarded his son with admiration.

'You had better stay,' Hadji Murat had said. 'You are the only one at home now. Take care of your mother and grand-mother.'

And Hadji Murat remembered the look of youthful spirit and pride with which Yusuf, pleased and blushing, had replied that, as long as he lived, no one would harm his mother or grandmother. Yusuf had then, after all, mounted and gone with his father as far as the stream. There he turned back, and since that time Hadji Murat had not seen his wife, mother or son.

And this was the son whose eyes Shamil was going to put out. Of what would happen to his wife he preferred not to think.

Hadji Murat was so agitated by these thoughts that he could not sit still any longer. He jumped up and limped quickly to the door. He opened it and called Eldar. The sun was not yet up, but it was fully light. The nightingales still sang.

'Go and tell the commissioner I want to go riding, and get the horses saddled,' he said.

24

BUTLER's only consolation at this time was the romance of military life, to which he surrendered himself not only when on duty but also in his private life. Dressed in Circassian costume, he performed the riding tricks of the natives and with Bogdanovich had twice gone out and lain in ambush, though on neither occasion did they catch or kill anyone. These daring deeds and friendship with Bogdanovich, who was well known for his bravery, seemed to Butler a pleasant and important part of life. He had paid off his debt by borrowing the money from a Jew at an enormous rate of interest – which meant that he had simply deferred settling his still unresolved situation. He tried not to think about his situation and, as well as in military romancing, he also sought oblivion in wine. He was drinking more and more heavily and every day advanced his moral decay. He was no longer the handsome Joseph where Marya Dmitrievna was concerned, on the contrary he made coarse advances to her, and, much to his surprise, had received a resolute rebuff which put him thoroughly to shame.

At the end of April a column arrived at the fort under orders from Baryatinsky to make a new advance through all those parts of Chechnia which were considered impassable. There were two companies of the Kabarda Regiment and, according to established custom in the Caucasus, they were received as the guests of the units stationed at Kurinskoe. The soldiers were taken off to the different barracks and were not only given supper of beef and millet porridge but also served with vodka. The officers took up quarters with the local officers, who, as was customary, entertained their visitors.

The party ended with drinking and singing. Ivan Matveevich, who was very drunk and no longer red, but pale and grey in the face, sat astride a chair cutting down imaginary enemies with his drawn sword; he was swearing, laughing, embracing people and dancing to his favourite song 'In years gone by Shamil rose up, Ho-ro-ro, Shamil rose up'.

Butler was also present. In this, too, he tried to see the romance of military life, but deep down he felt sorry for Ivan Matveevich, though there was no way of stopping him. And Butler, feeling slightly drunk, quietly left and set off home.

A full moon was shining on the white houses and on the stones in the road. It was so light you could see every small stone, every piece of straw and dung on the road. As he approached the house Butler met Marya Dmitrievna wearing a shawl over her head and shoulders. After the rebuff she had given him Butler had rather shamefacedly avoided her. But now in the moonlight and under the influence of the wine he had drunk Butler was glad to meet her and tried again to make up to her.

'Where are you going?' he asked.

'To see what the old man is up to,' she answered amicably. She had been quite sincere and positive in her rejection of Butler's advances, but she was displeased that he had been avoiding her of late.

'What's the point of going after him? He'll get home.'

'But will he?'

'If he can't, they'll carry him.'

'That's just it, and it really isn't good enough,' said Marya Dmitrievna. 'You think I shouldn't go then?'

'No, I shouldn't. We had best go home.'

Marya Dmitrievna turned back and began walking to the house with Butler. The moon was so bright that around their shadows moving along the roadside was a moving halo of light. Butler watched this halo round his head and wanted to tell Marya Dmitrievna that he found her as attractive as ever, but did not know how to begin. She waited for him to speak. Walking thus in silence they had almost reached the house when round the corner appeared some horsemen. It was an officer and escort.

'Who on earth is that?' said Marya Dmitrievna, stepping to the side. The moon was behind the officer and it was only when he was practically level with them that Marya Dmitrievna saw who it was. The officer was Kamenev, who served at one time with Ivan Matveevich and so was known to Marya Dmitrievna.

'Peter Nikolaevich,' she said. 'Is that you?'

'In person,' said Kamenev. 'Ah, Butler! How are things? Not asleep yet? Walking out with Marya Dmitrievna, are you? You look out or you'll catch it from Ivan Matveevich. Where is he?'

'You can hear him,' said Marya Dmitrievna, pointing to where there was the sound of singing and a bass drum. 'They're having a binge.'

'Your chaps, is it?'

'No. A column is in from Khasav-Yurt and they're giving them a party.'

'Ah, a good thing. I'll get to it myself. I only want to see him for a minute.'

'Is something up?' asked Butler.

'Just a small matter.'

'Good or bad?'

'Depends who for. It's good for us, but tough on others.' And Kamenev laughed.

The couple walking and Kamenev had meanwhile reached Ivan Matveevich's house.

Kamenev called one of the Cossacks:

'Chikhirev! Here!'

A Don Cossack moved forward from the rest and came up to them. He was in the ordinary Don Cossack uniform, wearing knee-boots and greatcoat, and had saddle-bags slung at the back of his saddle.

'Get it out,' said Kamenev, dismounting.

The Cossack also got off his horse and from one of the saddle-bags drew out a sack with something in it. Kamenev took the sack from the Cossack and put his hand in it.

'Shall I show you the latest, then? You won't be frightened?' he said, turning to Marya Dmitrievna.

'What is there to be afraid of?' said Marya Dmitrievna.

'There you are then,' said Kamenev and he pulled out a man's head and held it up in the moonlight. 'Do you recognize him?'

It was a shaven head, with prominent bulges of the skull over the eyes, trimmed black beard and clipped moustache; one eye was open, the other half-closed; the shaven skull was split and hacked about and the nose covered with black clotted blood. The neck was wrapped in a bloody towel. Despite all the wounds on the head, there was in the set of the now blue lips a childish, good-natured expression.

Marya Dmitrievna took one look and without a word turned and went quickly into the house.

Butler could not take his eyes off the terrible head. It was the head of that same Hadji Murat with whom he had recently spent his evenings having such friendly chats.

'How did it happen? Who killed him? Where?' he asked.

'He tried to make a break for it and they caught him,' said Kamenev, and handing the head back to the Cossack he went into the house with Butler.

'He died like a real man,' said Kamenev.

'But how did it all happen?'

'Hang on a minute. When Ivan Matveevich comes I'll give you all the details. That's what I've been sent for. I have got to go round all the forts and villages showing them.'

Ivan Matveevich had been sent for and came back to the house drunk, with two other officers also much the worse for drink, and began embracing Kamenev.

'I have come to see you,' said Kamenev. 'I have brought you the head of Hadji Murat.'

'Go on with you! Has he been killed?'

'Yes, he tried to escape.'

'I always said he would do us down. Where is it then? His head – let's see it.'

The Cossack was called and came in with the sack containing the head. The head was taken out, and for a long time Ivan Matveevich gazed at it with his drunken eyes.

'He was a fine fellow just the same,' he said. 'Let me kiss him.'

'He was a daredevil chap, that's a fact,' said one of the officers.

When they had all inspected the head they gave it back to the Cossack. The Cossack replaced it in the sack, dropping it carefully so as not to bump it too hard on the floor.

'What do you do, Kamenev – do you say something when you show it round?' asked one of the officers.

'But I want to kiss him,' shouted Ivan Matveevich. 'He gave me a sword.'

Butler went out on to the porch. Marya Dmitrievna was sitting on the second step. She looked round at Butler and at once turned angrily away.

'What's the matter, Marya Dmitrievna?' Butler asked.

'You are just a lot of butchers. You make me sick. Butchers, that's what you are.'

'It can happen to anyone,' said Butler, not knowing what to say. 'That's war.'

'War!' cried Marya Dmitrievna. 'What's war? You are butchers, and that's all there is to it. A dead body should be decently buried and they make mock of it. Butchers, that's what you are!' she repeated and went down the steps and into the house by the back door.

Butler went back to the parlour and asked Kamenev to tell him in detail what had happened.

And Kamenev told him.

It happened like this.

25

HADJI MURAT was allowed to go riding in the neighbour-hood of the town provided that he went with a Cossack escort. There was only one troop of Cossacks altogether in Nukha; of these a dozen were detailed for staff duties and if, according to orders, escorts of ten men were sent out it meant that the remaining Cossacks had to do duty every other day. Because of this, after the first day when ten Cossacks were duly sent out, they decided to send only five men, at the same time requesting Hadji Murat not to take his whole party of *nukers*. However, on 25 April all five of them accompanied Hadji Murat when he set off for his ride. As Hadji Murat was mounting, the commandant noticed that all five *nukers* were preparing to go and told Hadji Murat that he could not take them all, but Hadji Murat, appearing not to hear, spurred his horse, and the commandant did not insist. One of the Cossacks was a corporal, Nazarov, who had the St George's Cross, a young, healthy, fresh-faced fellow with light-brown hair cut in a fringe. He was the oldest child of a poor family of Old

Believers; he had grown up with no father and kept his old mother, three sisters and two brothers.

'See he doesn't go too far, Nazarov,' shouted the commandant.

'Very good, sir,' replied Nazarov. Then, rising on his stirrups and steadying the rifle across his back, he set off at a trot on his big, trusty, long-muzzled chestnut stallion. The other four Cossacks followed him: Ferapontov, who was lean and lanky, the troop's leading pilferer and fixer – he it was who had sold powder to Gamzalo; Ignatov, who was middle-aged and nearing the end of his service, a healthy peasant type who boasted how strong he was; Mishkin, just a weedy boy, too young for active service, of whom everyone made fun; and Petrakov, young and fair-haired, his mother's only son, who was always amiable and cheerful.

It was misty first thing but by breakfast-time it was bright and fine with the sun shining on the freshly burst leaves, the young virginal grass, the shooting corn and the swift, rippling river on the left of the road.

Hadji Murat rode at a walk. The Cossacks and his *nukers* followed, keeping pace with him. Thus they rode out along the road behind the fort. On their way they met women carrying baskets on their heads, soldiers on wagons and creaking carts drawn by oxen. When they had gone a couple of miles Hadji Murat spurred his white Kabarda horse to a fast amble, and his *nukers* went into a quick trot. The Cossacks did the same.

'Ay, that's a good horse he's got,' said Ferapontov. 'I'd have him off it, if he was still a hostile like he used to be.'

'Yes, mate, 300 roubles they offered for that horse in Tiflis.'

'But I'd beat him on mine,' said Nazarov.

'That's what you think!' said Ferapontov.

Hadji Murat continued to increase the pace.

'Hi there, *kunak*, you mustn't do that! Not so fast!' shouted Nazarov, going after Hadji Murat.

Hadji Murat looked back. He said nothing and went on without slackening pace.

'Watch out, those devils are up to something,' said Ignatov. 'Look how they're going!'

They rode like this towards the mountains for half a mile or so.

'Not so fast, I'm telling you,' Nazarov shouted again.

Hadji Murat did not answer or look back. He simply went faster and put his horse into a gallop.

'Don't think you'll get away,' shouted Nazarov, stung by this.

He gave his big chestnut stallion the whip and, standing on the stirrups and leaning forward, rode flat out after Hadji Murat.

The sky was so clear, the air so fresh, Nazarov felt so full of the joy of life as he flew along the road after Hadji Murat, merging into one with his powerful, trusty horse that the possibility of anything wrong or sad or terrible happening never even occurred to him. He was delighted that with every stride he was gaining on Hadji Murat and getting close to him. Hearing the hoofbeats of the Cossack's big horse getting nearer Hadji Murat realized that he would very soon catch up with him and, seizing his pistol with his right hand, used his left to steady his excited Kabarda which could hear the beat of hoofs behind.

'Not so fast, I say,' shouted Nazarov, now almost level with Hadji Murat and reaching out to seize the bridle of his horse. But before he could catch hold of it a shot rang out.

'What's going on?' cried Nazarov, grasping at his heart. 'Get them, lads!' he said as he swayed and fell forward over the saddle-bow.

But the mountaineers were quicker with their weapons than the Cossacks and fell on them with pistols firing and swords swinging. Nazarov hung on the neck of his terrified horse which carried him in circles round his comrades. Ignatov's horse fell and crushed his leg. Two of the mountaineers drew their swords and without dismounting hacked him across the head and arms. Petrakov dashed to his aid but before he could reach him was struck by two bullets, one in the back and one in the side, and he toppled from his horse like a sack.

Mishkin turned his horse back and galloped for the fort. Khanefi and Khan-Mahoma chased after him, but he had too good a start and the mountaineers could not overtake him.

Seeing they could not catch up with him Khanefi and Khan-Mahoma returned to their companions. Gamzalo dispatched Ignatov with his dagger and pulled Nazarov down from his horse before slitting his throat too. Khan-Mahoma took off the dead men's cartridge pouches. Khanefi was going to take Nazarov's horse, but Hadji Murat shouted to him to leave it and set off down the road. His murids galloped after him, trying to drive off the horse of Petrakov which followed them. They were already in the rice-fields two or three miles from Nukha when the alarm was sounded by a gunshot from the tower.

Petrakov lay on his back with his stomach slit open, his young face turned to the sky, gasping like a fish as he lay dying.

'Merciful heavens above, what have they done!' cried the commander of the fort, clasping his head as he listened to Mishkin's report and heard of Hadji Murat's escape. 'They've done for me! Letting him get away – the villains!'

A general alarm was raised. Every available Cossack was sent off in pursuit of the fugitives, and all the militia from the peaceable villages who could be mustered were called in as well. A thousand-rouble reward was offered to anyone bringing in Hadji Murat dead or alive. And two hours after Hadji Murat and his companions had ridden away from the Cossacks more than two hundred mounted men were galloping after the commissioner to seek out and capture the fugitives.

After travelling a few miles along the main road Hadji

Murat pulled in his panting white horse, which was grey with sweat, and stopped. Off the road to the right were the houses and minaret of the village of Belardzhik, to the left were fields, on the far side of which was a river. Although the way to the mountains lay to the right Hadji Murat turned left in the opposite direction, reckoning that pursuers would be sure to head after him to the right. He meanwhile would make his way cross-country over the Alazan and pick up the highway again where no one expected him, take the road as far as the forest, then recrossing the river go on through the forest to the mountains. Having made this decision, he turned to the left. But it proved impossible to reach the river. The rice-field which they had to cross had just been flooded, as happened every spring, and it was now a quagmire in which the horses sank up to their fetlocks. Hadji Murat and his *nukers* turned right and left, expecting to find a drier part, but the field they had struck on was evenly flooded and sodden all over. The horses dragged their feet from the sticky mud with a sound like popping corks and every few paces stopped, panting heavily.

They struggled on like this for so long that when dusk fell they had still not reached the river. To the left was a small island with bushes in first leaf, and Hadji Murat decided to ride into the bushes and stay there till night, resting their exhausted horses.

When they were in the bushes Hadji Murat and his *nukers* dismounted, hobbled their horses and left them to graze. They themselves ate some of the bread and cheese they had brought with them. The new moon that had been shining sank behind the mountains and the night was dark. There was an unusual abundance of nightingales in Nukha; there were also two in these bushes. In the disturbance caused by Hadji Murat and his men as they rode into the bushes the nightingales fell silent, but as the human noises ceased the birds once more burst into song, calling and answering each other. Hadji Murat, straining his ears to the sounds of the night, listened involuntarily.

The singing of the nightingales reminded him of the song of Hamzad which he had heard the previous night when he went to get the water. Any time now he could find himself in the same situation as Hamzad. It struck him that it would indeed end like that and his mood suddenly became serious. He spread out his cloak and said his prayers. He had scarcely finished when sounds were heard coming towards the bushes. It was the sound of a large number of horses' feet trampling through the quagmire. The keen-eyed Khan-Mahoma ran to one edge of the bushes and in the darkness picked out the black shadows of men on foot and on horseback approaching the bushes. Khanefi saw another large group on the other side. It was Karganov, the district commandant, with his militia.

We'll fight them as Hamzad did, thought Hadji Murat.

After the alarm was sounded Karganov had set off in hot pursuit of Hadji Murat with a squadron of militia and Cossacks, but he could find no sign of him or his tracks anywhere. Karganov had given up hope and was on his way back when towards evening they came upon an old Tatar. Karganov asked the old man if he had seen six horsemen. The old Tatar said he had. He had seen six horsemen riding to and fro across the rice-field and then go into the bushes where he collected firewood. Taking the old man with him, Karganov had gone back along the road and, seeing the hobbled horses, knew for certain that Hadji Murat was there. So in the night he had the bushes surrounded and waited till morning to take Hadji Murat dead or alive.

Realizing that he was surrounded, Hadji Murat discovered an old ditch in the middle of the bushes where he decided to make his stand and fight as long as he had ammunition and strength to do so. He told his comrades and ordered them to raise a rampart along the ditch. His *nukers* at once began cutting off branches and digging earth with their daggers to make a bank. Hadji Murat joined in the work with them.

As soon as it began to get light the commander of the militia squadron rode up close to the bushes and called out:

'Hey there, Hadji Murat! Surrender! You're outnumbered!'

By way of reply there was a puff of smoke from the ditch, the crack of a rifle and a bullet struck the horse of one of the militiamen, which shied and fell. After this there was a rattle of fire from the rifles of the militia positioned on the edge of the bushes. Their bullets whistled and hummed, clipping the leaves and branches and landing in the rampart, but none of them hit the men behind. All they hit was Gamzalo's horse which had strayed off. It was wounded in the head but did not fall; snapping its hobble, it crashed through the bushes to the other horses, nestling against them and spilling its blood on the young grass. Hadji Murat and his men only fired when one of the militiamen showed himself and they seldom missed. Three militiamen were wounded and their comrades not only hesitated to charge Hadji Murat and his men, but dropped farther and farther back, firing only random shots at long range.

This went on for over an hour. The sun had risen half-way up the trees and Hadji Murat was just considering whether to mount and attempt a break for the river when the shouts of a fresh large force of men were heard. This was Hadji-Aha of Mekhtuli and his men. There were about 200 of them. At one time Hadji-Aha had been a *kunak* of Hadji Murat and lived with him in the mountains, but he had then gone over to the Russians. With him was Akhmet-Khan, the son of Hadji Murat's enemy. Hadji-Aha began as Karganov had done by calling on Hadji Murat to surrender, but as on the first occasion Hadji Murat replied with a shot.

'Out swords and at them!' cried Hadji-Aha, snatching his own from its sheath, and there was a sound of hundreds of voices as men charged shrieking into the bushes.

The militiamen got among the bushes, but several shots in succession came cracking from the rampart. Three or four men fell and the attackers halted. They now opened fire from the edge of the bushes too. They fired and, running from bush to bush, gradually edged towards the rampart. Some managed to get across, while others fell to the bullets of Hadji Murat and his men. Hadji Murat never missed; Gamzalo's aim was no less sure and he gave a delighted yelp each time he saw his bullet strike home. Kurban sat by the edge of the ditch chanting '*La ilaha illa allah*'; he took his time in firing, but rarely got a hit. Meanwhile, Eldar was quivering all over in his impatience to rush the enemy with his dagger; he fired often and at random, continually looking round at Hadji Murat and showing himself above the rampart. The shaggy-haired Khanefi continued his role as servant even here. With rolled-up sleeves he reloaded the guns as they were handed to him by Hadji Murat and Kurban, carefully ramming home the bullets in oiled rags with an iron ram-rod and priming the pans with dry powder from a horn. Khan-Mahoma did not keep to the ditch like the others, but kept running across to the horses to get them to a safer place, all the time shrieking and casually firing without resting his gun. He was the first to be wounded. He was struck by a bullet in the neck and collapsed backwards spitting blood and cursing. Hadji Murat was wounded next. A bullet went through his shoulder. He tore some wadding from his jacket to plug the wound and went on firing.

'Let's rush them with our swords,' urged Eldar for the third time. He rose above the rampart ready to charge the enemy, but was instantly struck by a bullet. He staggered and fell backwards across Hadji Murat's leg. Hadji Murat looked at him. His handsome sheep's eyes stared earnestly up at him. His mouth, with its upper lip pouting like a child's, quivered but did not open. Hadji Murat freed his leg and went on taking aim. Khanefi bent over Eldar's dead body and quickly began taking the unused cartridges from his *cherkeska*. Meanwhile Kurban went on chanting, slowly loading and taking aim.

The enemy, whooping and screeching as they ran from bush to bush, were getting nearer and nearer. Hadji Murat was hit by another bullet in the left side. He lay down in the ditch and plugged the wound with another piece of wadding from his jacket. This wound in his side was mortal and he felt that he was dying. One after another images and memories flashed through his mind. Now he saw the mighty Abununtsal-Khan clasping to his face his severed, hanging cheek and rushing at his enemies with dagger drawn; he saw Vorontsov, old, feeble and pale with his sly, white face and heard his soft voice; he saw his son Yusuf, Sofiat his wife, and the pale face, red beard and screwed up eyes of his enemy Shamil.

And these memories running through his mind evoked no feelings in him, no pity, ill-will or desire of any kind. It all seemed so insignificant compared to what was now beginning and had already begun for him. But his powerful body meanwhile continued what it had started to do. Summoning the last remnants of his strength, he lifted himself above the rampart and fired his pistol at a man running towards him. He hit him and the man fell. Then he crawled completely out of the ditch and, with his dagger drawn and limping badly, went straight at the enemy. Several shots rang out. He staggered and fell. A number of militiamen rushed with a triumphant yell towards his fallen body. But what they supposed was a dead body suddenly stirred. First his bloodstained, shaven head, its *papakha* gone, then his body lifted; then, holding on to a tree, Hadji Murat pulled himself fully up. He looked so terrifying that the advancing men stopped dead. But suddenly he gave a shudder, staggered from the tree, and like a scythed thistle fell full length on his face and moved no more.

He did not move, but could still feel, and when Hadji-Aha, the first to reach him, struck him across the head with his great dagger, he felt he was being hit on the head with a hammer and failed to understand who was doing this and why. This was the last conscious link with his body. He felt no more, and the object that was trampled and slashed by his enemies had no longer any connection with him. Hadji-Aha put a foot on the body's back, with two strokes hacked off its head and rolled it carefully away with his foot so as not to get blood on his boots. Blood gushed over the grass, scarlet from the neck arteries, black from the head.

Karganov, Hadji-Aha, Akhmet-Khan and the militiamen gathered over the bodies of Hadji Murat and his men (Khanefi, Kurban and Gamzalo were bound) like hunters over a dead beast, standing among the bushes in the gunsmoke, gaily chatting and celebrating their victory.

The nightingales, which were silent while the shooting lasted, again burst into song, first one near by, then others in the distance.

This was the death that was brought to my mind by the crushed thistle in the ploughed field.